T0210048

SS
INDIGO

SS INDIGO

TWELVE'S COMPANY

WILLY MITCHELL

SS INDIGO
TWELVE'S COMPANY

iUniverse books may be ordered through booksellers or by contacting:

iUniverse
1663 Liberty Drive
Bloomington, IN 47403
www.iuniverse.com
844-349-9409

ISBN: 978-1-6632-2896-3 (sc)
ISBN: 978-1-6632-2897-0 (hc)
ISBN: 978-1-6632-2895-6 (e)

Library of Congress Control Number: 2022916537

Print information available on the last page.

iUniverse rev. date: 11/10/2022

To my wife, my daughter, and my son.
This book is for you, with all my love and continued
reading for years and generations to come.

To my beloved Uncle Billy Mitchell, ever encouraging,
ever supportive, illuminating the lives of all those who had
the honor to meet you – you will be
forever in my thoughts.

Bravely & Truly, Boldly & Rightly.

ACKNOWLEDGMENTS

SS Indigo is dedicated to all those people in my life who have taught me so much along my journey so far. There are those who have taught me the good and the right, Bravely & Truly, Boldly & Rightly, and then there are those who have shown me contrasting values and behaviors.

I always hoped that the former would prevail, but that was when I was young and naive and believed that there was more good in the world than bad. I realize now that the balance between good and evil is a much finer one than I had ever imagined and is almost always fueled by the quest for power and money—by greed.

I would like to thank all those who have been positive influencers in my life, helping me steer through challenges, always trying to do the right thing.

Of course, and as always, this book is dedicated to my wife, my daughter, and my son. Also, to my mother, my sister, and my father, God bless his soul.

To all my family and friends. Thank you.

To my best friend, Gary, and to Hans, Charles, and Jay. A big thank-you to my new octogenarian friend, Jim, and the amazing teacher, creative writing coach, and mentor Alta Wehmeyer.

The list is long. Thank you to all I have mentioned and all who I have missed.

www.willymitchell.com

AUTHOR'S NOTE

From an early age, I enjoyed reading. It wasn't until I was in my preteens and got beyond the Secret Seven and the Famous Five that I journeyed through to Roald Dahl and his wonderful imaginative adventures; J. R. R. Tolkien and his complete fantasy worlds, people, and languages; and Wilbur Smith and his accounts of empires, hardships, and adventures in Africa.

My reading, just like my music, has been an eclectic mix and a journey of discovery.

Ten or so years ago, when I first contemplated writing, I thought of the unsung hero and a collection of short stories. I didn't want to get stuck in a singular genre or create a long-running series, but I treasured the opportunity to wrap true stories around fiction and bring those tales to life.

Both *Operation Argus* and its sequel, *Bikini Bravo*, address maskirovka and how the art of deception is more prevalent than you think in the murky world of politics and organized crime, rarely mentioned in the same sentence.

Cold Courage tells the epic tale of bravery, grit, determination, and survival in the face of adversity during the Imperial Trans-Antarctic Expedition of 1914.

Northern Echo features two boys growing up in the North of England during the punk rock era, and then *Gipsy Moth* follows aviatrix heroines during the golden age of aviation.

With this, my sixth book, *SS Indigo*, I wanted to explore the world of mystery—an eclectic group of characters, from all walks of life, united by one common thing. A luxury steamship in my favorite part of the world collects its passengers and embarks on a journey of mystery and discovery as it sets sail across the Caribbean.

I hope that you enjoy the story of *SS Indigo: Twelve's Company* as it unfolds in the following pages.

"The road to hell is paved with good intentions."

PROLOGUE

I'd been anticipating this trip for a long time. I had the sense it was going to be important. We'd been in business for a couple of years now, and I figured this could possibly be the big break we'd been looking for. Lithuania joining the European Union meant an influx of qualified and soon-to-be-legal workers for a much-needed gap in the UK hospitality market. It's not as though business was bad, not at all, but this was the potential of finding a seam during the gold rush.

Most of the weekend, I'd been hanging out with Kipper and Jimmy at the Drovers, drinking beer and playing pool and poker. It was Sunday afternoon, and I was in the middle of a game of Brag. Amanda, my adopted admin, had popped into our office upstairs and brought down a fax that had arrived, and I folded my ace high to meet her. She had always been my favorite, ever since I'd taken her on—a young girl, a groom, no qualifications, but sweet and full of enthusiasm. Three years on, she'd grown, and she was very grateful for my investment in her.

In her riding outfit, she handed me the fax with her usual sweet smile. "I thought you should see this."

I went over to the snug and sat down to read it. For fifteen minutes, I pondered, reread it, and reread it again before carefully folding it up and placing it in my back pocket as though it were a winning betting slip from the Grand National.

I walked over to the bar where the stuffed Gentleman Fox that Diesel and Mick had once held ransom sat and ordered myself a glass of Liddesdale. It was only four in the afternoon, but why not? I'd been right—this trip was going to be a game changer.

Twenty-four hours later, I landed at Schiphol, left the terminal, and caught a cab right next to where the big red AMSTERDAM letters are and headed into the city. I asked the driver to drop me off in the main square. It was full of the usual stag parties, football fans—full of beer and likely stronger substances, singing their way into an evening of debauchery, no doubt.

Last time I'd been there, I'd found a locals' post just down an alley a couple of blocks away, so that's where I headed. It was quiet in Amsterdam, and apart from the tourists, it didn't get busy for locals until much later into the night, often into the early hours and sunrise.

With little giving it away that it was a bar at all—dark wood door, black facade, no sign—the No Name Bar was just as I remembered, and I walked inside.

Amsterdam is a truly international city, so I shouldn't have been surprised to hear the barman's Northern Californian accent as he greeted me with what was obviously his standard question: "What can I get you, my friend?"

I paused for a second and looked him up and down. "I'll take a Lagunitas?"

He looked at me, paused, and then smiled knowingly. "Not in Amsterdam, my friend. Wrong country. Where are you from?"

He was clearly impressed that I had spotted his accent after having heard barely a sentence, but what he didn't realize was that this somehow had become my thing. Spoofing accents from my home country was kind of easy— the grate of Glaswegian, the pronunciation of Edinburgh, the poetry of Ayrshire. Across the sea, Dubliners were easy to establish against Belfasters. South of the border, it was even easier—from the hardly audible Newcastle drawl, across to the "Manchestor," "Liverpooool," and then Birmingham, Coventry, Londoners. But some of the accents, like those of specific Australian territories and US states, were harder to define.

For some, it was not just their accents that gave them away but also their dress and demeanor. The boxer-like swagger of a Scouser versus the bold confidence of a Cockney. The over-the-top glitz of the nouveau riche Russians versus the more utilitarian style of former Soviets. The straight-to-the-point New Yorker versus the bright-smiled Angeleno. The surfer-dude types of Northern California.

The bartender's name tag told me I was speaking to Zach. As I mentioned, his accent gave him away, but his looks also fit the stereotype of a typical Northern Californian—although I suspected that he'd seen more than Sonoma County in his life. After all, he was five thousand miles away in Holland.

"Glasgow," I said. "What about you?"

"That's no Glasgow accent," he said and smiled.

"Yep. I've been around a bit."

He looked at me and nodded knowingly.

I already knew I liked Zach—it was another one of those *things*; I could immediately tell whether I would like someone or not. There were plenty of warning signs of who I likely would not like, and they were relatively easy filters: mullets were out, as were Bulgari watches, shell suits, sovereign rings, and Botox.

Over the course of my stay, and with the benefit of my being the only one in the bar, I got to learn more about Zach.

I'd always been a great believer that there's a lot to learn in the confines of a bar, no matter where you are in the world. And today it was no different in the No Name Bar in Amsterdam.

Turns out that I was right, with Zach's roots being in Sonoma and Marin Counties. He'd worked in Sausalito on the boats and taken his marine engineer qualifications at the Maritime Academy. After graduation, he'd traveled a bit, including in the Caribbean, Virgin Gorda, and made mention of Necker Island and how he and his brother had acted as hosts, tour guides, and, of all things, water instructors to Sir Richard, his kids, family, and visitors.

The mention of Jet Skis, powerboats, scuba, and his Caribbean knowledge made my ears prick up.

Zach looked like he should be on a film set—not a modern-day *Love Actually* or a *Gone with the Wind*, but with his mustache and his square jaw, he reminded me of one of those pilot characters in the old World War II movies, who sat around the piano in the officers' mess, waiting for the scramble call, raucously singing "Roll Out the Barrel" before donning their gear and calling for "Chocks away!" as they sailed into the blue skies to have a dogfight or two with the Hun.

"What brought you to Amsterdam?" I asked.

He explained his travels from one city to another, mainly following beautiful girlfriends who never quite worked out how he'd expected. I could empathize with that. And how he was "in between girlfriends right now and looking for his next port of call."

After half a dozen Heinekens, I gave him my business card. He gave me his number and email and held out his hand, revealing the Golden State Warriors tattoo on his forearm, one of his giveaways—the other a simple search on Facebook and reference to the Californian barman with a mustache, Zach.

I shook his hand. "Nice to meet you, Zach Carter." I smiled, nodded, and headed out for something to eat, to line my stomach for the night ahead.

It was May 8, 2003, Vilnius. The referendum to join the EU was just two days away, and the air was full of anticipation. A sense of nervousness prevailed. Was this Lithuania's chance to finally recover from the grasp of the former Soviet Union, the threat of another invasion in the country's long history of occupation? Was this an opportunity to return the country back to its status as the garden of the Baltic? Was this a chance to get a nation back to work?

I got on the Lithuanian Airlines flight after my night out on the canals. After my Ronson-lighter all-nighter, I was a little worse for wear as I boarded the LY-SBD Saab 2000 and took my seat: 4A, at the front of the plane, but hardly a premium experience.

Despite my state, I noticed an extreme state of orderliness during boarding—how quiet it was, the passengers obediently boarding and taking their seats. I rested my head on the window and fell asleep, or at least closed my eyes in a semiconscious state.

My subconscious heard the twin turboprop engines spring to life after a little coaxing from the pilot. An initial splutter and cough, then a gradual ease into the familiar hum as they climaxed to full operating speed. The aircraft lurched forward as the brake was released and started the taxi toward the runway. Up, up, and away.

Eyes still closed, I thought back to my crossing the Atlantic years earlier in an old army Hercules, in my *maggot*, lying on the webbing down the center of the otherwise empty hull, like a hammock, listening to the drone of the engines as we flew.

On reflection, I'd spent quite a bit of time in the air—as a kid in the Air Training Corps, summer camps, Bulldogs, Chipmunks, doing barrel rolls and loop-the-loops at the tender age of fourteen. Family holidays to the Algarve, back in the day, when smoking was allowed in the rear rows. In the army, several flights on the good old Hercules, but, more interestingly, in the helicopter versions of flight, hedgehopping in a Gazelle over the fields of Ireland, the plains of Africa, and the rain forest of Central America. Abseiling from the Westland Wessex in the Arctic Circle. Then, more recently, my trips to Australia and the tortuous slog of a journey—almost twenty-four hours in the air, with a brief stop in Singapore.

I awoke from my shallow snooze, looked around me at the still strangely quiet and subdued payload, and reached for the brochures in the pocket in front of me. I needed hydration.

The first document was the safety card for the Saab 2000. On the back, the Crossair logo with the familiar Swiss flag was crossed out, but still visible, and a Lithuanian Airlines sticker had been carelessly placed alongside it.

I had heard the stories about *sloppy* airlines, especially in the former Soviet Union and in Africa. I remembered my old mate's jibes at Aeroflot, or *Aeroflop*, as he would say, and his alternative name for Air Afrique, *Air Tragique*. That brought a smile to my face.

Ninety minutes into the flight, I managed to get a double serving of orange juice and a much-needed shot of vitamin C for my constitution before the Saab started its descent into Vilnius, the capital of Lithuania, one of the three Baltic states. The other two are Estonia and Latvia.

Coming into land, I looked out at the gray skies and the even darker gray buildings below. Large apartment tower blocks sprouted around—as did the bizarre-looking chimneys painted with red and white bands, looking like something from a Pink Floyd video.

The tarmac appeared close below; the wheels touched down one by one; and after the plane shuddered, the passengers burst into a round of applause, some of them disregarding the safety brief and standing up in their seats. Seems they were just genuinely pleased to have touched down safely and alive—this was a first for me despite my airborne experience.

I remembered the humorous references. I thought of Totalitarian Airlines. I didn't have the natural wit and turn of phrase as my friend Gary Mackay.

My phone lit up. A text. Gary letting me know he was on the other side of security waiting in his newly acquired Land Rover 110. What else? Everywhere I had ever met him around the world he had got hold of his favorite workhorse. We're all creatures of habit.

I made my way down the steps of the plane to the tarmac below, my fellow passengers back to their obedient silence as the airport staff ushered us toward the terminal.

I approached immigration amid the ominous silence of the airport and the still extraordinarily quiet crowd of passengers. I handed over my British passport to the uniformed officer, and the National Guard soldier stood by his side complete with Kalashnikov, at the ready, menacingly staring at me as if I had just gotten off a flight from Mars.

"What you do in Lithuania, Mr. Mitchell?" the immigration officer sneered.

"Visiting a friend," I said.

He looked down to inspect my papers. "You are in business?"

"Yes, sir!"

"What business?" He continued his emotionless, intimidating stare.

"Recruitment" was my limited response—although there was much more. I didn't want to overcomplicate the situation, especially as the soldier looked more than capable and willing to use his rifle.

"Is RekruitUK?" asked the officer.

I paused for a second, trying to work out how the hell he knew the name of my business. "Yes, that's correct," I said, trying to hide my surprise behind a poker face.

He approved my passport with a forceful stamp and slid inside of it a copy of one of my ads that had been in the local paper, along with a telephone number, a name, and 500 litas, around $150, in local currency. I looked him in the eye.

"He my uncle. I want you to call him. He looks for job." The officer grinned, an attempt at a smile in that Eastern European sort of way that the old guard simply hadn't quite got the knack of—it came across as even more intimidating.

"Yes, sir! I'll call him."

I put on my own version of a smile, picked up my papers with the new additions, and went on my merry way to meet Gary. I made my way to baggage claim, picked up my bag from the carousel, and hurried from the terminal to the arrivals pickup area in front of the building. I saw Gary's Land Rover immediately, shot him a big smile, threw my bag in the back of the car, and climbed into the passenger seat. We exchanged the usual small talk as Gary navigated through the airport traffic.

"I hope things change if they get in the EU," Gary said.

"What do you mean?"

"They know everything that goes on here and especially keep an eye on who comes in through the airport. Especially persons of interest—like you, Willy!" He looked over and grinned. "These people live in fear. They don't like outsiders."

Gary passed me a newly lit Marlboro Light. I thanked him, took the fag, and deeply inhaled the harsh smoke as I looked out the window. Ironically, a Philip Morris factory was in the industrial district we were passing. It stood all gleaming and new. I remembered the theory that they load their products with all the things that are bad and addictive for the human being, especially in emerging markets—makes them eat more, drink more, and smoke more and fattens their corporate coffers regardless.

Lithuania is nestled southeast of Sweden and Denmark with Belarus to the east and south, Poland to the south, and the Russian enclave of Kaliningrad Oblast to the southwest. At the time, the country's population was just shy of three million. My reason for being there? I was leading a recruitment drive for workers to come to the UK. We had a lack of people willing to wash, clean, cook, and wait, and assuming that the referendum result was yes, then Lithuania would be in the European Union and the citizens able to fill these entry-level jobs and earn money. For many, that had been a thing of the past, and they were desperate for these new opportunities.

"You see, once upon a time, Lithuania, or the Grand Duchy of Lithuania, was the largest country in Europe, but that was a long time ago—over five hundred years, to be precise," Gary said.

Over the years I had known him, Gary always knew the lowdown of his latest home, temporary or not, and there had been many in his time. Originally from Scotland, Glasgow, with his roots in the Highlands, he had lived in some of the most dangerous places in the world, and I had either been with him or visited him in many of those countries.

"You see, since the late 1700s, they've been occupied, first by the Russians, then again at the start of World War II, then the Nazis, then the Soviets again, until they got their independence after the wall came down in 1990."

I nodded, taking in the information like an in-country briefing from my former combatant, soldier, and friend from the UK's Special Air Service, the British equivalent of American Special Forces.

"With the Russian muscle flexing in Georgia, Belarus, and Ukraine, the Lithuanians have been paranoid ever since that they would once again wake up one morning with Russian tanks on the streets, reoccupying what they, the Russians, believe is their rightful territory. And hence the paranoia!"

"And then you have the Russian enclave of Kaliningrad right around the corner." I was referring to the isolated island of land under Russian control and officially part of the sovereign state of Russia. This clearly added to the paranoia.

We pulled onto the cobbled streets at the bottom of the city center and headed to the familiar Shakespeare Hotel across from the cathedral. After entering through the archway, like an entrance to a fort, I dropped my bag off at reception, and then we ventured by foot to the main square for a beer and a bite to eat.

"You look like shite, Willy. Good night in Amsterdam?"

"Thanks, mate. You don't look too clever yourself."

We walked up the cobbled streets past the stalls of vendors selling their wares—everything from the works of local artists and painters to handcrafted jewelry; knockoff old Soviet uniforms, hats, and badges; and the ubiquitous babushka Russian dolls.

Clapped-out old Soviet-built relics as excuses for taxis hustled by with little to no regard for pedestrians. The residents of Vilnius obediently walked, mostly in twos, looking straight onward, seemingly nervous of distractions or the ever-watchful police keeping the peace and ensuring social calm and tranquility.

"We got an amazing response from the ads," Gary said.

"I saw that," I said, thinking of the immigration officer.

"Almost one hundred and twenty for each of the sessions."

"I better get busy finding them jobs, then." I pulled out the piece of paper the immigration officer had handed me. "Is this guy on the list?"

Gary unfolded the paper, the money still in it. "Who's Igor Bromovich? And what's the money for?"

"Just a little gift from homeland security."

Gary pulled out his phone. Sasha was helping coordinate the expedition and within a couple of minutes confirmed that Bromovich, an unemployed but nonetheless fully qualified ship's captain, was on the next morning's session.

We meandered to the city square, past the Russian Orthodox church on the left, with the City Hall looking down on us from the top of the sloping cobbled square. We sat down in one of the several pop-ups in the center and ordered a couple of steins of Švyturys, and the waitress shared the menus.

"I could eat a bloody horse."

"You might have to, mate."

"Pigs' ears left or pigs' ears right?" I said, remembering an amusing menu translation from the past.

We stayed safe and ordered a pair of cheeseburgers and sat in the late-afternoon sun as the evening closed in.

We sat and watched the locals strolling the cobbles in earnest, in pairs, staying focused, looking forward, compliant with the laws of the day—any groups of more than four constituted a civil disturbance, with the penalty of being locked up and receiving a heavy unaffordable fine. Threes were legal, but if you happened to bump into another group, you were over the limit and in danger of jail. Hence, twos were the acceptably safe norm for wandering the streets, as many seemingly liked to do, especially at this time of day.

I remembered Gary's wedding a couple of years earlier: how Tom Tom the Piper's Son had made the trip over from Scotland in his kilt and with his pipes; how the men of the wedding party, including me, donned kilts; and how we made the local television news that evening.

"How's business on your end?" I asked.

"It's OK. Making a living, doing all right."

We had both spent a lifetime *doing all right*. Lots of hard work, opportunity, and fun, but neither of us had achieved anywhere near the ambitions we'd once held.

"Things will pick up and get better" was always the optimistic response.

There was no point in anything else. Without optimism and hope, we have nothing, and I had learned that from my travels to some of the most desperate places around the world.

Soon the burgers arrived. The waitress, a beautiful Lithuanian woman wearing the traditional national dress of a plaid skirt and white starched shirt, seemed intrigued by us two Westerners—a novelty in Vilnius back in 2003, the year of the referendum that set the stage for the nation's entry into the EU the following year.

"I might have a job for our friend Igor." I pushed another paper over the table as we began digging into our burgers.

Gary opened the fax Amanda had handed to me in the Drovers and read in silence.

Highly Confidential: Ship's Crew Needed

Mr. Mitchell:

We are seeking key personnel for our luxury steamship *Indigo* and an upcoming private cruise around the Caribbean, leaving from St. George's Caye, Belize City, on July 16, 2003.

We are looking for the following crew members:

1. Qualified ship's captain
2. Michelin / AA Rosette chef
3. Front-of-house hostess
4. Tour guide / host, with knowledge of the Caribbean

Upon your acceptance of this retained search, we will provide you with a full job description, required qualifications, and experience for each of the positions for your review.

Mr. Mitchell, you come highly recommended, and we understand that you have a good network of connections. We hope that you can help. Upon your acceptance of the project, we will wire US$10,000 for each position as a retainer for you to find the right candidates. Upon successful placement, we will pay you a further US$40,000, a total of US$80,000.

Please contact me when you find the right candidates. I am confident you will not let us down.

Mr. N. Waring
Litions Industries

Gary looked up at me as I was into my second mouthful of burger.

"Who the hell are Litions Industries?"

I shrugged. "No clue, but if they want to pay me eighty grand, I'm not sure I care! What do you know about our man Igor Bromovich?"

It was an unfair question. I knew that Gary was a professional but also knew he wouldn't know the answer to that. As I asked the question, the pretty blonde waitress arrived back at the table, this time with an envelope for Mr. Gary Mackay. He sat there and ceremoniously opened it in front of me with a big grin on his face and pulled out what was obviously a résumé, with IGOR BROMOVICH in big bold black print at the top of the page. I couldn't help but smile back in admiration of my old friend.

"You don't hang around, do you?"

"The early bird catches the worm, my friend," he said as he scanned the document.

I recalled a time I'd been on the phone with him years earlier. I was in Hereford, he in Iraq, when I heard an explosion in the background. After a split-second silence, all Gary said was "Och, I better go, Willy. There's been an explosion. Catch up soon." Gary Mackay was a character for sure.

Burgers finished, we ordered another couple of Švyturys. The hair of the dog was proving its truth beyond the myth.

We caught up on all things since last time we had been together, a few months ago in Perth, Australia. We caught up on our wives—and girlfriends.

"And may they never meet" was the usual toast. "To wives and girlfriends!"

"What about the other positions?"

"I think I have them covered."

We had a big day the next day. Despite the urge to carry on, around nine, we headed back down the cobbled streets, traders packing up for the night, back to the Shakespeare. I waved Gary off in his 110 and headed to the hotel bar for a nightcap.

Last time I had stayed at the Shakespeare, I had persuaded them to stock a bottle of Liddesdale whisky, and sure enough, the bottle was still there on the top shelf, filled to the same level as last time.

I didn't recognize the barman. He looked shocked that someone had ordered it. I smiled to myself at the satisfaction of knowing more than he. It was a thing. Having superior intel, deeper insights, a better knowledge platform, gave one an advantage, and although this may sound trivial, it became a thirst for me—and one that had proven helpful over the years. Knowledge is power.

I sat at the bar sipping my Liddesdale on the rocks while checking out the résumé.

Bromovich had qualified at the Klaipeda Naval Academy twenty-five years previously and had worked himself up in the merchant navy to captain several ships, including freight and transportation, and he had traversed both the Atlantic Ocean to the Americas and the South China Sea and the Pacific Ocean to Australia, New Zealand, Hawaii, and California.

Interestingly, after the collapse of the Soviet Union and the devastation of Klaipeda, its shift from major trading port to an empty one, Bromovich had worked for a couple of years as captain of a luxury steamship in the Baltic until that closed because of an accelerated bankruptcy and dodgy dealings of the Russian mob owners—a story I was familiar with and a reminder from the past, of one Mr. Dmitri Dankov.

I ordered another whisky. "Make that a double."

I looked at the note from Litions Industries to double-check I hadn't misread it.

Earlier that day, I had confirmed that there was $40,000 already in my account and that another $40,000 would be on the way if I found the suitable candidates, which I already had, at least on paper. "Bingo!" was my celebratory conclusion. That money would come in handy. *Very handy*, I thought as I saw the clock clicking to ten.

The next day, 7:00 a.m. alarm, curtains open, sunrise. I grabbed a coffee and a pastry from the hotel coffee shop and set off walking up the cobblestones, this time past city hall and on to the Radisson Blu. The street vendors were already setting up for the day, and old women were sweeping the streets in the absence of sufficient civic resources and funding. The Baltic sun shone down on the crisp morning. It was a good morning to be alive.

Gary was already at the Radisson. Sasha had done a great job organizing the road show; a crowd was already assembled. The candidates sat nervously clutching their portfolios, résumés, and credentials. I had a sense of their desperation, and that made me feel sad, but also hopeful that maybe I could help them too.

Promptly at 9:00 a.m., we kicked off, with Sasha giving opening remarks in Lithuanian and introducing yours truly. Assuming the country's accession to the EU, I set off explaining the opportunity to work in the United Kingdom and potentially anywhere in Europe—I had to work that one out yet. Placing potentially a thousand folks in the UK was enough of a challenge, never mind expanding across Europe.

Sasha had set up computer stations around the perimeter of the room and instructed the candidates to log on and submit their details online. Sasha busied around the room helping them, from the cleaners and cooks to the lawyers, doctors, surgeons, and, today, ship captains.

I had spotted Igor Bromovich as he arrived. He looked as nervous and apprehensive as most. I would make time later in the day for a one-to-one.

At my request, Sasha had arranged for plenty of food and refreshments all day. Our guests didn't quite know what to do with the apparent opulence of the spread—they were proud, humble, anxious people, afraid and probably hungry too. I made a point of walking round with the platters to encourage them to eat, never mind see my investment being thrown in the trash at the end of the day because everyone was too proud to eat it.

I met with a qualified surgeon who had been out of work for four years and didn't care what she did to earn money to support her children, her husband—also out of work—and her parents. There was also a professional accountant, a former businessman who ran the state oil business, an architect, a former auditor—all totally desperate for any work, any income, no matter what it was. All these people were prepared to swallow their pride and more out of desperation. It was a very sad experience and a situation where I thought that I could actually make a difference, help them, and maybe do good for once in my life.

As my good friend would say, "The road to hell is paved with good intentions." I had learned over time that Gary had been right all along. It was a phrase that I would become all too familiar with over time.

Then there was the ship's captain, Igor Bromovich.

He sat there facing the now empty stage, almost looking like he was waiting to be dismissed from class, clutching his black leather portfolio with a long-faded logo on the front—*probably from too much spit and polish*, I thought to myself.

His right leg bounced up and down restlessly as he sat in his dark blue, almost black, suit, which looked as though it might have been from his wedding years earlier. A thin red tie on his starched white shirt also showed the wear and tear of age.

It was difficult not to feel sorry for these people. I had come into this as a potential moneymaking venture within the bounds of the law and immigration, but it was quickly turning into something else. Maybe I could help these people. It was obvious that they needed all the help that I could give and probably more.

"Igor. You come highly recommended, sir."

He greeted me with his deep, sad mahogany-brown eyes and his carefully groomed mustache. I noticed his hand shaking slightly, another sign of his nervous state, and just maybe a signal of his capitulation to do almost anything to survive, not for himself but for his family.

I had learned over the years that it's often the smallest things that give someone away, and I was by now an avid spotter of these signals: the shaking hand, the tapping of a foot, the tiniest beads of sweat, the dilation of pupils—all signals of sorts, all things to be observed and noteworthy.

We sat there as he nervously went through his résumé, and I did all that I could to bolster his confidence, especially at one point, when tears welled from the eyes of this clearly proud and accomplished man.

"I think I might have a job for you, Igor."

He looked up from his well-rehearsed pitch. "Mr. Mitchell, I would do anything," he said, hopeful but seemingly in disbelief.

"How about the captain of a luxury steamship in the Caribbean?" I pushed him the job description from Litions.

He looked through it, slowly met my gaze, and beamed. "Are you serious?"

"Yep, this is a perfect fit for you. Ten thousand dollars a week, maybe up to six weeks."

He looked at me not believing what I had just said and the enormity of the potential paycheck. I was pretty sure that ten grand amounted to more than he had earned in the last four years combined.

"When would I start—if I got the job, of course?"

"The ship sails from Belize in mid-July."

We concluded the interview a short time later. The session ended for the day. Gary and I headed for a beer. Interviewing wasn't as easy as it may seem. Especially if you paid attention. The bar was quiet pre-evening, and we sat in the corner nursing a couple of steins and ordered some beer snacks. Sasha joined us, and we casually summed up the day.

It was dark when we left and strolled together back down the cobbled streets, with the vendors packing up for the day, until the morning. We turned the corner and into the familiar archway of the Shakespeare.

I had a nightcap with my friend, the Liddescale feeling like I had done some good. It was a nice feeling.

The next morning, I emailed Igor's résumé, his name and contact details blacked out, to Litions Industries. Within an hour, I heard back from them—deal done. Another $10,000 was on the way to my bank account, and another $30,000 was coming soon. Three to go.

In that moment, life was good.

I would meet with Igor to let him know and have Sasha complete the final details and travel arrangements to Belize City.

It's funny. With every good intention, there is consequence, and as I had learned from the past, it's not always necessarily positive. I hoped that this would work out for Igor and his family. Of course, I didn't have a crystal ball to tell me that I would be swept up in murder. I would have to wait for events in the near future to play out before I discovered that the cruise from Belize was far from what you'd consider an average pleasure trip.

This is the story of SS *Indigo*.

PART I

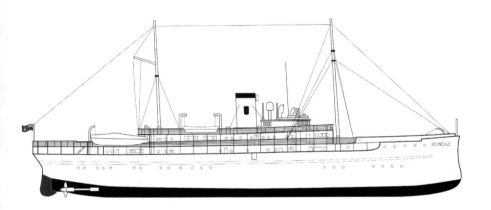

I

I.
Fort George Hotel, Belize City

SIR JAMES PARSONS STARED UP at the ceiling fan whirring above his four-poster bed in the Fort George Hotel. The alarm clock on the nightstand next to the bed began beeping at 7:00 a.m. Groaning, he leaned over and silenced the obnoxious thing. He'd been awake for at least two hours in the hot, humid room, and he'd found himself lost in thought about his past, present, and tenuous future, the theme tune playing in his head all the while, "When I was a child, I had a fever. My hands felt just like two balloons. Now I've got that feeling once again. I can't explain—you would not understand. This is not how I am ..."

He'd made his money—and a lot of it. What was it in him that left him still wanting more? He had often tried to work that out but had never really come up with a solid answer.

1

He recalled how his father had been a perfectionist—how, as a boy, he would help his father with the various chores and projects around the house and how nothing he ever did was ever quite good enough.

Even painting the gate at the back of the house. A simple task, yet his father would take over halfway through and finish the job off for him.

"If you're going to do a job at all, make sure you do it right, James" was his regular taunt—meant with good intention, but it had caused permanent scars, Parsons now realized.

They'd spent many an hour on various projects with the same pattern repeating itself. He recalled his father's frustration at his not being able to tie his shoelaces for school, at his riding his bicycle without stabilizers. As a result, he'd taught him to be self-sufficient, work things out, and just get stuff done, and that's what he had done and was grateful for.

The best conclusion Parsons came to was that he had spent his life on a treadmill chasing the acceptance and recognition of his father. That chance was long gone, his father long since passed.

"... There is no pain—you are receding. A distant ship, smoke on the horizon. You are only coming through in waves ..."

His father had been in the war, Normandy invasion, seen and shared the horrors of the beach landings and beyond through France, German, North Africa, and Palestine. He'd talked about friends and heroes and the alternate on all sides.

Parsons had grown up learning not to tolerate mediocrity, and definitely not *the despicables*, of whom he had come across many.

It wasn't that his father was a bad man—far from it. He was a great man who had taught him so much. Never to give up, never to let go, and always to do the right thing, no matter what.

Parsons went to a military school, then Imperial College to study material science—a subject that bored him, but with patience and determination, he had completed before heading to the Royal Military Academy Sandhurst. After graduation, he joined the Royal Engineers and served three years as a young officer before completing P Company and joining 9 Parachute Squadron RE—that was the last time he was in Belize, jungle survival training.

He rolled out of bed and padded across to the small desk at the window and reached out to his attaché, past his papers, his dossier, and other photos, and pulled out an old black-and-white photograph that reminded him of those times. There he was, in the front row in his combats and with his face painted, cradling his self-loading rifle. Next to him was Harry, his old friend. He tapped on the images of Vince and Tom, both gone now. Then there were the two Macs, the instructors, one gone, one to go. And then their platoon commander, Austin, also now gone.

Parsons wasn't sure if he'd had his fair share of losses or more than most. He suspected the latter. From the time he was a young boy, he'd seen tragedy, and throughout his life. And now, even with those remaining, he felt alone. He remembered the old saying "You enter this life alone, the

3

way you leave it," and he was beginning to understand the wisdom in those words.

After six years, he left the service and transitioned into the world of investment banking, working in London for four years before setting up his own investment firm, placing investments into institutions and eventually investing in some of them himself.

He had built up a nice business and a very nice nest egg indeed. He had purchased his country estate in Surrey twenty years previously, along with most of his other investments, which had flourished too.

He missed his mother. She had passed away nearly five years before, in a nursing home, apparently sprightly one day, then died in her sleep. She was eighty-six, but he hadn't expected her to pass that suddenly. He was too busy with his life and hadn't gotten to say goodbye. He regretted that. He was at the age now that he regretted a lot of things.

With the kids growing older and farther apart, the same was true with his marriage. He hadn't even told Emily his news. It wasn't good. A rare form of cancer—hereditary, according to the specialist. Affects the brain. He stared at the wall thinking why, and then he remembered his grandmother and her sad demise long before he was on the scene.

He had decided months ago that this might be his last endeavor, his swan song. He was ready to hang up his boots, and why not? This way he could do it in style and pay one last homage to his father in the process—ever in the shadow of the man he loved so much and still to this day yearned for his approval.

Like his father, Parsons had grown to be a perfectionist. He wasn't naturally that way; it was the teachings of his father. The older he got, the more steadfast he became in the pursuit of perfection. His career had shown that, and his achievements were the proof—still longing for the long overdue recognition.

"Do you think he ever knew what he was doing, or was it by accident?"

He explored that question in his mind, weighing up the odds of each point of view. Either way, by accident or otherwise, his father had taught him values that had made him to where he was today, and for that, Parsons appreciated him.

His thoughts were rudely interrupted by a commotion dockside, below his window. He jumped up and pulled the Victoriana lace curtain, and there she was, standing proudly before him, the Princess of the Seas, dressed in white, with the flag of Grand Cayman on her stern, polished and gleaming in the morning sun, ready for her journey.

"You are indeed a sight to behold," he whispered as he admired her brilliant bright white hull, her pair of masts fully dressed in her crisp white sheets, the Jack and the crest of the Caymans, with the words "He hath founded it upon the seas."

Her lifeboats and tenders dangled from the sides like decorations, her name proudly emblazoned on her bow: SS *Indigo*.

He smiled to himself as he looked down and averted his gaze to the new arrivals on the quayside.

A water taxi was pulling up with an unlikely array of passengers, including domestic workers coming in from the Cayes for their day's work, as well as a couple of local businessmen in their impossibly hot-looking suits, clinging on to their worn leather briefcases. Then two other passengers who looked distinctly out of place: two men, in their forties, both in blue jeans, desert boots, and burgundy T-shirts, carrying canvas holdalls. It seemed to him that the men were distinctly military in their gait.

"The Parachute Regiment arrives," he whispered.

A Triumph motorbike and sidecar had pulled up onto the quay, a woman driving, a man in the sidecar. After dramatically skidding to a halt, they pulled off their helmets in synchrony right in front where the *Indigo* was majestically poised, waiting for her passengers.

The Para men walked into the front of the hotel. The woman and the man on the classic Triumph each lit up from a packet of Marlboro Reds.

"It's like the scene out of some sort of movie. Like an Agatha Christie movie. But who shall be the Hercule Poirot?" He smiled.

He was talking to himself again. It was a growing habit. He had noticed it increasing in frequency over recent years and even more so in recent months.

This was a gathering of sorts—a different type of gathering. He knew that this one would be distinctly different from his previous experiences.

He recalled his first proper birthday party as a child, his eighth. His mother had invited a dozen or so kids from the school to join him for reception sandwiches, jelly, and ice cream and Battenberg, which was his favorite.

The night before the party, he'd had a nightmare that no one showed up. He was the posh boy at the school, an implant, an outsider, as it was his first year at the school since he and his family had moved.

He recalled staring out the window, looking out at the driveway, looking at his watch, anxious to see whether anyone would turn up. As it happens, they all did, but the anxiousness was so much it turned him off holding parties for most of his adult life, except for when he had to. He felt this was one of those occasions.

Parsons had recently experienced the same intense level of anxiety, and many nightmares, but this time it was different. They all had a reason to be there, his nightmares and the passengers.

His children had grown up and gone off to university in search of their own lives. He and his wife of thirty years had drifted apart.

He had himself, his own thoughts, and the voice of his father that had been with him throughout, cautioning him, steering him, advising him. His father had become noticeably more vocal of late.

Parsons concluded that he still loved Emily as a companion, but they no longer had anything in common. The more time Parsons spent on business trips, in hotels around the world, in airport lounges, hotel lounges, even his own lounge at home, he spent more and more time in his own company and more and more of that time talking to himself, often aloud, and sometimes talking to his father.

He enjoyed his own company. For the most part, he simply found other human beings annoying. Especially those disingenuous, lacking worthiness of trust—of whom there were many—the distasteful, the selfish, the greedy, and the despicables.

Parsons had come to realize that the only people who he really liked were those who had no edge, nothing to prove, contented with their own lives, not for their riches but for their wealth of happiness. He would find these people in the doormen at hotels, the waitresses of the world, old men sitting on street corners smoking pipes, sometimes the homeless.

Often over the years, Parsons in various cities around the world, under the disguise of nightfall, frequently into the early hours, would traipse the streets seeking out such people, engaging with them, talking to them, and often parting with life-changing wads of cash.

He never told anyone of these unsung encounters.

However, he didn't do it for charity. It was as much as his own therapy—the richness of the stories he would hear and the contrast to his own life. He got a buzz from these clandestine activities.

He had concluded over the years that he was a complex character, and that was becoming more evident the older and nearer to the grave he became.

The venue was set. The guests were arriving. He was ready for this.

2

I.

ZACH CARTER HAD ARRIVED EARLIER that week. After his encounter at the No Name Bar, he'd quickly agreed to the opportunity, signed up for the gig, left Amsterdam, and headed west back to Sonoma County for a while to get over his latest would-be bride.

Recharged, he left SFO for Miami and traveled on down to Belize City, where he hung out on San Pedro until it was time to meet his new boss, Captain Bromovich, and join SS *Indigo*.

Zach was tall and handsome, his mustache still intact as he stood on the lower deck in his white pants, linen shirt, and boat shoes. He looked and felt at home.

From the time Zach was a little kid, his father would take him down to Sausalito, and they'd hang out on his dad's Monk McQueen motor yacht, the *Lady of the Bay*, as he'd take the tourists on trips around the bay. Zach would serve as the host and entertainer, pointing out the various points of interest as they sailed as far as the Bay Bridge, past Alcatraz, and skirted the city, the marina, and Crissy Field before heading to the Golden Gate herself, standing diligently like a guardian overlooking the bay, and taking the old dears to lunch, often at either Cavallo Point or Sam's at Tiburon.

The guests were always generous—out-of-towners from across the States and overseas. He liked the Texans and the Japanese as they would tip the most. On their way home in Dad's Ford Bronco, Zach would count their takings and their tips, and his father would call in at the local bar for a drink. Zach would sit and listen to the radio in the Bronco, his father no doubt telling the tales Zach had heard a thousand times of his adventures around the world in pursuit of the next fixation of potential hidden treasures.

As he caught himself back to the *Indigo*, Zach gazed out from the majestic steamship onto the passengers as they assembled on the quayside. He saw the woman on the motorcycle, who had already caught his eye. He wondered who they all were, why they were there, and where they had come from.

For a moment, he thought of his latest dalliance, Eva. They'd met in Virgin Gorda. She was a real estate agent; he was the host. She was touring some wealthy Europeans around the island's top property investments; he was taking them on Jet Ski safaris, sailing, scuba diving. They'd fallen in love—or at least *he had*, he thought to himself and shook his head.

Like the woman on the motorcycle, Eva was tall, athletic, and blonde, and to his disappointment, he found out she was also fiercely independent.

It's not as though he wasn't good with women—he was. As a host, he'd learned to talk to anyone from when he was a kid. He had a rich repertoire of stories and tales and no lack of charm. Only thing was that, on occasion, and mainly in front of beautiful women, he got tongue-tied and tripped over his words and usually made an ass of himself. He shook his head once more thinking about it.

Zach had a knot in his stomach. Deep down, it had been bothering him since his return to the region, and he had pushed it to one side, mind over matter. But his swift departure last he was here preyed on his mind, and although years prior, it still did.

Ever the smiley, optimistic, and hopeful Zach, he knew that everything would work out fine, that he would one day find the right one, move on from the past, and one day settle down, probably back in Sonoma, among the vines and the great food, with a short walk to the town center, a picket fence, a clapboard house, and 2.2 children.

She was out there somewhere. Turned out that Eva just wasn't the right one or at the right time. Besides, his pockets weren't deep enough, but there wasn't much he could do about that. If only his dad had found that lost treasure, things might have been different for Zach, but as with his father, so far, all Zach had done was traverse the world looking for his own type of illusive treasure. Perhaps this trip on the *Indigo* might have been destiny and about to change all that.

He took one last glance over at the quayside and let out a soft wolf whistle under his breath. He smiled and turned to the stern to check on his equipment one more time before joining the guests for the boarding.

II.

Captain Igor Bromovich stood proudly in the pilothouse looking down on his ship. The Princess of the Seas was ready to sail. That morning, each hour, he would go for a walkabout to get closer to the preparations to be sure that everything was just perfect. This was important to him. This was his first trip in longer than he cared to remember, and he was determined that this was just the beginning of his revival and better fortunes.

He stood there with his brand-new tailored uniform, all white, starched, and pressed, his big trimmed mustache and mahogany eyes framed with a peaked cap complete with gold embroidery and a crest of the SS *Indigo* at the front. He had purchased a pair of aviator sunglasses at the Miami duty-free, protecting his eyes from the glare of the morning sun rising from the ocean before him.

He was a very proud man and had now managed to land what had once been just a hope, a dream. He was not only returning to work after way too long, but he was back to where he belonged.

In his right-hand trouser pocket, he clutched at his lucky charm from the naval academy, long worn and rounded but nevertheless always reassuring; it had been his strength over the years.

He looked down at the hustle and bustle on the quayside and the interesting array of passengers. In his hand, he had the passenger list with his research notes on each person— some sketches more complete than others, but none as complete as he would have liked.

From what he had gathered, they were all personal invites from Waring on behalf of Litions. It was a small group, an eclectic assortment of characters, seemingly from all walks of life. Bromovich pondered the scene, still trying to put his finger on what was bothering him with this high-profile, seemingly no-expense-spared excursion, a bunch of strangers who had never met each other joining a luxury cruise across the Caribbean. He shook his head and packed his thoughts away, returning to the job in hand and the $10,000-a-week pay packet.

He had seen Simpson and Sharp arrive, and there was something familiar about them. He had read their profiles and had been racking his brain since.

Many years ago, Bromovich had captained a boat that somehow had got involved in extracting some mystery men just off the coast of Sosnovy Bor, close to Saint Petersburg, whisking them across the Baltic to Finland, close to the town of Kotka, no questions asked. He had no idea to this day what they had been up to, or who they were, but there was something familiar about these two, and he wondered whether fate was that possible.

He shook off the thought with a slight shudder and took a final sip of his warm tea and set off on his last tour of the decks before he would greet his passengers on board.

He wasn't too concerned about the lack of crew—himself as captain, Zach a seemingly well-qualified maritime engineer and seafarer, and the cook and stewardess. After all, it was only a five-hundred-mile sail to Grand Cayman, a thirty-six-hour passage, but taking their time, as instructed, Bromovich had planned the route, including anchoring up in the evenings, and, along with a couple of excursions, planned to arrive in George Town five days later. *Should be plain sailing*, he thought.

He had taken well to Zach, which was saying something for Bromovich, as he wasn't the sort of person who took to anyone swiftly. It was his Eastern European way growing up in the Soviet shadow, but Zach was a cheery, happy-go-lucky sort of guy full of optimism and enthusiasm. Bromovich admired that in people and sometimes wished he had been blessed with the same.

He wasn't so sure about the cook and his girlfriend hostess. They were both a pair of whiners—he'd spotted that almost immediately as they'd joined the ship to stock her up and get ready for her passengers.

He thought of his wife and the kids back home. Tatiana had been with him through thick and thin—they'd both been through a lot—and this was his big break after desperately trying for so long to make ends meet and put food on the table.

He was looking forward to setting sail, captaining his ship, the SS *Indigo*, Princess of the Seas. He finished his solitary thoughts and headed out of the pilothouse for one last tour of the ship before going to greet his passengers.

III.

With her tan riding boots, Lady Helen Bailey strode up and down the quay stretching her legs with a Marlboro Red in her hand. It had been a long and adventurous ride across from Teakettle Village, Belmopan, almost fifty miles to the southwest. She and her travel mate, an Australian named Sal, had left at the crack of dawn to get to the quay and fulfill the request of the letter they had both received weeks earlier.

She was inquisitive by nature, a risk-taker. The letter was short and to the point. A luxury cruise? She was always up for those. It was free, so why not? She looked up Litions— he seemed legit—but then again, she didn't look too hard. An investment opportunity, maybe. But her friend Sal was invited too. Why the hell not? It had never really crossed her mind why.

Lady Helen Bailey was a lady of sorts. Along with the inheritance from her father and the land above the village, she had also inherited a small piece of land in Scotland that came with the title. It was a scrappy plot in the highland town of Tong with not much use beyond grazing sheep, but she liked the title. It suited her bright, airy, and carefree attitude.

She'd been on many adventures for someone of her age. At just thirty-six, she had had her fair share—in Africa, traversed the Silk Route, and from Perth to Sydney all on her

Triumph Thunderbird with sidecar intact. It was in Australia she had met Sal.

James "Sal" Salmond was from outside Sydney, the Central Coast, the industrial port town of Newcastle—his mother came from a fourth-generation farming family and his father from a mining family. They married their fortunes together, and Sal was the result. In his late thirties, he had never worked a day in his life, just jaunted around the world from one free invitation to another. He had received the letter from Waring a month or so back and was not surprised that his old friend Lady Helen had also received an identical invite, so that made the decision to travel to Belize a lot easier—not that he would have declined anyway.

They had been in-country a week already and taken some time to take in the sights that Belize had to offer. And indeed there were many—from the deep, rich sprawling jungle to the coastline and to the stunning Cayes beyond. But even for Sal, the Australian, the grizzly bugs, mosquitoes, spiders, and snakes were a bit of an overkill.

Lady Helen made the arrangements for her beloved Triumph to be taken aboard and stowed carefully. They grabbed their small leather bags and headed to the hotel lobby for a well-earned breakfast and to freshen up before boarding.

They noticed the two now familiar military-looking men in the breakfast room. She had seen them before on their travels in Punta Gorda and San Ignacio and on Caye Caulker.

The two nodded in their direction as they walked in, recognition and acknowledgment of their presence. Lady Helen Bailey, in her usual exuberant way, bellowed her best "Good morning, gentlemen!" and let out a big smile, catching the two men by surprise. They averted their gazes to the plates of English breakfast before them—a reminder of the colonial history of the hotel and the city.

IV.

Belowdecks in the galley, Perry was in his chef's whites working away on the first luncheon of the cruise: a chilled spring-pea-and-mint soup as a refresher; then Crab Louie with grapefruit, mandarin, and shaved white truffle, topped with Russian Osetra Golden caviar; followed by a poulet printanier.

He was in his element—an unlimited budget to delight his twelve passengers.

Perry may have been rough around the edges, but one thing he did know was how to cook, and he took great pride in doing so.

Kayla was busy readying the champagne cocktails for the welcome: Dom Perignon P3 Brut and its Rose cousin, with a choice of additions, including fresh peach puree, freshly squeezed orange, or crème de cassis for a Kir Royale.

They'd both arrived a week earlier in time to receive the ship provisions. Perry had chosen the best that the world had to offer, including an abundance of local fruits and vegetables that arrived the morning of departure.

They had been nervously excited as they left Gatwick bound for Miami. In their matching tracksuits and Nikes, they had gone through their newly acquired Lonely Planet guide, Kayla turning her already upturned nose up at the thought of the heat and the bugs—but she relished the thought of the white sand beaches.

"Perry, do yer think we'll be getting any downtime to spend on the beach?" she asked in her high-pitched, whiny voice that grated at Perry's bones. "Perry?"

He looked at her and shrugged. "We're going there for work, Kayla, not a bloody holiday. We'll have plenty of time for that after, when we get to Benidorm."

His cigarette hung out the corner of his mouth as they crammed into the smoking cabin inside the terminal. She looked back at him and rolled her eyes in disappointment. He reminded her of their balcony view at their favorite resort on the Spanish Mediterranean. He also reminded her of the new kitchen and much-needed bathroom he'd ordered too.

"Perry, why don't we just save our cash, sell up, and go somewhere else? Perry?"

She had a habit of using his name in every question she posed, and it annoyed the hell out of Perry. This time he just completely ignored her.

V.

At 10:00 a.m., the horn of the SS *Indigo* sounded, the signal for the passengers to make their way on board. Simultaneously, the sound of a string quartet could be heard up and down the quay, heralding these very special guests onto the *Indigo*. Zach was waiting at the top of the slightly inclined wooden ramp onto the ship, waiting to meet the guests.

One by one, the passengers boarded. To the right was the group of musicians playing the distinctive "The Arrival of the Queen of Sheba" by Handel.

The sight, the sound, and the majesty attracted more than just the passengers. A crowd of locals, dignitaries, and tourists quickly gathered along the quayside to witness the pomp and circumstance on display.

At the top of the ramp, Kayla, dressed in her newly starched white shirt and a black pencil skirt, was seeing to the welcome cocktails when Dr. Bronwyn Brown insisted on her usual tipple.

"I'm sorry, Dr. Brown. We don't have any lime cordial on board."

Much to Dr. Brown's obvious disapproval.

Zach stepped in and with his warm Californian smile suggested that they could get some from the hotel bar before they set sail, pointing at the St. George's Bar across the way, trying to appease what he thought was a difficult customer to get any sort of smile on her face. She reminded him of the annual Women's Guild tours he and his father would host back in Sausalito—it had become a sport for him over the years to see whether he could make the women smile and increase the pair's measly tip each year.

Dr. Brown just took a glass of the Dom Perignon without saying a word. The shake of her head was sufficient to prompt Zach to make sure that Kayla picked up a bottle of Rose's lime cordial before they set sail. He knew it to be an old favorite of the Women's Guild, and he automatically placed Dr. Brown in that same bracket.

He noted that the doctor was completely overdressed, in more of an outfit she would wear at the annual Victoria sponge baking competition at the village show, rather than one for a Caribbean cruise. Her handbag, a sort of satchel, was over her shoulder, her glass in her hand, and her straw hat shading her bloodshot eyes from the equatorial sun.

"Funny old cow," Kayla whispered under her breath just loud enough to hear.

Zach shot her a stare and a smile at the same time.

Kayla averted her gaze and went on to greet her next guests, Lady Helen and Sal.

Zach stepped up. "Welcome aboard, Lady Helen. May we interest you in a refreshment?" He pointed to Kayla and let out a big, warm, hostest-with-the-mostest kind of smile. From a distance, he'd not been wrong—close up, she was stunning—and Zach could feel his normal paralysis of tongue and brain come on, so he quickly moved on to Sal, right behind her.

As Dr. Brown flashed a glare toward Kayla unnoticed, Lady Helen Bailey and her Australian friend Sal were much warmer—not that that was difficult—full of smiles, *thank yous*, and *fair dinkums*.

Zach watched on, noting Lady Helen Bailey's air of confidence and the almost regal manner in which she sailed through the reception and floated like a breeze around the assembling passengers. Zach had to pinch himself, reminding himself when he had first met with Eva. "What the hell is wrong with you, Carter?" he whispered to himself.

One by one, the passengers boarded, gathered their drinks, and soaked in the music, cautiously observing one another until the last two of the passengers boarded, Keith Simpson and Tony Sharp. Both men were now in a change of clothes, still a uniform of sorts: beige chinos, polished Church's brogues, blue blazers with brass buttons, and Thomas Pink double-cuffed shirts—one pink check, the other blue—each with a color-coordinated silk square in his top pocket.

"Very dapper boys." Lady Helen winked and smiled at the pair. She had a way of disarming even the strongest characters, which these men clearly were. She was young, tall, slim, beautiful, and very charming indeed.

Both men were in their forties, with short cropped hair— military grade 1 on the sides—and the kind of leathery skin that had been in hot and cold climes. They had the air of a pair who had seen the rougher side of life in their times. Both were ex–2 Para. One had gone on to Scotland Yard, where he made detective inspector, and the other stayed on and made it to squadron sergeant major of D Squadron, 22 Special Air Service.

They each took a glass of the Dom Perignon Brut Sec, bowed, and raised their glasses to Kayla and Lady Helen, quietly gathering at the back of the group next to, and in stark contrast to, the not-so-sprightly figure of Quentin Perkins lurking at the back of the group, disengaged, nervous, and looking even more out of place than the rest.

As Zach mingled, he spotted Angela Chalmers, ever the socialite, clearly used to mixing among strangers in crowds and business meetings. She'd quickly latched on to Stuart

Jacobs—*birds of a feather flock together*, he thought—and they were each making their introductions and reiterating their own self-importance to their new acquaintance.

"So, Ms. Chalmers, how's business?"

This was obviously Jacob's standard opening question, which Zach interpreted as really meaning "Tell me about yourself," but more subtle.

Thing is, Zach had been in these types of situations for years, ever since he was a kid. In Sonoma, he'd also worked in bars, including the Bounty Hunter in downtown Napa, where he'd met all sorts of characters, from the local farmers, ranchers, and growers to the rich and famous and Silicon Valley's *finest*. Jacobs reminded him of the latter.

He'd seen it all before, the modus operandi of an opening salvo that left the recipient assuming that he'd done at least some homework—which he probably had, to an extent—giving them an opportunity to talk about a subject in the third party, about their business, and not necessarily about themselves.

Chalmers was different from most, however. She clearly had no hesitation professing her own self-importance or talking about herself. Jacobs looked impatient as he listened, obviously awaiting the "And what about you?" which eventually came, clearly to Jacob's delight—it was his turn to talk about himself.

"Well, I was at the consulate general's regular soiree, and I received an email from Litions inviting me to this jaunt."

Chalmers nodded, acknowledging the similarities of their invitations.

He rattled off the list from his résumé of various leadership positions, his wealth building from his various stock acquisitions, and explained how the British Airways first class was not a match for Emirates, where he was a lifelong Platinum member.

Chalmers was nodding politely—obviously feigning her engagement, Zach surmised—her eyes dancing around the other passengers, targeting who she would latch on to next. It was clear that she was already bored with Jacobs.

"I'm an American Airlines gal myself. Last year, I flew over one hundred thousand and made ConciergeKey." She winked and raised her glass.

Jacobs returned the wink and smiled. "Did you, by golly?" he said, looking momentarily deflated, temporarily outdone by the Florida woman. "I'm currently using ExecAir for my travel," he said and beamed, referring to the fractional Gulfstream jet fleet operating out of San Francisco.

Chalmers couldn't beat that as she looked for someone else to engage with.

It was these levels of social observance and interpretation that often shocked Zach. He found it almost comedic, but he also saw a more sinister side to it too. These types of people, like Jacobs and Chalmers, only engaged with people to see what was in it for themselves. He found that hard to understand. Throughout his life, he'd grown up to be curious, genuinely interested in other people and their stories, not for gain but in a way as a self-education. He wanted to understand more about the world, others' perspectives. That was important to Zach. That made him a good listener, and in turn, that's what people liked about him—he listened and most of the time cared too.

Zach had no issues hobnobbing with anyone, apart from when it came down to good-looking women. It wasn't even that—it was more defined. It was women he was attracted to and about whom he somehow automatically thought, *Is this the one?* Ridiculous. It's not as though he was a teenager; he was thirty-four, had traveled the world, and was socially adept. And yet this was his Achilles' heel.

He shook his head at himself again as he found his gaze wandering in the direction of the soft British accent he guessed from somewhere up north—a soft and well-spoken Yorkshire, he concluded.

Sheldon stood alone, tall, gangly, and obviously awkward, looking down at his glass of champagne. He muttered to himself too loudly, "Fucking froggy shite. Anything proper to drink on this tugboat?"

Everyone could hear, and all turned to look over. He'd obviously tried to dress up for the occasion, wearing a pair of crumpled chinos; a Marks & Spencer button-down shirt, probably that his wife had bought him for the trip, Zach guessed; a beige box jacket, probably from ASDA, that barely fit him; and a pair of brown leather dealer boots. He looked like one of the ranchers in the Bounty Hunter bar.

Sheldon looked around the audience nervously as he clearly tried hard to assimilate. He obviously wasn't used to this level of social engagement down at his local, the Bingley Arms.

All the guests had heard Sheldon's blast, but it was Lady Helen and Sal who sniggered aloud.

Zach was enjoying the comedy around this clearly dysfunctional group. The faux priest, the faux doctor. The whining Australian businessman, Bland; the snobbery of Chalmers and Jacobs; and the stewardess Kayla's apparent distaste.

Lady Helen and Sal were clearly having a church moment—one of those moments when you shouldn't laugh but can't help it.

Paul Bland was adorned in Amani with his big gold Bulgari watch and his Gucci man bag and had navigated his way over to Sheldon to make conversation. You could have mistaken him for a nouveau riche Russian. In fact, he wasn't much better: Bland was a nouveau riche Okker.

Bland and Sheldon greeted each other, and having got the pleasantries out of the way, they stood in contrast to each other, Sheldon tall and gangly, looking like a schoolboy on a field trip, and Bland short, round, and dressed to the nines. Their brashness was in contrast to the rest of the passengers, and that was their starting point.

"So, what brings you here, Bruce?" Sheldon asked, using the ubiquitous nickname that most Australians loathed.

Bland went through the invitation, his thought process about joining the ship, his international jaunts and adventures, and his own self-importance, explaining how he ran the facilities services business for the mining industry of Australia and beyond.

With Sheldon's background in plumbing and property maintenance back in Yorkshire, the men established at least some basis of common ground.

"The problem with the bloody Californians is that they're too polite, to be honest. It gets in the way of them telling the truth," Sheldon said, looking Bland in the eye with his menacing tone and demeanor as if Bland himself were one of the wine country property dealers in Sonoma County who had apparently ripped Sheldon off.

Moving on from the awkward conversation of Sheldon's woes north of the border, Bland switched gears. "So, how do you know Litions?" he asked, looking around at the other passengers.

Sheldon didn't reveal the nature of his invitation. He skirted the question. "I don't, really. How about you?"

Bland went into an onslaught, saying that, when invited to such an event, he expected at the very least the host would be in attendance, embarking on a "Where the hell is Litions?" rant for all to hear.

VI.

Zach stood next to Bromovich for the formal welcome as they gave their introductions to the passengers.

Zach was the official tour guide. He liked that role, one he'd played many times, but looking at this crowd, he was skeptical that it would be as much fun as it had been in the past.

By this time, he'd got a gin and tonic in his hand, "purely for medicinal purposes" and to keep up with tradition. He had checked and thanked God when he found out that they were stocked up on board with Plymouth Gin and Schweppes, his staples.

"Lemon, not lime, young lady," he said to Kayla as she gave him what was a very generous pour. Zach winked and smiled.

Why couldn't he be more like that with all the girls? he thought.

Zach held court with the group of passengers, explaining the traditions of gin and tonic and that it was always six o'clock somewhere in the world, raising his glass with a big beam. He related that the drink had been invented by the British Army in colonial India as an alternative to drinking the local putrid water, and as a cocktail that apparently protected the men against malaria, with the combination of juniper berries, quinine, and lemon juice.

By this time, Kayla had found Sheldon a beer of his liking while Zach continued his lecture, talking about how the empire had developed IPA for the other ranks, a hop- and alcohol-heavy form of beer that lasted the sail to Indian shores and also acted as an alternative to the local water.

Sheldon looked down at his boots, having been pigeonholed as a mere foot soldier; Jacobs rolled his eyes at the trivia he had heard a thousand times before; and Perkins, still detached at the back of the group, was red-cheeked and visibly perspiring in his black suit, his white collar looking like a noose around his neck about to cut off what remaining blood flow there was to his brain.

The string quartet continued with Brahms's String Quartet in C Minor as Parsons made his rounds, politely introducing himself, shaking hands, exchanging small talk on guests' various journeys to Belize, the weather, how beautiful the ship was—he found himself talking through her history and the incredible detail that the owners had undertaken in her refurbishment, with his photographic memory and eye for detail on full display.

He listened to the music, one of his favorites, marveling at how somehow the instruments played in conflict with one another, showed the struggle among them, the sadness, yet the size of the moment, the tension between the musicians' parts. What better backdrop to this scene on the SS *Indigo*, he thought and smiled, the moment lost on most of the audience before him, but not Parsons, or Lady Helen Bailey, who recognized the tune from long ago.

"Well, the suites themselves are quite a thing," he started as the individual conversations quickly subsided and everyone seemed to have an interest in what he had to say.

"Horace Dodge was the original owner of the *Indigo*, and I believe that's where Mr. Jacobs will be staying, in the Horace Dodge Suite."

Jacobs raised his glass and offered a silent thank-you.

"Then we have Ms. Chalmers in the delightful Marilyn Monroe Suite. Lady Helen Bailey is in the Vettriano Suite, an homage to Scotland's greatest living artist."

"He's the one that painted the butler on the beach," Sal whispered in Helen's ear.

"Then, Mr. Simpson and Mr. Sharp, I believe you are in the MacArthur and Churchill Suites."

The two former military men seemed happy with that.

"Captain, do you want to take us through the rest of the accommodations allocation?"

Standing straight like a guard on parade, Bromovich cleared his throat and lifted the clipboard in his hand. "Of course, Sir Parsons," he said and looked around the gathered audience. Then he leafed through the boarding instructions.

"Mr. Parsons, you are in the Dauntless." Bromovich nodded, seeking acknowledgment, and Parsons raised his glass, signaling for him to continue.

"Mr. Zach Carter here is in the Liddesdale Suite; Mr. Salmond in the Monaco; Dr. Brown, you are in the Marie Curie; Father Perkins in the Oscar Wilde ..."

Perkins shuffled his feet and looked down at his shoes.

As Bromovich continued, Parsons observed each reaction.

"Mr. Bland, you're in the Delphine, and, finally, Mr. Sheldon, you are in the 1921 Suite."

"What the bloody hell does 1921 mean?" Sheldon demanded accusingly.

The other passengers turned to look at him, then back toward Bromovich. Parsons stood next to him.

Parsons cleared his throat. "That was when the *Indigo* was commissioned by Horace Dodge, built by the Great Lakes Engineering Works, and then she was launched in the year of 1921."

Sheldon blushed with embarrassment for asking.

"Anyway, never mind that," Bland said. "Where the bloody hell is Jemol Litions?"

3

I.
The Previous Evening

SITTING IN THE CORNER OF the St. George's Bar, Sir James Parsons, chairman of Watershed Investments, puffed on his cigar and ran his eye through the latest *Financial Times*, keeping a close watch on his stock portfolio and the performance of his various companies and investments. It was just a ritual of habit by now. He had spent a lifetime watching his investments and spotting opportunities like a hawk.

His now gray hair was flicked over to one side, revealing his vanity and the memory of his youth. Dressed in his linen Rhodes Wood suit, leather boat shoes, and red-and-blue-striped Polo Ralph Lauren shirt, his panama hat on the mahogany table in front of him, Parsons sat in the carefully chosen most secluded corner of the bar.

He laid the pink newspaper down in front of him and gazed out of the window at the old colonial city and its harbor, and he wrinkled his face at the humidity even at this time of night. His piercing steel-blue-gray eyes glanced at his Patek Philippe timepiece: 9:00 p.m. Belizean time. It had been a long flight from London via Dallas–Fort Worth and into Belize International. Thankfully, he had stopped in overnight to see an old friend, Harry, which broke up the trip nicely.

It was good to see Harry, although the man was a shadow of his former self. Not the same as when they had met all those years ago just down the road in the jungles of Belize. Parsons reflected on the long late lunch at the Adolphus, their conversation, the bottle of Chateau Palmer from his personal cellar—a sign of times past—the hesitation to pay the bill. Of course, Parsons stepped in. He knew that Harry wasn't in a good place, and in fact, he also knew that he wasn't either.

Parsons had gotten in that afternoon and headed straight to the hotel.

He went over in his mind the labor of love that was the SS *Indigo*: launched in 1921, back then $2 million, she was one of the largest and most expensive steamships of the time, built by the Great Lakes Engineering Works.

She had originally been powered by three Babcock & Wilcox boilers producing 1,500 horsepower to its quadruple expansion engines. After her refurbishment, these had been replaced with more modern, even more powerful equivalents to propel her 1961 tonnage, 258 feet, and 35-foot beam at a cruising speed of 12 knots.

She'd had an interesting history. The SS *Indigo* had caught fire and sunk in New York in '26, to be recovered and restored. In 1940, she suffered damage as she ran aground in the Great Lakes, and then she was acquired by the US Navy in 1942. After World War II, she was retired back to civilian life and restored to her former glory, then changed hands several times before landing in the hands of Litions Industries.

The Lloyd's Register cataloged that the then weary steamship was transferred in ownership at a sale price of $5 million. At the time, it had certainly raised some eyebrows in the boating community of who would pay such a huge amount of money for such an antiquated ship, never mind investing a further $60 million in its refurbishment.

The SS *Indigo* was now registered to Litions Industries and the secretive billionaire for his leisure, entertainment, and business.

He fumbled around in his attaché case, passing by the oncology report, and pulled out a printed copy of an email.

I am writing on behalf of Litions Industries, of which you may have heard.

We would like to cordially invite you to a small group of select passengers to join the SS *Indigo* in Belize City, departing July 16, taking in the sights of the Caribbean. During this time, you will have the opportunity to learn of a world-changing opportunity, in which your interest and involvement would be greatly appreciated.

We are certain this will be of a high level of interest to you.

Please RSVP, and we look forward to welcoming you on board the SS *Indigo*.

Sincerely,

Mr. N. Waring
Litions Industries

Of course people had heard of Litions—who hadn't? Parsons knew more about it than most.

There were many rumors—several holding companies hidden in deep, dark places with a web of legends of mysterious and well-shrouded investments. These included Yahoo, Google, the more established Apple and Microsoft, and wild bets, such as in the upstart electric car company Tesla run by some tearaway from South Africa, but also in more mysterious places, like the burgeoning cannabis industry, links to the oil fields of Russia, gold and diamond mines of Africa, Mexican retail operations, government, military contractors, and far beyond.

Litions Industries had many fingers in many pies.

Parsons had played this thing over in his mind repeatedly.

He had made his money and enjoyed his life, for the most part. He was satisfied that he had set his family up for life and many generations to come. Along with the liquid assets he had accumulated and distributed through his will, he had the house in Surrey and had had a portrait of himself commissioned that now sat above the fireplace in the main lounge.

He smiled to himself, thinking about how he would be ever present, looking down at his children, grandchildren, and their children's children to come. It was like something out of an old *Tales of the Unexpected* from years gone by. He found that highly amusing.

The whole notion of this trip was just too much of a temptation, and he had reached the conclusion, and that was his decision, his final decision—and Parsons always stuck to the decisions he made, no matter how sometimes difficult or unpopular they may be.

He could hear the distinctive Yorkshire voice that he had heard at the back of the BA first-class cabin on the way down from Dallas. Parsons glanced over the room. The tall, gangly, balding, brash, and loud Yorkshireman was sat at the bar with a glass emblazoned with Belikin Beer in front of him, talking and gesticulating at the barman.

Parsons knew exactly who the man was.

"Yer see, the thing is, where I come from is that yer bloody well know where yer stand. What yer see it was yer get. Not like some of them bloody hippies in California."

It was by now an old story. Parsons, and the rest of the first-class cabin, had heard his rants throughout the flight from Dallas about how a California wine property deal had gone south. He was apparently content to share his business with anyone who would listen—the air stewardess, his fellow passengers, and now the barman, no doubt the taxi driver from the airport too, or anyone else in earshot, for that matter.

Parsons observed the lanky six-two man in his fifties, with his puffer jacket, jeans, and what looked like construction boots. He was one of those types who you kept a safe distance from. Loud, brash, opinionated. The Yorkshireman had an intimidating look about him. Parsons was keen not to hold eye contact, and certainly not engage. He was simply not his type, and Parsons wanted to keep it that way. He had made it a lifetime habit to avoid unwanted acquaintances, and he wasn't about to change that best practice.

"Fucking moron," he whispered under his breath.

Parsons pulled out the dossier from his old attaché. He knew the Yorkshireman was Andrew Sheldon, and he probably knew more about the man than he probably did himself as he listened to his rants from the other side of the room.

Parsons pointed his finger at the photographs of the passengers as he reread each of their stories. He had done this many times now. He wasn't sure why. He had what many had described as a photographic memory. Not that long ago, he could remember details about almost anything, he could recite dozens of poems and quotations, and he didn't need to read things a second time. But this document he kept getting drawn back to.

He looked down the dossier. Dr. Bronwyn Brown. He stared at the mug shot–like photo of her. Of Simpson and Sharp in military uniform somewhere hot and dusty. Bland from an article in the *Sydney Morning Herald*. Chalmers from her online résumé. Then there was Lady Helen Bailey. He paused, settling his index finger on her face. Then he tapped slowly as he gazed back out the window at the harbor lights.

Henry, the barman, according to his proudly adorned name badge, just politely nodded and apart from his cheek-to-cheek smile was left with a blank expression, with no realization whatsoever what the Yorkshireman was speaking of. Sheldon had no filter at all and waffled on about his various business interests, mainly a landlord to hairdressers and a plumbing supply business, and he was a self-confessed intimidator of his tenants if they didn't pay their rent on time, or if they didn't rise to his whims, of which apparently he had many.

Parsons took another double puff of his cigar and carefully refolded the papers back into his attaché.

They would be boarding the *Indigo* in the morning. He would get a good night's sleep, his usual eight hours; get through the jet lag, and be bright-eyed and bushy-tailed in the morning. He wanted to have his wits about him. His survival instincts were in overdrive, reminding him of his last time in Belize, jungle training as a young subaltern with the Royal Engineers, and his old friend Harry.

Upon that thought, Sir James Parsons retired quietly to his room, leaving the Yorkshireman at the bar with his captive audience of one.

II.
San Francisco, Weeks Earlier

That evening at the consulate general's had been a pleasant occasion as usual. Drinks, canapés, and a gathering of expats and dignitaries from the latest UKTI trade mission promoting transatlantic connections and commerce.

The consulate general himself was waxing lyrical about the strength of the connection and collaboration. The mission tonight was a delegation of tech entrepreneurs and investors from Wales.

Jacobs was a regular invitee, former chairman of the local chamber of commerce, involved for more than twenty years, and now part of the furniture.

One of his many claims to fame was how he had been appointed to the voluntary organization to effect the removal of one of the founders and long-term leaders. That is what Jacobs had done multiple times during his career and life— remove people out of his way—and it was something that he had come to enjoy and perfect as a master Machiavellian.

He especially enjoyed the receptions at the CG's home. The bite-size treats were always delicious and usually included his favorite, miniature fish-'n'-chips served in an ice cream–size newspaper cone. It reminded him of the home he had left many decades earlier.

He ordered the taxi and headed toward home but figured he'd have maybe a couple of drinks before bed. He had arranged to meet some of his regulars at his favorite, the Fly Trap, within an easy stumble of his apartment a couple of blocks away, close to the ballpark.

Sat in the back of the yellow cab, he pulled out the envelope that had been passed to him earlier that evening by his office manager. He looked at the typed envelope and noticed the postal mark, Washington, DC, and an imprint of the White House behind. Maybe this was the letter he had been waiting for all these years. Finally, recognition for his efforts in transatlantic relations. He had set his heart on a Queen's Honors List mention, but in the absence of that so far, a call to Capitol Hill would be equally gratifying.

He also recognized the mailing address, right in the center of DC and close to the corridors of power he so yearned for.

Preparing to read, he put on his half-moon spectacles, and then he carefully opened the sealed envelope and let its contents slide out.

The cab passed through the flashing lights of the city as Jacobs focused on the type on the page. He read it once, then reread. A potential global investment opportunity with strong cross-Atlantic ties—maybe, just maybe, this was his ticket after all.

He didn't know too much about the sender, but he had certainly heard of them, and their reputation certainly preceded them. Why wouldn't he? was the question rattling around his mind as he looked out the rear side window at the traffic flashing by in the opposite direction, the lights almost hypnotic.

"Sir! Sir! Excuse me, sir. We are here, the Fly Trap," the driver—a New York transplant, Jacobs guessed—called from the front.

"Yes, yes, of course. Sorry, old boy." Jacobs reached to the inside pocket of his beige suit jacket, grabbed his wallet, and handed over two twenties.

"Do you want change, sir?" The driver looked at the meter showing twenty-five dollars.

An old trick—embarrass the customer into saying, "No, keep the change," and that was not the response this driver got from his passenger tonight.

Jacobs stuffed the full fifteen dollars in change back in his wallet; jumped out of the taxi, fleeing the driver's disgruntled murmurings; and headed into the bar.

To the right of the entrance was his usual tall table, reserved, sufficient to seat ten.

The table was almost full already, with one space remaining. He was the only one of the group with the honor of being invited to such elevated and prestigious soirees at the consulate general's. Jacobs knew that, and he rubbed it in every chance he got to elevate his own standing in his world. Stuart Jacobs was a very important man, and he let everyone around him know how important.

Although he exuded the air of an air chief marshal, Jacobs was a former flight sergeant in the Royal Air Force, an aircraft communications engineer serving nowhere with any form of danger attached to it whatsoever. He had left after ten years and started a hard slog to the top of his tree, not caring who he trod on along the way. First in sales, UK, then Europe, then a handful of C-suite jobs culminating in the CEO role at a French software company, before he was cashed out and, in most recent years, in pursuit of his MBE.

Cindy, the waitress, greeted him with her usual bright smile and flash of cleavage and tattoos. Jacobs was in his midsixties, but that didn't stop him from letching at the younger women. The waitress was in her late thirties, married, but he didn't care, and neither did she.

Jacobs liked to splash the money around when people were watching, and in exchange for the VIP treatment and perks, he would kitty together with his crowd, bullying them into at least a forty- or sixty-dollar tip each. This meant that each time Jacobs went in, Cindy walked away with a tip haul from anywhere between $400 and some nights up to $1,000. It was a form of low-level prostitution, absent of sex, but sufficiently gratifying for both of them to be part of the transaction. Jacobs took every opportunity to get his monies worth every time Cindy came near, and she obliged with a silent smile.

Jacobs's crew was a collection of former employees, software engineers, subordinates, admins, and former secretaries, including a couple of old flings. Every one of them he had something on, some secret, indiscretion, or major favor. They all in some way or another owed him. He knew that, and so did they. As in a harem, he strutted around, fluffing his feathers, tending his flock, and feeding his own oversize ego in the process.

Tonight, though, the letter was never far from his mind as he beamed from ear to ear. He sensed that this could be the big one. And so did Cindy as she tolerated Jacobs's roaming hands and accepted the collective $1,000 tip.

III.
Philadelphia

Angela Chalmers sat in the window booth of the restaurant at Loews Hotel, Market Street. Outside, the jungle went about its usual evening routine—a nightly performance of police cars, flashing lights, sirens, news of another shooting, yet another mugging, violence in the street. In fact, just another typical night in downtown Philadelphia.

It was a far cry from Chalmers's roots, a beach girl from Florida made good. She had joined Coca-Cola straight from university and had transcended through what was predominantly a man's world using her charms—her skills of cunning and bending the truth, as well as an unwavering vindictiveness should anyone decide to cross her, also reserved for people she just didn't like.

Her reputation in her current company preceded her, but someone far above in the tower strangely appreciated her style. At least she kept getting promoted, and the more she did, the more she became emboldened and justified in her own actions.

Thing is, she knew that to succeed in a man's world, she had to be twice as ruthless, twice and cunning, and willing to go to almost any lengths to get to her end game and use all her available assets. For Chalmers, it was all about her and her own goals—me, myself, and I, or Memyi, as her coworkers would call her behind her back.

Tonight, although her team was in town, she had opted for a more strategic meeting with one of her coconspirators, a regional vice president in the business. Equally mediocre at getting the job done, but also equally cunning, ruthless, and vindictive, both focused on their own careers, bonuses, and growing pension pots, regardless of anyone or anything else. Chalmers didn't care about what collateral damage she caused; it was all absolutely 100 percent all about her.

As she sat there waiting for Matt, she received an email on her phone, an invitation, from an apparent former executive at Coca-Cola, Neil Waring. She vaguely remembered the name as that of a mover and a shaker, but she had never met him back then—he was far too elevated at that time. But she took pride in the fact that he was extending an invite to her to join the SS *Indigo*. She would check with Jason back at home, but in her mind, there was no doubt. She was not one to look a gift horse in the mouth and turn down opportunities. She had racked up plenty of air miles traversing the country on the company dime, and she could easily get down to Belize business class on her accumulated points.

As Matt walked past the window, she flurried her fingers and typed, "Of course I would be delighted to join the group. Thanks for thinking of me. I will be there on July 16." She finished the email and hit Send.

Of course she would like to steer the investors and take a cut as the invitation had described. That's what she did. She was a master manipulator, after all.

"Good evening, Matt. How are you, darling?"

She smiled and embraced her colleague, consciously allowing her bosom to contact Matt's chest. She saw him blush slightly, and she smiled at him and to herself. Chalmers liked to be in control and for the most part of her life was.

"So, Matt, what are we going to do about that pest Martin Baker?" She grinned her cold, heartless assassin smile she had perfected over the years.

"But how are we going to do this without Frank's buy-in? You know he's a big fan," Matt protested.

"Don't worry about Frank. I have that covered," she said, maintaining the smile on her face like a mask.

Over the past couple of years, she had engineered the dispatch of several key players in the business. She had made it her early priority to get close to the COO and the president of the business and had won them over as a trusted adviser. And that in place, she fully leveraged it—and always to her own advantage.

The pair sat down to hatch their plan of the demise of their latest chosen victim. Chalmers willingly and naturally took the lead. She was an expert in this field, dispatching people.

IV.
London

Quentin Perkins sat at his antique mahogany desk in his Georgian house overlooking Fairholt Street, Knightsbridge, London. He was on the phone, an art auction bidding call. He liked his art, and especially this type of art.

Perkins wore his signature white collar, and although having never become a practicing priest, after leaving Eton, he went on to St. Mary's College to take the cloth before things got in the way of that career option.

From his home office, he gazed out of the window to the street and the shoppers and the tourists below with their Harrods bags full of things they likely couldn't afford, or, if they could, why shop at Harrods anyway?

When his father, a merchant banker, had died, he left the house to Perkins, then in his twenties. That was nearly forty years ago now. Since then, he had upgraded the town house but was careful to maintain its historical charm. In addition to the upgrades, he had added a cinema, a pool and a Jacuzzi, an elevator to all floors, and built up a collection of art unique to his taste.

He sat patiently as the auctioneer went through the lots. He had a one-way live video feed to the auction room and knew that his lot, 514, was just a few lots away. He took a sip of his Earl Grey tea as he leafed through the Christie's catalog until he came to the earmarked lot.

From an Austrian estate, the series of three life-size paintings was the work of a father who had painted his children with their blonde hair, the two girls in braids and pigtails, the boy with a short crop and blue eyes, and all with shorts on, and had set the Austrian Alps in the background. In one of the oil-on-canvas paintings, the three children were sat on a wooden fence; in another, in a glade in traditional lederhosen; and in the third, stood poolside by a cabana with swimming outfits on. In all the paintings, the children were wearing red lace-up shoes.

The estimated value was £75,000. High, he thought, for the quality of the art but underpriced, he knew, for the content. His heart started to race as lot 513 flurried through its crescendo and the auctioneer's hammer came down with a bang. It had gone for £5,000 more than estimate. That had been a trend so far that day.

This was it, the moment, the time for the kill, the opportunity to get what he wanted and desired. Thanks to his father's investments, Perkins usually got what he wanted.

He listened intently as the auctioneer described the lot and monitored intently the number of phone bidders as they joined, six—probably some dealers and probably some directs like Perkins. Nothing unusual. For some, this genre was very niche, and many people prepared to pay plenty to add to their collections, much like Perkins.

"So, we start this lot off at seventy thousand pounds … fifty … forty … thirty. What about twenty-five thousand pounds to start the bidding? Any bidders?"

A hand went up from one of the telephone auctioneers in the room.

"Twenty-five thousand pounds I have," the auctioneer said, looking around the room. Then he pointed his gavel. "Twenty-six I have. Twenty-seven in the corner. Twenty-eight with the gentleman in the hat."

Perkins was paused, ready for the kill. He knew from experience it was far better than fueling the bidding to back off completely, to let that take its course and come in with the killer bid when it was almost over. Great in theory, but he knew there would be a lot of interest among his fraternity for these oil paintings.

The bidding continued.

Perkins was on the edge of his seat, enjoying the excitement of the moment, the adrenaline rushing through his veins. He liked these moments. It was these sensations that he lived for, and those he chose over fully taking the cloth all those years earlier.

"Going once"—the auctioneer paused for a microsecond—"going twice." He paused a bit longer and then nodded at one of the phone operators. "We have seventy thousand pounds on the phone."

He once again nodded in the direction of the operators and the anonymous phone bidders as it started up again like a resurgent wave.

"Eighty bid, eight-five bid, ninety-thousand-pounds bid on the phone." He pointed his gavel in their direction.

Perkins felt a discomfort below.

"Ninety-five bid, one-hundred-thousand-pounds bid."

Perkins could sense the tension in the air in the auction room, more than two hundred miles from his office. He remained silent.

"Back in the room at one hundred and five thousand pounds."

Perkins assumed the mysterious man in the hat.

The flurry of phone bids kicked in again, taking the number up to an astonishing £125,000. Bidding was slowing right down now. The man in the hat was clearly above his limit, and Perkins calculated that there were just two left in the race, one more keen and with deeper pockets than the other. *A private collector*, Perkins thought, nodding slowly.

"OK, at one hundred and twenty-five thousand pounds," the auctioneer called. "Any advances on one hundred and twenty-five thousand pounds?"

"Going once—"

Perkins didn't allow for a second call. He really wanted this. Raising the stakes, he figured beyond reach of the others and boldly bid £150,000.

The silence was thick in the auction room. The counter of £155,000 came through from a bidder on the phone. Perkins knew he had won—it was time for the kill. Go in too low, and then it encourages the bidding war; go in too high, and you are bidding against yourself. Perkins knew this. He had done this many times. Despite being a priest of sorts, he enjoyed the thrill.

"One hundred and seventy-five thousand pounds," Perkins called over the phone, bringing to a halt the auction room and the other phone bidder.

"Going once ... going twice ..."

Perkins was physically shaking. A long pause, a heartbeat—

"Sold. To the bidder 4810 on the phone, one hundred and seventy-five thousand pounds."

The hammer came down with a deafening thump, and that was that.

Perkins had sweat coming from his brow. He was pale. He had won the race, the auction—he had prevailed, got his prize—and that filled him full of self-satisfaction. He looked down at his hands and realized he was shaking.

After a few moments and a couple of sips of tea, he opened his email and saw the letter inviting him to a soiree in the Caribbean. He always liked mystery get-togethers with his brethren and wasn't fazed by the secrecy of the note. He was used to that—they had to be in pursuit of their type of fun, especially given the status and standing of many members of the group.

Relieved, his veins still full of adrenaline, Perkins announced to himself with a big Cheshire cat smile on his face, "Of course I'll be joining you in Belize."

V.

Sydney

Paul Bland sat in his corner office on Kent Street overlooking the Opera House and the approach to the Sydney Harbour Bridge while gripping the phone tight enough to whiten his knuckles. His latest dalliance was sat on the leather sofa opposite—he had picked him up in a bar in Rome on his latest recreational travels. "You're wrong!" he shouted into the phone. "Just plain wrong!"

Bland made sure that all the company travel bookings were made with his personal frequent-flier card, and therefore he traveled first-class everywhere and often, to Thailand, Morocco, to Los Angeles, San Francisco, London, and anywhere he thought he could pick up a new muse. Mario was his latest, a nineteen-year-old from Rome lured by the opportunity to go down under in more than one sense of the phrase.

He blasted over the phone, strutting his power in front of Mario, "You listen to me, Bryan, and listen to me only. You're wrong!"

He went silent for a few moments as the person on the end of the line, a vice president of operations, was trying to plead his case and maintain his employment status.

"Listen, Bryan. This is my ship. I call the shots, I make the rules, I wrote the Bible. If you don't like it, then I can easily find someone else to replace you tomorrow. So what's your decision, *Bryan?*"

The call went silent again as Bryan was clearly making his case to stay and save his job.

"That's better, Bryan. There's a good boy. I knew you would come to the right conclusion."

Shortly after the call hung up, the door closed. Five minutes later, Bland came out all flushed, red cheeks, with his chops smacking as if just delighting some delicacy.

Adrienne despised, him but she also needed the job. She was a single mother and, as with many things, turned a blind eye in preference to feeding her two kids and putting a roof over their heads. Her husband had been killed working in one of the company's mines. They'd received some compensation but not enough for what they needed to survive.

Recently, on Thursday and Fridays, she had taken to working late nights at a nightclub in Kings Cross. She would make more in two nights than she would in a month. She was ashamed. She appreciated the money, but for the most part, she enjoyed the work too, especially when the young visiting sailors were in town. Lonely, and with her husband long gone, she had found a way to enjoy the carnal pleasures and make good money at the same time, although it was something she kept as a dark and heavily guarded secret.

In the club, wearing her stage clothes, a wig, and makeup, almost unrecognizable, she had seen Bland a couple of times up to his no-good ways, picking up Sydney's young and innocent boys from the street to take to his apartment in Darlinghurst around the corner. She knew what that felt like as a woman, never mind imagining what it was like for a young boy with a dirty old man like Bland.

She passed the invitation to Bland. She had already read it and provisionally booked flights and the hotel in Belize

City. She knew him well enough to know that this was right up his alley.

He took a quick glimpse, then did a second take, and flashed her his gummy smile. "Thanks, Adrienne. You know me too well, darling."

She hated it when he called her that. She watched as he flitted off to do his rounds of the office and annoy and intimidate anyone he found on his tour.

Adrienne drilled a hole in his back and whispered under her breath, "Fucking creep." And she meant it.

VI.

Andrew Sheldon was a tradesman made good—well, sort of. He was a plumber turned builder, turned property investor of sorts. He had grown a portfolio of properties in the Bingley-Otley-Ilkley area of West Yorkshire—mainly hairdressers. For some reason, that eluded most, but not Sheldon. His rationale was simple. Restaurants came and went like the wind, as did retailers, but hairdressers stood the course.

At the size of his investments, the safest bet was hairdressers for two reasons: (1) they rarely, if ever, went bust, and (2) they always had a vested interest to make it work and pay their bills, as it was their livelihoods at stake.

Sheldon made sure he let them know that and had bullied his way to the top of his own tree, albeit a small tree, the king of hairdressing landlords in West Yorkshire.

He was immensely proud of his achievements from his roots as the son of a binman from Bradford. He rarely told the latter, but he let all and sundry know about the former.

He was tall and gangly, but from a life growing up as a binman's son in Bradford, an apprenticeship on the construction yards of the city, and progress through the ranks, he had learned how to intimidate, and he let everyone know that too, especially the weaker than him, the smaller than him, the vulnerable, and the more polite.

He'd received the letter in the post a few months back.

Apart from the ubiquitous mailers, invoices, and bills through his mailbox, Sheldon rarely received any personal communications, and this one was very strange, very strange indeed. He looked up the sender, and that further intrigued him. How had they heard of him? But then again, he justified that in his own mind because of his standing in the community and, hey, maybe now even worldwide.

Standing in his office at his yard in his usual attire, he shook his head at the thought as he took a mouthful of builder's tea from his Sheldon Plumbing Supplies mug.

The letter described the investment opportunity but also the need for a strong man should the situation arise.

> "You see, the problem is, Mr. Sheldon, that with the amount of potential at stake, often people can become irrational and unreasonable, and despite wanting to extend the opportunity to you personally as a potential investor, having you aboard, we believe you will also help us keep the peace."

Sheldon liked that. His self-professed reputation as a hard man played to his ego. He had a repertoire of stories about how he had dealt with errant customers who had not paid their dues, of evicting tenants indiscriminately, even being the strong arm to oust people from their own companies for him and his associates to steal.

Sheldon didn't have many friends, if any, but he didn't know that. He spent time hanging around his hairdressing salons, flirting with the hairdressers, making suggestive comments, being overly tactile, and now and again fitting out a kitchen or bathroom here and there in exchange for favors.

He had taken a trip the previous year to the United States, to Alabama, South Carolina, and central Florida, and he was impressed with the amount of acreage available for the price. That appealed to him, the prospect of owning a few hundred acres. "Andrew Sheldon, the son of a binman, lord of the manor of a thousand-acre plot," with nothing on it but useless swampland and few alligators as a bonus. He didn't even see the land or the alligators—he just saw the size of the acreage and the stories he could tell to further boost his fragile ego.

He looked back at the invitation letter and concluded that he could certainly accelerate his trip to Napa, look at the scorched acreage there due to the latest wildfires, and then head down to Belize. At least on the same continent, or almost.

His mind was made up. They needed him, and he liked that. He finished off slurping his tea, wiped his mouth dry with the back of his hand, grabbed his keys, and jumped in his bright red Toyota pickup truck on his rounds to his properties.

He would of course tell all and sundry about the invitation to remind them of his own self-importance, in his own little world.

4

I.
Back on the *Indigo*

FOLLOWING A QUICK TOUR OF the ship, the guests were shown to their cabins, and each was given a map and left to their own devices to settle in before they set sail. They would have luncheon on the main deck as they broke harbor.

Simpson and Sharp were the first volunteers for the tour and headed to their cabins. It was instinctive for them both, and although they had already studied the *Indigo*'s deck plans in detail beforehand, they were keen to acclimatize and familiarize themselves with their new surroundings. They had both been invited under separate cover, but the essence was the same:

Sergeant Major Sharp,

Upon speaking with General Sir Peter de la Billière, and upon his highest recommendation of your service, I am contacting you to invite you to help us control potential security risks during an upcoming event.

We are assembling a world-class group of investors for a cruise around the Caribbean, and given your background, we would like to invite you and your former colleague and Scotland Yard DCI Simpson to join us.

We will be very happy to reward you for your duties at a rate of US$5,000 a day plus travel and expenses.

The SS *Indigo* will be in Belize City, departing July 16, but we request that you check in one week prior to observe any potentially unusual activities during the buildup to the event.

We would appreciate your confirmation of acceptance of this operation.

Sincerely,

N. Waring
Colonel (retired)
Litions Industries

Neither of them knew the retired colonel, Waring, although Sharp seemed to vaguely recognize the name from the dim and distant past. Simpson was shown to the Churchill Suite and Sharp the MacArthur Suite. Very appropriate for these two military men through and through.

II.

"Wow, what a beautiful room," announced Lady Helen Bailey as she entered the Vettriano Suite—dark, mysterious, yet vibrant, with a color scheme of black, deep red, and chrome, and adorned with paintings from the Scottish artist himself. She paused briefly at the door to admire it all. "It's beautifully decorated," she said. "Are these originals?" she asked Bromovich as she pointed to the canvas above the king bed. In it, a women lay down on the deck of a yacht in her red-white-and-blue-striped bikini, a bottle of champagne in a bucket of ice, listening to an old gramophone by her side.

"That's going to be exactly what I will be doing tomorrow, Captain." She smiled as she stuck out her hand to shake his as he was midway through swinging up a salute.

"Now, are you sure that my Thunderbird is all safe and sound?"

Bromovich nodded and smiled, pulling his hand down from the awkward salute.

"Safe as houses on the *Indigo*," he said before stepping back out, almost tripping up, into the hallway. "Enjoy the cruise, Lady Helen," he said and gently closed the door behind him.

She walked into the bathroom—black marble and more chrome—and looked at herself in the mirror, her blonde hair more vivid after a week in the equatorial sun. "That I will, Captain. That I will," she said and smiled.

She was well aware of the effect she had on the male of the species. She was very conscious of that power that she held, and it gave her a great sense of confidence. Often she didn't even have to wield it—it just happened. She thought of the interaction with Bromovich and let out a giggle.

At thirty-six, she was full of life and still brimming with adventure. She had done plenty, and she knew there was more to come. Although finding her soul mate had eluded her so far, she was hopeful that day would come soon. She patted her belly and reminded herself of her yearning to have babies, one day, maybe.

The two military men she had spotted that previous week, Simpson and Sharp, were mysterious. There was something about them that appealed to her. Clearly both were real men—confident, fit, lean, and not bad looking either, she thought as she pulled out her brush from her leather bag and began running it through her golden locks.

She always liked the slightly older men, and these two certainly fit the bill—especially Sharp, she thought. She smiled at herself in the mirror once more.

She'd also spotted Zach, the cute Californian. She'd noticed his shyness, and she liked that in an endearing sort of way. Lady Helen knew when she had the upper hand, and she often did when it came to the opposite sex.

She would take a quick shower and get into something more comfortable, perhaps her blue caftan she'd picked up on the Silk Road with her bikini underneath in case there was an opportunity to dive into the ocean, or, if not, take a dip in the Jacuzzi.

She lay down on the bed to test it out and looked around at the other Vettrianos in the room, taken aback by the obvious and meticulous level of taste and detail behind, as well as the expense invested in, her cabin.

She thought about her real father. Her stepmother had told her about him moments before she fell to her death. The woman had taken great pleasure in letting Helen know the family secret that apparently everyone knew apart from her.

A wealthy businessman, a secret dalliance, a pact of secrecy. She had tried to extract the details and the identity before her own mother had died, but to no avail. The secret was locked deep down and was never to be revealed unless she found out for herself, and that's what she had been working on of late.

Instinctively she had been getting closer, working out the timings of things, her own birth date, the adjacencies to her mother's trips to London, the card and flowers at her funeral. She was getting closer; she knew that, and perhaps so did he.

She didn't know what she would do when she found him. She just knew that she needed to, and to get to the bottom of the many mysteries in her mind—*why*, just plain and simple: Why didn't they ever get together properly? Why didn't he come and see her? Why was it as secret as it was? Why didn't she ever know? In hindsight, why was she so different from the rest of her brothers and sisters?

These were all questions running through her mind. She wanted to track him down to ask the questions as much for herself as for her mother.

She was the one person in her life Helen had ever really connected with. She missed her. She yearned for her. She longed for her warm smile and touch and how they would cuddle on the sofa in front of the open fire at home—just the two of them, together. She had longed for that intimacy and probably would always do so.

She shook away her train of thought and looked around the suite.

"Wow, this really is very beautiful indeed," she said to herself, thinking how it was so appropriate for her.

She liked Vettriano and was fascinated by his style, one she described as a form of voyeurism: if you carefully study his paintings, there is often a figure in the background—a reflection in a mirror, someone in the scene who is a little out of place, someone watching.

"Always someone watching," she said and turned her mind back to the present. She slipped on her bikini, the blue silk caftan, and flip-flops; double-locked the door to the Vettriano Suite; and headed to the sundeck.

III.

Just Paul Bland and Zach were left on the deck, with all the other passengers escorted to their quarters. Zach continued to take his host responsibilities seriously, and Bland started showing his true character.

"So, where is Litions, then?" he said to anyone who was listening.

Zach just investigated his gin and tonic and slowly shook his head.

"I expected him to be here," Bland said and looked at his Bulgari watch. "We're setting sail in just under an hour. I can only say he'd better be here before we do"—he nodded at Zach as though it was his problem—"or I'm heading right back to Australia."

"Well, listen, Mr. Bland—we couldn't have chosen a nicer ship, or a more beautiful part of the world to explore with her." Zach tapped the teak handrail by his side as if he were patting a thoroughbred in the winner's enclosure.

Bland just looked at him and asked loudly, "Is someone going to get around to showing me to my quarters?" He looked at his watch again and started tapping it as the captain walked up.

"This way, Mr. Bland. Let me show you to your quarters," he said and ushered Bland away down the stairs and belowdecks.

Zach could hear Bland ranting as he followed behind Bromovich, shuffling along as though he was holding something between his knees.

"Strange little man," Zach muttered, just loud enough for the stewardess to hear.

"There's a few of them around here, sir." She winked.

Zach looked at her sharply, pursed his lips, and shook his head.

Kayla blushed, embarrassed, realizing she had stepped over the line.

"We keep our opinions to ourselves, young lady," he said with a smile. "No matter if sometimes you might be right." He winked.

IV.

Angela Chalmers was keen to get to her quarters. She had email to check and catch up with, calls to make—ever the busy bee. Some would confuse this for her work ethic when all it really was was her yearning to be in control, of everything, and at all times. Even if she was away on travel, on vacation, on the weekends, she needed to know everything that was going on in her domain. Less of a queen bee and more of a black widow sat in the middle of her web, and even the slightest movement she would know about. And God forgive those who entered her domain without permission or ever put a single foot wrong.

In her late forties, a former beach girl and cheerleader for her college football team, she didn't look too bad for her age. In fact, some would say she looked pretty good. It wasn't her looks that were the mark of her attractiveness or otherwise, but she had the swagger and confidence of a former athlete and a fine figure to go along with it.

She had married her high school sweetheart. That had been nearly thirty years ago, and apart from the occasional calculated indiscretion to help her up the corporate ladder, she had always been at least emotionally faithful to her husband.

She pressed the call button on her cell phone, and as she was waiting for Matt to answer, she looked at herself in the full-length mirror, pouted, smiled, and swung her hips like the cheerleader of old.

"So, Matt, I was thinking: Why don't we just get HR to act on that rumor that he doesn't like working for women? That'll take care of him. He won't be able to survive."

On the other end, Matt was talking himself through to agreement, and Chalmers patiently nodded her head, smiling in the mirror and rolling her eyes. But after a few minutes, she lost her patience.

"Look, Matt—you've got to decide what you want to be when you grow up. Do you want to be my chief operating officer or not?"

That was the end of the conversation. Of course he did—they both knew that—and that's how she played people. By understanding what really drove them and dangling the big fat carrot right in front of them.

Still looking in the mirror, she smiled to herself. "There's a good boy."

Mission accomplished. Her latest rival was on the way out of the door, thanks to Angela Chalmers and the techniques she had honed so well.

V.

Dr. Bronwyn Brown in the Marie Curie Suite opened her second suitcase with its secret code. She didn't want anyone prying into her business. She never did like that at any time. In fact, she did all she could do to conceal her business and transactions. That was hers and hers alone. Nobody else's business.

She pulled out one of the bottles of Grey Goose VX carefully cushioned between layers of clothing and set it alongside one of the Rose's lime cordials she had commandeered from the stewardess. Then she poured a four-finger nip and added a splash of the syrupy sickly-green liquid.

From the compartment at the back of the case she pulled out a capsule of pills—*codeine* was typed on the label, as was the name of a patient who had long since died. She disregarded the advised dosage and ignored the familiar prescribing doctor's signature, her own.

She took a deep gulp of the spirit, closed her eyes, and then with the flat of her palm piled three white pellet-shaped tablets into her mouth. Another swig of the vodka. And then, motionless, looking up at the ceiling of her cabin—an ode to Marie Curie, one of the greatest names in medical history—she sat there feeling ashamed of her deception and the things that she had done. She often felt that way, trapped in her loneliness and isolation and the terrible things that she had done, although she had repeatedly tried to justify them in her own mind.

She was the victim of their weakness. She was there for them as a savior, removing their pain, providing them relief and light to the other side. The fact that they bestowed much of their remaining wealth to her was their choice, not hers. She simply laid out the possibilities for release from their misery and obliged when they agreed.

Why should she feel guilty, after all? She was giving them what they wanted. They were old enough to make their own decisions, right?

She regained her focus on the ceiling, caught herself for a moment, and sat up, bolt upright, recovering from her moment of weakness.

She wasn't weak, she told herself. She was the savior— she was stronger when others were not so, and that was something she should be proud of, and not feel guilty about, right?

5

I.
Vilnius, Lithuania, Weeks Earlier

IT HAD BEEN SOME TIME since Igor Bromovich felt such a sense of purpose and hope. He had received his travel papers from a courier three days before, and he was all packed and ready to go. In the package was also an advance of $10,000, more money than he had seen in years. He would leave most of it with his wife while he was gone.

The next morning, he would have breakfast with his wife and children and then head to the airport in a taxi-bus to get on his flight from Vilnius International to Schiphol, then on to Miami and down to Belize International Airport to take charge of his ship, the SS *Indigo*.

He felt a twang of apprehension. It had been a while since he had captained a ship, but he leaned on his education and training from the academy and his years of experience on the seas. He knew he would be fine, but the last few years had dinted his confidence.

Igor's wife, Tatiana, had been busy in the kitchen from early that morning and was cooking up a feast for his farewell breakfast: *varškės apkepas*, fried curd cheesecakes; *cepelinai*, a type of fried potato dumpling; some *bulviniai blynai*, potato pancakes; and *spurgos*, traditional Lithuanian doughnuts.

He could smell the delicious aromas coming from the kitchen, and it reminded him of his childhood, of better times, but this morning he had this sense of optimism that even better times were ahead of them. *And about time too*, he thought, although he was still cautious, by nature, by culture, to fully believe what appeared to be his good fortune.

They sat at the dining-room table tucking into the feast before them with cups of tea and, as a special treat, some imported orange juice.

Igor, Tatiana, and their two girls all hugged before Igor grabbed his holdall, left through the front door of the apartment, and went down the seven flights of stairs. He looked back up, and his three girls were all waving. Igor gulped back his tears of pride and headed to meet the taxi-bus, on his way to the Caribbean.

Atsisveikinimas, su grožybėmis, he thought. *Farewell, my beauties.* And then he took a seat in the back of the cramped bus full of passengers heading to their own destinations.

II.

Rainham, Kent

Perry had received the letter that morning from the recruitment agency. He put it in his pocket and headed to the Cricketers for a beer and a bite to eat and to meet his long-term partner, Kayla. The arrival of the letter and its contents had put a spring in his step.

As he walked, every step reminded him of the town that he had the misfortune to be born in, and now, nearly forty years later, and after a stint in the army, back in. "The apple doesn't fall far from the tree," his mother had always reminded him, and every time she said it, he felt like taking his driving wood and a big tee shot to the head and putting her out of her misery.

Since his return, he had tried everything, from serving as personal chef to the sultan of Brunei to working as executive chef in London at a large investment bank, with the painful daily commute on the train; to running the clubhouse and hospitality suites at the local municipal golf club, until he got stabbed by one of the customers; to painting and decorating—and that's what he was doing now.

He was keen to change that.

They had a little two-up, two-down at the end of the high street, and since he had bought it nearly twenty years ago with the proceeds from his father's will, he had piece by piece tried to improve and update it. It still wasn't ideal though. "Not enough room to swing a cat" was what his father would have said.

Perry despised his father. He hadn't left much for the family. Beyond the cash, there was a lot of cleaning up to do after he passed. At the wake, Perry slept with his widowed girlfriend, twenty years his father's junior. He didn't feel guilty. In fact, he despised her too, but he made the most of the one-night stand and gave her what for, as the Kentish saying goes.

"Imagine shagging your own father's girlfriend at his own funeral. Shame on you, Perry Kirkham."

At that, he kicked a pebble down the road, emulating a recent sensational goal from his team, the Gills, and feigned, kicked, and scored into the top right-hand corner of the net, giving his own commentary along the way.

"He picks it up at the halfway line; he surges forward; he dribbles; he passes one, then two, and then a third; he looks up; he shoots; and he scores! *Goal!*"

Perry feigned the celebration as he ran down Rainham High Street pumping his fist in the air. No one noticed, no one cared. That was Rainham and the Medway towns.

He had updated the front room with a new fire, decorations, and carpet, and gotten some new furniture from IKEA. The kitchen too—his mate Dave the builder was replacing the kitchen at a well-to-do house, and Perry had taken advantage of the bargain with the exchange of a monkey, £500 in layman's terms.

Similarly, upstairs, the two tiny bedrooms received coats of paint, new carpets, and more build-it-yourself furniture.

The back garden was his pride and joy. He had turfed it and planted flowers, even his own grapevine, which fruited each year thanks to the Kentish summers, once called the Garden of England for a reason.

He'd never gotten around to updating the downstairs and the one and only bathroom, still with the toilet whose cistern you had to open in order to flush and the shower that had only one setting, drizzle, and two heat settings, red hot and icy cold. Each morning when he took a shower, it would really make him angry, but it was kind of a reminder for him of his roots—to never expect too much and to always remember where you came from. For Perry, it was the Medway towns, specifically Rainham, Kent, in the South of England.

Perry strolled up the high street, past the Rose Inn, where he and Kayla would go most Sundays for their version of Sunday lunch: meat, usually beef, lamb, or pork, roasted to death, just to make sure; potatoes roasted in fat; and vegetables boiled sufficiently to ensure that they lost their color and probably any remains of nutrition. Nevertheless, it was a tradition, and Perry liked his traditions.

Past ASDA, Paddy Power, and the Tandoori Parlor, next the United Services Club where for as long as he could remember, when he was home, Perry and the boys would go for their regular Friday-night game of snooker.

He remembered the kebab-shop incident and how his fellow footy teammates turned on a drunken and arrogant customer and all but killed him. He recalled the old guy with the leather jacket who Dave took exception to with his fists, so much so he lost control of his bodily functions—number one and number two.

He passed by the shopping center on the right, St. Margaret's Church on the left across the junction, and on to the Cricketers.

It was Tuesday, twelve o'clock, and the town had already settled into its mediocrity of the day—people having already collected their dole checks, many of whom had gone to the nearest off-license to stock up and take their alcohol home. But more and more were just drinking themselves into oblivion, some in public view on the street—they no longer cared, clearly.

Perry hated this place.

Some would try their luck at the local bookies with the hope of turning their £50 into £5,000 but for the most part come out with nothing, maybe enough for a pint in the pub. In the Cricketers, that was preserved for the front bar, smelling of stale beer, sweat, and other unthinkable odors. Perry headed to the back bar and dining room. Those with a little more sensibility chose to spend their weekly cash courtesy of Her Majesty by getting a good meal and a drink.

Perry was meeting Kayla to talk about their big break. He waited patiently at the hostess station until seated and got out the letter once more.

The envelope was typed, with the Glasgow postal mark dated three days earlier. It was headed with *Hospitality Recruiter* and went on to describe how Perry had come highly recommended—he assumed from the chef work he had done in Brunei, London—and Kayla, too, who for a time had worked at Barings Bank in the Square Mile.

They needed a couple, a chef and front-of-house staff member to look after the guests and crew on some luxury steamship sailing the Caribbean. He squinted his eyes again looking at the £5,000 each a week, plus travel and expenses, and shook his head at the number. In a month, they could save enough money to have the bathroom upgraded, and some change. Maybe they would go to their favorite destination, Benidorm, for a short break. This time, they could afford the ocean view with a balcony. He shook his head again as Kayla appeared at the hostess station, spotted him, and sat down opposite just as the drinks arrived, a pint of Carling and half with black currant.

Kayla still had her uniform on. She had just left the nursing home, morning shift, looking after the residents, making their beds, bathing them, dressing them, and whatever else she had to do as part of the job. Perry never asked; too-vivid details just made him feel sick. He preferred not to know.

He pushed the letter over to her as he nodded down, a prompt for her to read.

She looked at him. "What is it, Perry?"

He just stared and pointed.

"What is it, Perry? Don't mess about."

He realized that she might think it was bad news, so he read the letter aloud as she sipped her drink.

"What does that all mean, Perry?" she asked with her shrill and mostly annoying voice.

"It means we can get out of this shithole," he said and looked around him and at Kayla's green scrubs. "Well, at least for a while." He didn't want to get too far in front of himself.

He had already figured out in his own head, reading between the lines, that if they did a decent job, then why wouldn't it continue? A luxury steamship needs a crew, and the guests need feeding, right?

"Oh, Perry, I'm not sure about this, not after that last bloody scheme of yours."

They both looked at each other and then averted their eyes in embarrassment and shame.

It wasn't something they talked about, and certainly not since the truck full of immigrants had been found just off the M20 with all its occupants inside.

"There were women and children in that truck, Perry," Kayla whispered.

Perry flashed a look of paranoia around the bar and glared at Kayla. "Shut the fuck up, will yer?"

In the following silence, he kept his head down. There was really nothing to say.

It had been one of those plans plotted over a few beers down the pub with Dave and some of the former London gangsters who for some reason made the Medway towns their home, mostly after completing a stretch.

It sounded straightforward when presented and an easy way to make a bit of cash.

"Pel, this is fucking bulletproof," he remembered Pikey Rob telling him over the table at the Rose, complete with his gold-toothed grin.

What had seemed like a good idea at the time certainly wasn't Perry's finest moment—was one he chose to forget.

After a few minutes, he said, "This is our chance, Kayla, the one we've been waiting for. With ten thousand quid a week between us, we could finish off the house, go for a holiday, maybe even go back to New Zealand to see your mum."

She started to nod, ever so slightly. He knew that would get her. Her lit-up eyes and nodding indicated she was sold. They had been together eight years now, and she had been back to her homeland only once in that time, and that was the first year they had met. So a visit was overdue, and most Sundays at the Rose, she would remind him.

"When do they need us there?"

"Ninth of July."

"That's only six weeks away," she said, a look of fear in her eyes.

"That's plenty of time. You're on two weeks' notice." He could see her pain.

She had become attached to several of her residents, but the draw of seeing her mum was greater. Anyway, she could send them postcards. And, who knows, maybe when she returned, she could always go back there.

They were always short of staff anyway. Perry had always observed that there was plenty of demand and a reluctance of supply in that market, and when that imbalance arose, it always created opportunities.

The deal was done, but as they walked back home, Perry couldn't help remembering the terrible scene at the truck and the bodies, especially the children. He would have more nightmares that night. He was haunted by the memory but fearful of consequences—it could never be spoken about, ever.

III.
Harrogate, North Yorkshire

Dr. Bronwyn Brown was finishing up her shift at St. Mary's Hospice, seeing her last patient of the day. Charlie Hoggs, an eighty-seven-year-old World War II veteran, could barely remember his name or what he had for breakfast but could still remember both the horrors and adventures of his service years, from the Normandy landings to the liberation of Belsen camp.

Weekly, Dr. Brown would check each of her patients' vitals and blood pressure and assess their progress or otherwise. She had been doing the job for so long now that she had become detached from the individual inside, just focused on their physical being and existence.

She'd never married, no kids. Both of those dreams had long since evaporated—working long hours in the National Health Service had taken care of that, and her own mother's needs as she slowly expired with dementia. Having had a couple of short-lived, failed flings a very long time ago, Dr. Brown long since had given up even trying.

She had done quite well for herself, especially after leaving the NHS and since arriving at St. Mary's. She had taken good care of her patients, and in the last decade, several had also taken care of her as they departed this earth.

Brown had a small but well-kept cottage in the Yorkshire Dales, a little village, Birstwith, with its local pub, the Old Station Inn, and despite the vibrant and sociable local village crowd, she kept at arm's length to avoid the prying eyes and the gossip.

She had become a very private person, and she wanted to keep it that way, especially considering her growing bank balance—a combination of increased income and legacies and her ever-diminishing outgoing expenses—her only passion her growing collection of gold coins kept under lock and key in her secret walk-in safe in her cottage.

Dr. Bronwyn Brown would spend many an hour locked in her secret place in her cellar, just her, a bottle of vodka, and her treasure.

That evening, as she drove home, she decided to call by the Station Inn and sat in her usual place, the corner of the snug, sipping on her vodka and lime. There was the usual crowd: Clive, a local construction contractor and businessman, with his ever-amenable smile and bright-eyed welcome; Diesel, the local agricultural worker, spreader of local gossip; Kevin, another businessman, selling his kitchens; Claire and Paul, an actress and the son of a wealthy local family; James, a barrister; and the owner—Mr. Burns, as Brown had nicknamed him, after the character from *The Simpsons*—and ironically also once the owner of a nuclear power station. That always made her laugh, one of the few things that did nowadays.

She quietly watched the crowd through the bottom of her glass, almost unnoticed by the others. She liked it that way.

She pulled out the letter from her handbag one more time.

She had already made the decision. When she got home, she would book the flights to Belize City.

"Why the hell not?"

6

I.
Back on the *Indigo*

PARSONS WAS AN EX-GIGGLESWICKIAN. YEARS later, he had secured an old Parachute Regiment friend the job of bursar at the school. Parsons was on the board of governors and would regularly make the trip up north to the Yorkshire Dales to fulfill his duties and spend time with Denis.

Denis was a real character and a lot of fun. They would jump in his blue Sunbeam Alpine, top down, goggles on, and speed across to Kirkby Lonsdale for lunch at the Snooty Fox before heading to Thompson's art auction. With the absence of a speedometer and serviceable window wipers, the ride was always an experience, as were the lunches and copious amounts of Timothy Taylor's and Chateau Musar, Denis's favorite.

On one of their trips, they poured into the auction house having targeted their lots for the day. It was the first time he had become aware of what he found a strange penchant for what on the face of it seemed an innocent form of art, but with seemingly much more sinister undercurrents.

They made their purchases for the day's bidding—Denis an oil on canvas of a canal scene by Belgium artist Jacques François Carabain, and Parsons a watercolor of Grasmere by Lakeland legend William Heaton Cooper. But it was the set of paintings of children that caught Parsons's eye, not for the content but because of what seemed the ridiculously high figures they were being auctioned for, and mainly from agents and phone bids.

Denis had explained the phenomena back in the Snooty Fox over a whisky before the ride home.

It was one of those mysteries that was impossible to comprehend.

Parsons sat at his desk in the Horace Dodge Suite and remembered those years back—Perkins skulking at the back of the auction room, showing far too much interest in the portraits. He sat there flicking through the dossier, the most recent turn of events in London, and his own horrors as a child with the local priest at his youth club. He shivered for a moment, stole himself, reached for the pills on his desk, and swallowed a handful with a glass of water.

He knew Perkins's background all too well, and that really bothered him. A lot.

II.

For those who knew Paul Bland, it was well known that he wasn't the most savory of characters. His signature war cry—"You're wrong, you're wrong, you're wrong!"— regularly came from his gummy mouth as he inadvertently splattered the victims of his rants with his anger and saliva.

That was what he was known for: getting his own way, bullying his own way, using any levers necessary, and wielding his power over the weaker or less powerful. Bland liked to be in charge, always, and left a long list of victims in his wake.

"If someone invites me to an event, then I think it's just plain courtesy that he's here!"

Bland was all but foaming at the mouth like a rabid dog.

"Sir, sir, Monsieur Litions will be joining us when we get to Grand Cayman," Bromovich said.

"You're wrong, you're wrong, you're wrong!" Bland continued to wag his finger and splatter Bromovich before him, Bromovich politely standing back from the increasingly belligerent onslaughts.

As Bland stood in his white linen Armani suit, Gucci tie, and alligator-skin shoes, clutching his Louis Vuitton luggage by his side, his portly form and obnoxiousness shone out across the deck like a bad smell.

Bromovich was trying his to placate him, with Zach in support, and he followed Bland's repeated gaze to the quayside and the smiling bright-eyed youth, where there was an obvious connection.

With his Louis Vuitton carry-on case in hand, Bland glanced over at the quayside, where his previous night's conquest was obediently waiting for him, waving with a big boyish smile. He was only sixteen, and a "darling," according to Bland, the night before slipping him $1,000—a lot of money for a Belizean.

That was it, mind made up. Bland turned right and headed down the wooden boarded gangway with his carry-on case rattling behind him like a train.

"You're wrong, you're wrong, you're wrong!" he shouted as he left the *Indigo*. "Stick yer treasure where the sun don't shine" was his last insult as he walked up to his conquest and kissed him on the lips, the boy shrugging him off nervously and looking around for witnesses to what was taboo in those parts and carried often harsh consequences.

Another set of eyes on the quayside observed intently, taking in all the details of the scene. Zach looked across at the captain and shrugged his shoulders. Bromovich mirrored the gesture and went about pulling the walkway, ready to sail.

"Gangway up. Let's set sail. One down, eleven to go," Zach said sarcastically.

III.

Stuart Jacobs shuffled through his papers and found the invitation he had been looking for. He still had the envelope with the DC postmark and the address. He read through the invitation once more, signed by Mr. N. Waring on behalf of Litions Industries.

He'd heard of the latter, but there was something that rang a bell with him. *N. Waring.* He stared at the letters on the page. He was a crossword buff, had been all his life, usually the *Independent,* representing his more liberal leanings, but frankly any crossword would do. He had a desire to constantly push his intellect as far as he could.

He then looked at Litions Industries in the same light, then Jemol Litions—was it possible these had a hidden meaning?

Jacobs, the youngest son of a mining family, hadn't had the opportunity to go to university, and that had always been a cause of deep regret for him. He was better than that, deserved more than that, and although he escaped the pit for the Royal Air Force as an *other rank,* he had managed to work himself up the noncommissioned ranks and get himself a technician's position on communications. "Not bad for a miner's boy," he would tell himself.

Now in his late sixties, he had run his career's course and was now just looking to keep busy. He still fantasized about getting the recognition that he deserved, one day, from Her Majesty herself. He had positioned himself well, and through his proxy diplomatic-corps alignment, he was poised for his life goal—to be recognized for his service to queen and country—and all that would bring for his fragile ego.

He pondered an earlier comment from Parsons about Austin, apparently his old platoon commander, and how he had been evicted from his place for life at the head of the chamber of commerce. Jacobs considered the connection, how he himself in fact was the accused assassin, and how Austin had died of a heart attack less than a year after his unceremonious removal.

Over the years, Jacobs had built up justifications as to the reasons and rightfulness of his actions. He stood by them today. Of course he did. The right thing—that's what he told people anyway.

That's what everyone justifies to themselves, that they did the right thing—the list of which through history was a long one. Jacobs had joined that club in a big way.

He had justified this trip for its clear opulence, the opportunity of an investment of a lifetime, but the treasure hunt and the *Ella Sophia* intrigued him also.

A once-in-a-lifetime opportunity, he had thought. And now, at this time of life, his counting the years down instead of up meant he was even more ruthless than he had been in his earlier career. For many, they mellow with age; for Jacobs, the ticking clock just accentuated his sense of urgency.

IV.

Angela Chalmers sat in her cabin. She had just got off a call with her boss, or at least that's what he thought he was. There was only ever one person in control when it came to Angela Chalmers. She always got her own way, no matter what.

Another coworker was getting in her way, and she had set her sights on his demise.

Her modus operandi was quite simple, but the amount of skill, technique, and cunning it took to execute was quite extraordinary and something she had been perfecting ever since she had started school. Never the obvious bully on the playground, Chalmers had developed a process of undermining, bending the truth, spreading falsehoods, and just creating new versions of reality. The more people she told, the more they believed, the more vulnerable her targets became.

She proved herself in her art, and the foundation was her charm and her believability. Without those two, the potency of her methodology would not work to its fullest effect.

She was cool and calm in her execution, never dropping her guard in public, always the team player, the convivial host. It was only when one carefully observed her actions that she might be identified for the black widow she was.

It took patience too; these things took time. Like flooding the foundations with quicksand, fanning the flames on a bushfire, slowly filling up the water until the target could no longer breathe.

She maintained the momentum with multiple sources. People may be able to survive a one-off attack, but Chalmers knew that a sustained campaign from multiple directions over time resulted in her victory.

Sometimes she got found out and people recognized her craft and how she was the wielder of these barbs. This latest target had done just that, and she had to take him out before he got the opportunity to reverse the tactics on her. She could not allow that. She had to destroy him, and that is what she'd do.

The call with Frank went well. She dealt her cards to him one after another.

She'd spotted early on that he was perhaps overly concerned and sensitive to what others in the organization thought of him, that he was indecisive probably as a result. He was impressed by her wisdom of the organization, including her relationship with the big boss, her former boss at Coca-Cola. She had connections and influence, and therefore her counsel had perceived value.

Frank needed allies, and she was happy to help in that regard in exchange for some benefits for herself, a kind of friends-with-benefits type of arrangement, although Frank wasn't her cup of tea in that regard, no matter how ruthless she was.

Chalmers took great pride in her craft, sharing her insights with him, sufficiently fueling his paranoia, and ensuring that he saw her at the forefront of her allies.

Although she didn't rate him herself, she knew that type of positioning had worked to her benefit in the past. Chalmers engineered herself as the trusted adviser, meanwhile acting like quicksand around those in her orbit, ensuring their footing was never firm enough for them to leap away from her clutches and her world of influence.

At times, she regretted that she had gone into business instead of the world of politics. She was a hard-right Republican, but at the beginning of her career, there wasn't much room for women—a fact that she had worked hard to change in her realm of influence in business.

She got herself ready for dinner. She would make it short, bring back a bottle of wine. She would get an early night and read her latest book.

Her work almost done for the day, she headed out of the Marilyn Monroe Suite to go schmooze with the others, identify the real opportunities. She'd already worked out that probably Jacobs and Parsons were her best bets.

V.

Perkins in the Oscar Wilde Suite sat at the Victorian walnut dresser contemplating his life and how on earth he had got to this place. He looked at his reflection in the mirror, sweat rolling from his brow, his chubby red chops, and his white collar. He ripped off the collar in rage and remembered when he was younger, leaner, even vaguely good looking, in his time.

He continued staring in the mirror. "What the hell?" He shook his head, then put his head in his hands.

He heard the turbines of the *Indigo* crank up, the horn, and the shudder of the vessel as they started to move away from St. George's Caye. He had one last glance out of his window and spotted the police car, officers watching intently.

He went to the bathroom and started running the water. He would take a bath.

Over the decades, things had been going well for him, although he had always walked a fine line—a very fine line.

His last party at his home in Kensington had been a disaster. One of the boys was found drowned in the pool.

He sent the guests out at four in the morning and called his friends at Scotland Yard. In hindsight, it had been a very big mistake, because even the men at the very top found it hard to cover up a sixteen-year-old's body full of a cocktail of cocaine, heroin, and semen.

Two days later, an overenthusiastic young detective sergeant came knocking at the door asking questions, hoping to come into the house, look around. Of course, Perkins complied, thinking that not to would be too obvious, hiding behind his white collar and holy intentions.

The morning he left for the airport, his butler called him and let him know that the police had been by again, this time with a warrant for Perkins's arrest. He had seen the police arrive at the quayside as they sailed. The noose was getting tighter—he could almost feel it. He was sure that they would be waiting for him in George Town.

He looked back at the mirror, shook his head, his fingertips pressed against his temples.

"What the hell am I to do?"

He knew not only that it was serious but that a lot of people in very high places would be nervous as hell, and that could mean dire consequences for the self-proclaimed priest.

Thankfully, he kept all his records in one place, in his little black book, safe at all times dressed as a Bible in his jacket pocket, never to leave his side. He needed to get rid of it, destroy it, but it felt a bit like Gollum destroying the ring in the fire: it had become him, he had become it, and he couldn't think of his life without it. He would suddenly become irrelevant to everyone, and quickly expire from this earth, in one way or another.

He took his Bible, arranged it in the bottom of the shower with some papers and a candle, and set it alight, watching the flames take hold and the evidence go up in smoke. He had deactivated the smoke alarms and made sure that there would be no remnants remaining. He made sure the red lace-up shoes were packed up safely in his case. Shoes from when he himself was a child. He packed the rest of his belongings back into his case and zipped it up as if he were departing.

He stepped into the hot bath, the mirrors and glass all steamed up, wearing swimming trunks and a T-shirt. He wouldn't want to be found fully naked—that would make him vulnerable, and he had been there too many times before.

He braced the initial heat of the bath as he stepped in and then slowly eased himself down, where he sat and laid his head back. He closed his eyes, thinking about his impossible predicament.

7

I.

In the Galley

THE SPRING-PEA-AND-MINT SOUP WAS READY to go as Kayla walked in the galley, red-cheeked, chin rigid, her eyes staring straight into the bowls of soup.

Perry recognized the look. "What's up, Kayla?"

She turned her gaze up to him. "What's up? What's fucking up, Perry? I'll tell yer what's fucking up."

She started telling him about the "rude" Dr. Bronwyn Brown, the "obnoxious" Mr. Bland, the "lecherous" Mr. Sheldon, and "that weirdo Father Perkins—now, he gives me the fucking creeps."

Perry diverted his attention and concentration and just stared back at her. "Kayla, get a fucking grip and shut the fuck up. Yer can't go foul-mouthing the guests like that—someone might fucking hear you. Now just pull yer socks up, suck it up, and keep quiet. This is all about our new kitchen, bathroom, and ocean-view balcony. Got it?"

Kayla slowly nodded.

"Right. First course. Ready to go—go, go, go!"

II.
The Upper Deck

Sheldon sat himself at the head of the table, set for twelve. That was just the type of man he was. He looked around impatiently for the others to join him as if still in his two-up, two-down in Little Horton.

Most of the passengers had risen above deck as they pulled out of the port and set off on their passage. Over drinks, they watched as the city of Belize diminished behind them and the beautiful clear blue oceans and Cayes opened up before them.

Zach was at the head of the viewing gallery and was pointing out the landmarks and the colonial history as they headed out past the Hicks Caye to the port side of the ship, around the top of Turneffe Atoll. Later they would anchor a near distance to Lighthouse Reef and the world-famous Great Blue Hole.

"We'll watch the sunset and, for the more adventurous among us, do some snorkeling." Zach smiled at his audience. He felt like a tour guide at Jurassic Park or something similar.

Ever the well-versed historian and host, Zach went on to explain the history of Belize—how it dated back thousands of years to the Mayans and how they flourished there between 1500 BC and around AD 1000.

"Many examples of Mayan ruins include Cahal Pech, Caracol, Lamanai, Lubaantun, Altun Ha, and Xunantunich—all examples of how advanced this ancient civilization actually was at the time."

He went on to tell his audience how it wasn't until the Spanish conquistadors in the sixteenth century that European influence arrived in this far-flung land.

"The availability of timber was a big attraction, including for the British too. Belize was formally termed as the colony of British Honduras in 1862. It became a crown colony a decade later, until self-government was granted in 1964, the name changed in 1973, and full independence granted in 1981.

"Back in the day, these beautiful oceans were a very dangerous place." Zach had a big smile on his face. He was enjoying this—he had everyone's attention, especially Lady Helen Bailey's, and that now familiar knot in his stomach returned.

"The Spaniards plundered and shipped their newly found treasures back to Europe. The Royal Navy policed and stopped the ships on their way, and the pirates, often an extension to the crown, attacking, fighting, sinking, plundering the treasure."

At this point, they were mesmerized, even Sheldon.

"It was the original Wild West, and if that wasn't enough, there were the reefs and the hurricanes too. There is many a lost treasure sitting on the ocean floor in this part of the world."

The audience looked impressed with the briefing—the awe of these lands and oceans on the other side of the world from home, for most. The guests, minus Bland, were all sat down, apart from one.

"Anyone seen Father Perkins?" Parsons asked.

The luncheon table was silent, just shaking heads as guests tucked into the pea-and-mint soup, all eyes down.

"He looked a little peaky to me earlier," Chalmers said.

"Maybe he's finding his sea legs," Zach said optimistically.

Sheldon looked around him and out to the calm sea. "It's as flat as a McDonald's bloody pancake out there!"

Again the company rolled their eyes at the Yorkshireman.

"What? What?" Sheldon looked around in appeal to the reaction.

Lady Helen Bailey struck up a conversation with Angela Chalmers about how women survive and excel in a man's world. Jacobs resurrected his experience of flying in different classes and cabins and managed to drop in his elite flier status once more.

For the most part, Sharp and Simpson just listened, nodded, and agreed, soaking it all up. Sal peppered the conversation with silence, or a "fair dinkum" when he agreed with something or someone's comments. Parsons just listened and observed as the conversations unfolded.

"So, Dr. Brown, what brought you to this wonderful ship?" asked Jacobs.

Dr. Brown looked up from her soup bowl and flashed her eyes around the table, looked back down, and cleared her throat. "Are you talking to me, Mr. Jacobs?"

"Yes, ma'am. What brought you to the *Indigo*?"

She hesitated again for a moment, and then she explained the invitation she'd received from Litions Industries, and her cottage and her life, hinting at her loneliness.

"And it just seemed a good idea at the time, I suppose."

"Sounds fair enough to me," Sal said.

"And what about you, Sal?"

Sal was happy to share. "Well, same as the doctor here. Sounded like a lot of fun, with a lot of fun people," he said and pointed around the table, then paused, realizing the unintended humor. "And besides, I fancied a little jaunt around the Caribbean with my very good friend Lady Helen Bailey."

She put on a big smile for the entire table.

Angela Chalmers put on her "Fuck you—you're prettier, younger, and wealthier than me" smile. Sheldon goggled. Simpson and Sharp looked on, seemingly amused, and Parsons just continued observing.

After a top-up of the wineglasses and Sheldon's beer, the Crab Louie arrived neatly displayed on the fine porcelain bowl on a delicate bed of greens and radishes, garnished with sweet grape tomatoes and a touch of Caribbean pineapple, and drizzled with Perry's signature sauce.

"Kayla, this looks bloody splendid. Thanks to the chef."

All the passengers agreed as Kayla passed around the freshly baked rosemary-scented rolls.

The small talk continued as guests sat on the deck enjoying the food and the wine; the glorious sunshine; and the views of the islands, the reef, the shoreline as it diminished, and the crystal-clear blue waters below. Even Sheldon seemed to appreciate the combination of the senses.

"Yer don't get water this clear, even in Yorkshire—I'll tell yer that for nowt!"

Apart from the odd squeal of approval and the sound of cutlery on porcelain, the table was silent, until a loud bang from belowdecks disrupted the tranquility.

"What the bloody hell was that?" Sheldon was the first to speak, as he often was.

The rest of the table frozen for a moment, Simpson and Sharp hurried off in the direction of the sound. Zach, ever present, kept a close eye on the guests' reactions to what had sounded distinctly like a gunshot.

Sheldon just kept on eating and didn't miss a beat. Lady Helen and Sal continued their conversation about when they were in some dry, dusty town in the outback. Dr. Brown looked nervous, her hands shaking, and ordered a vodka and lime from the stewardess. Chalmers was oblivious, emailing on her phone. Stuart Jacobs sat upright in his chair.

Ten minutes passed, and the two military men returned, accompanied by the captain.

Father Perkins was apparently dead.

"Bloody hell!" Sheldon called as he rocked on the back of his chair.

III.
Indigo Lounge

Sir James Parsons looked up from his newspaper as Stuart Jacobs sat down next to him in the Indigo Lounge, just off the promenade deck. The doors were open, the light breeze taking the edge off the humidity. Parsons was glad to be off the baking-hot, bug-ridden land and on the ocean.

"Much cooler out here," Jacobs said as he made himself comfortable in the winged armchair and plonked his straw boater on the coffee table in front of him, next to Parsons's panama.

Kayla appeared and took their order for tea for two and then scurried off to see to it.

"What do you make of all this, old boy?" Jacobs asked, diving straight in.

Parsons looked up from his pink *Financial Times* through his half-moon glasses. "Make of what?"

"Well, it's a bit strange, don't you think?"

"What, exactly?"

"This whole thing, really. The invite. The no-show of Litions. Who's in charge here? What is the purpose? The eclectic collection of passengers, and now Father Perkins dead."

Jacobs keenly eyed Parsons for his response as the man continued reading his newspaper without so much as a flinch.

"I guess we'll find out soon enough," Parsons said.

Kayla appeared with the tea tray, carrying a fine porcelain teapot with two cups and saucers, a choice of teas in a wooden case, sugar cubes, and milk.

Jacobs busied himself going through the selection and picked out a green tea. He poured over the piping-hot water, dropped in two lumps of sugar, and stirred rapidly and noisily.

When Parsons looked up from his paper again, Jacobs slowed and stopped stirring. Parsons refolded his newspaper and set about making his own selection, Earl Grey, with a splash of milk, and settled back in his winged chair.

"So, what was the context of your invitation, Jacobs?"

Jacobs was happy to be engaged. He retold the story of the consulate general's, why he was there, his connection with the chamber of commerce, his career and accolades, his property ownership in the exclusive St. Francis Wood area of San Francisco, his apartment on the trendy King Street, and his farmhouse in Tuscany. Jacobs was never one for missing an opportunity to tell people how important he was, with no care of the danger of repetition.

Parsons looked visibly bored with the answer. "So why did you come?" he asked, putting Jacobs on the spot.

"Investment opportunity, I guess. It sounded interesting … too good an opportunity to miss?" He was now asking questions, not giving reasons why he had accepted.

"Do you know Litions?"

Jacobs paused. "Does anyone?"

Parsons took a crunch of his shortbread biscuit and a sip of tea.

"Tragic about the priest."

"Yes, indeed. Looked like he was carrying a lot of weight on his shoulders to me."

The humor wasn't lost on either of them—neither was the underlying meaning.

Outside, Parsons heard the laughter of Lady Helen and the Australian having fun on the deck.

He and Jacobs turned to their cups of tea in silence.

IV.
Promenade Deck

Sitting on the promenade deck in the shade, Dr. Bronwyn Brown was reading her book. She'd brought an old Agatha Christie novel. It had always amazed her how Christie had written so many—in fact eighty in total, sixty-six detective stories and fourteen short-story collections, with more than two billion copies sold worldwide.

She knew as a wannabee author herself that that amount of productivity precomputers was very impressive indeed. *How was that even possible back then?* she'd often wondered.

She'd also been fascinated by Christie's mysterious, although temporary disappearance midway in her career, and she would often go to the Old Swan Hotel in Harrogate for afternoon tea to soak in the atmosphere, get into Christie's mind, and solve the mystery, which she never had yet, although she had her theories.

She had got as far as to when the group had arrived on the mysterious Soldier Island, off the South Devon coast of England. Who was the killer? She liked the Justice Wargrave character, wasn't too sure about Philip Lombard, or Dr. Armstrong. And then there was Vera Claythorne, the secretary—Bronwyn Brown never trusted secretaries.

Dr. Brown was feeling unusually relaxed on board the *Indigo*. She had surmised she felt that way because, given her observations, she was probably the least interesting character on the ship, and therefore she felt out of the limelight, which was exactly how she liked it.

She took a sip of her vodka and lime next to her. It was never far away. She winced as she swallowed and at the noise of the two young ones having fun. She didn't understand that. It had been a very long time since she had fun in her own life, and she sort of resented it when she saw and heard others doing so.

She flipped the pages of her book noisily as a mark of protest, but of course no one heard apart from her.

She paused and looked out across the ocean. Bland had certainly been a character for sure. Perkins, God bless him, was clearly deeply troubled. The two military men; the pompous Stuart Jacobs and equally obnoxious Yorkshireman; and the aloof Sir James, who she thought she recognized from somewhere in the dark and distant past. And then the annoying American, Chalmers.

She could hear Chalmers approaching again. This would be her sixth walk by in the past thirty minutes. She was still on her mobile phone, still scheming, plotting, playing some game of corporate politics. Bronwyn Brown despised people like her, especially when they had no regard for others around them. She found that of Americans—total disregard and lack of awareness of their surroundings, as if they believed that they lived in a bubble and they were the only ones in it.

"Frank, I told you this would happen. He needs to make more personal sacrifices for the business. He needs to learn how to fit in with the team …"

And the conversation continued in bite-size pieces, Bronwyn Brown getting snippets as Chalmers patrolled the ship, apparently oblivious to who was listening. Dr. Brown was piecing together the drama unfolding somewhere in some big office in Philadelphia.

Yes, this was Chalmers's sixth circuit—Dr. Brown had been counting. She put her book down on her lap and waited until Chalmers was passing right by.

"Excuse me, young lady," she bellowed loudly to make sure that Chalmers heard her. She'd chosen the words deliberately.

Chalmers stopped and looked at her as if she had just killed her first child.

"Do you mind being not so bloody obnoxious walking around here with that wretched thing? How about you at least take it off speakerphone; or, better, go to another deck; or, even better, go to the privacy of your own cabin to have your clandestine conversations?"

Chalmers glared, walked off, and switched off the speaker. She didn't return.

Dr. Brown was delighted that her suggestion had worked. She went back to her book and vodka and lime. "Bloody Americans."

V.

Lady Helen and Sal were playing badminton on the top deck. They were young and on the face of it carefree, and didn't ever worry about too much. They were at that stage of life where they were invincible and nothing would catch up with them. They were traversing through life with one purpose in mind—to have fun, and that often meant regardless of anyone else. Whereas some lived in a bubble of ignorance of those around them, Lady Helen and Sal simply didn't care.

After Helen Bailey's father died from a heart attack, his wife, Helen's stepmother, tragically died from a fall while walking at Brimham Rocks, close to the family home.

Helen had been with her that rainy and blustery Yorkshire afternoon. She had been there when she had *tripped*. She ran home, didn't tell anyone, just waited for her body to be found and the news of her accidental death. She couldn't explain why she hadn't told anyone and didn't choose to.

With every knock on the door, her heart raced. All she could think of were those final moments when she had confronted her and reached out—not a strike, but a push was enough to send her over the edge to her death. Two days of torture until the body was inevitably found and the news was out.

The headline of the *Nidderdale Herald*: "Tragic Accident: Local Woman's Body Found at Brimham Rocks."

The use of the word *accident* in the headline and the declaration by the local police were sufficient. She could breathe a sigh of relief and now play the role of grieving stepdaughter.

> "Mrs. Linda Bailey was an avid walker of the local dales and unfortunately on that day, with the high winds and heavy rain, had likely slipped to her tragic demise. There were no signs of foul play, and the Nidderdale police were treating this as a tragic accidental death."

The story went on to give statistics on how many walkers died each year in the Yorkshire Dales and how a healthy regard for the real and present dangers shouldn't be ignored. Traffic incidents were of course at the top of the list for most injuries and deaths, but there were also equestrian accidents, cycling accidents, climbing trips and falls, and even injuries and deaths from stampeding cows.

Despite the seriousness of the moment, Helen burst into a huge belly laugh at the thought of her stepmother's alternative demise at the hands or hooves of an errant herd of Friesian cows.

"Miserable old witch."

They were in the middle of a long rally. Sal hoisted the shuttlecock high into the air, and Lady Helen parried with a smash. Sal recovered and scooped it up over the net and to the far byline. Lady Helen stretched her backhand to the opposite side of the court, and Sal slipped, floundered.

"Game point!"

With the stepmother now out of the picture, her father's estate was split among her two sisters and brothers. Helen had done very well from the will—she had 25 percent ownership of the farm as well as the revenue it produced. She got another 25 percent of all his liquid assets, which turned out to be impressive. "Tight old bugger," she had said of him in the context of his frugal lifestyle compared with the size of his numerous bank accounts. Then she was a named recipient in his very generous life insurance policy, in addition to the plot of land in Scotland and her title.

All of a sudden, any financial concerns she may have had previously had completely evaporated, and the reality was, as long as she didn't go crazy, the combination of assets and income meant she didn't have to worry about money probably for the rest of her years.

She quickly purchased the Triumph Thunderbird and headed out on her travels.

Contrary to popular thinking, she didn't want to go back to the scene of the crime; she wanted to escape it, and frankly never go back there ever again, if she could avoid it.

She headed south to London, with no real plan, over to Calais and Paris, and then down through France and took the long trek across to Istanbul. After a couple of nights there, she continued through Persia to Baghdad. She was on a mission that was forming with each leg of the trip. She carried on to Mary in Turkmenistan, then Samarkand, Kashgar, and Dunhuang, and on to Lanzhou and Xi'an before eventually reaching Guangzhou, China, on the South China Sea. In just over three months, more than six thousand miles, she had tracked one of the several versions of the Silk Road in her wake.

Not content, and not ready to return home, she decided to carry on and sailed down to Perth and then started her traverse across Australia, and that's where she met Sal. Footloose and fancy-free and with plenty of cash to burn, they took the Triumph through the dusty outback.

Helen was impulsive. For all her life, she had done exactly want she wanted without any apparent fear of consequences. She was a maverick. She endeared people, but at the same time, she scared them, too, with her seeming lack of respect for protocol, or safety, including her own.

Playing for the game, Lady Helen served overhead, smashing the shuttlecock over the net to Sal's weak side, his backhand. Sal scraped the shuttlecock back over, high enough for Lady Helen to smash and take the game—2–2, one game to play.

Since as long as she could remember, Helen was second fiddle, and so was her mother. Her real father was never revealed, even from her own mother's deathbed—such a secret was impossible to imagine for her that it could never and would never be shared. She was determined to find out for herself one day.

One fateful night, at a stopover bed-and-breakfast, fueled by too much Bundaberg and weed, she and Sal fell into a stupor, then fell asleep. The pair awoke in the middle of the night when the candle had been knocked over and the hot wax and naked flame had quickly combusted into a full-on fire. It ravaged the curtains and then spread like wildfire, quickly eating into the tinder-dry wooden structure they were staying in, consuming the whole property in what seemed like the blink of an eye.

The pair stumbled out into the night, beneath the clear starry sky, with bleary eyes and foggy minds, the raging fire popping and bursting and crackling. The smell of burning wood and human flesh quickly sobered them up.

The mother and her two young kids burned to a crisp. Her husband was out in the mines. It was indeed a tragedy, but one the pair seemed to shrug off, compartmentalizing that memory and the guilt somewhere deep within their souls. They didn't show much sign of the burden.

Sal floated the shuttlecock in the air, and Helen parried. Sal hit it back in the air, and Lady Helen smashed it over the net to win the game.

"Match point. Champers?" She ran over to the Jacuzzi and took the plunge, shortly followed by Sal.

"Fair dinkum, you beauty." He beamed as they clinked their glasses and toasted.

VI.

Zach strolled into the pilothouse, where Captain Bromovich was waiting for him. He was completing the incident report following Perkins's death, an apparent suicide—the Webley revolver, single shot through the brain. Bromovich was even heavier browed than normal as Zach walked over to him and patted him on the back, a gesture of reassurance, the already printed out incident report ready for them both to sign.

Given the seriousness of the situation, he'd asked Zach as a qualified US maritime officer to jointly sign the report, and of course Zach was happy to oblige.

"It sure is a tragedy, Captain, but he obviously had his worries and demons," he said, trying to make Bromovich feel better.

It's not as though Bromovich was morose, sad, or even emotional—Zach knew enough about Eastern Europeans to understand that wasn't in their genes. But he also knew how seriously Bromovich took his responsibilities and how his captaincy of the *Indigo* was so important to not only him but his family and his pride.

"No one likes losing one of his passengers, Zach. It doesn't look good for business." He shot a look at Zach and slid the paper across the chart table for him to sign.

Zach pulled out his Paper Mate and scrawled his signature, Zach Carter, and as he did, the radio sprung to life with crackles and pops, and a man's voice came over the speaker. It was the Belize City Port Authority, probably wondering where the incident report was.

"BCPA calling SS *Indigo*" came the call, crackling on the radio.

"This is SS *Indigo*. Over."

"SS *Indigo*, we need a passenger list check. Over."

"Roger that. Over."

"We're looking for a passenger listed as Mr. Paul James Bland, an Australian citizen. Passport number *L*, for Lima, 1987542. I repeat: Mr. Paul James Bland, an Australian citizen. Passport number *L*, for Lima, 1987542. Over."

Both Zach and Bromovich of course immediately recognized the name, but needed to check the credentials and the passport number. Bromovich looked over to Zach as he pulled out the ship's log and the passenger list and confirmed with the port authority.

"Affirmative. The named passenger was on our original passenger list but decided not to join the ship at the last minute and disembarked yesterday morning at St. George's Caye. Over."

The radio crackled and hummed. Bromovich leaned on the console with the radio handset in his right hand, looking out at the ocean. Zach stood behind him, still at the chart table.

"Are we speaking to the captain of the ship? Over."

"Yes, sir. This is Captain Igor Bromovich. Over."

The radio continued to crackle and hum.

"Captain Bromovich, this is Chief of Police Walters of Belize City. We regret to inform you that Mr. Bland was found dead this morning. Over."

His face immediately wrinkled in disbelief, and he shot a look behind at Zach, who was the same.

Bromovich hit the console before him. "What? How did he die? Over."

A short silence.

"He was found nailed hand and foot to a door floating down the Belize River. Over."

Zach had come across this method of dispatch before, the last time he was in the Caribbean. He knew that in this part of the world, the ways people die, or are murdered, often mean something. The method of nailing the victim, with six-inch nails, to a door and throwing them into water was a sign that the victim had committed an ultimate betrayal or a heinous crime.

Zach reached for the handset. "Was he right side up or upside down? Over."

The police chief paused for a moment. "Facedown. Over."

Bromovich looked at Zach puzzled and in need of an explanation.

"The level of punishment fits the crime. You might survive the nails and the pain, and if the disease-ridden water doesn't get you, then right side up, you have an outside chance of survival if you're found before the sun bakes you.

"But upside down, you've got no chance whatsoever—drowned, and the sea creatures below eat you alive.

"How do you know this to be true?" Bromovich asked.

"Whoever and whatever Bland did, it must have been something very serious and taboo in the local street law."

"Seems there's more to you than meets the eye, Mr. Zach Carter." Bromovich turned back to the handset and the port authority. "Sending over special report on the Perkins incident now. Over."

"Roger that, Captain. BCPA out."

"SS *Indigo* out."

Bromovich grabbed the incident report, countersigned it next to Zach's initials, and placed it onto the fax machine. Dial tone; punched-in number; connection, followed by a pause; and the weird analog scream as the paper went through the feeder. Out the other side, a little more of the digital whining, and a double beep before hanging up. Job done.

Bromovich reached into his jacket, pulled out his flask, and poured them both a double-finger shot of vodka.

Ship's Log (Special Report)

SS *Indigo*
Captain Igor Bromovich
Klaipeda Naval Academy

Transmission: July 17, 2003: 9:11 a.m. CST

Incident: July 16, 2003: 12:35 p.m. CST

After we boarded the crew and passengers in Belize City and set sail in a northeasterly direction toward San Pedro, a loud blast was heard from the lower cabins and specifically in the ship's Oscar Wilde Suite.

Within the suite, the body of Mr. Quentin Leonard Perkins was found with a single bullet wound to the forehead. Mr. Perkins was declared dead at the scene, presumed suicide.

The body was found in the bath with just a T-shirt and a pair of swimming trunks. A military service Webley revolver was found on the floor beside the bath, and the remnants of a burned book were found in the shower area.

The appropriate photographs were taken and attached to this special report, the bagged revolver is in the ship's safe, and the body has been placed in the ship's morgue as per standard operating procedures.

The Belize City Port Authority was informed of the incident, and permission to proceed as planned was received.

Captain Igor Bromovich

8

I.
Dallas, a Few Days Earlier

SITTING IN THE FRENCH ROOM at the Adolphus, Harry ordered his second Dark 'n' Stormy of the day. He stared at his watch: 1:23 p.m. Tapping his foot on the barstool next to him, he looked out at Commerce Street and the downtown Dallas business going about its daily routine.

It was a far cry from his hometown, but Dallas was home now, or, more specifically, Highland Park, a fifteen-minute ride away. Unlike most of the other cities in the States, he liked Dallas and appreciated the more laid-back nature of business, although it lacked the character. And that's why, when he moved twenty years earlier, he had opted for Highland Park.

He stared again at his watch, an old blue-faced Breitling Aeromarine: 1:27 p.m. He took a generous swig of the mix of Pusser's Rum, his favorite, ginger ale, and lime juice with an orange-rind swirl. It reminded him of his own time on the high seas.

Harry had been a master diving instructor based out of Thailand and had many a fair story to tell of his adventures. In fact, his adventures went back far beyond there too, and he remembered meeting Parsons during jungle training back in Belize. The boy had done well for himself.

He toasted the air. "The boy did very well for himself indeed."

He looked in the mirror facing him behind the bar and squinted, barely recognizing the man he had become. All those memories long gone, and all he had to show was a big old empty house; Christine's ashes on the mantelpiece; and the occasional email from his two sons whenever they remembered him, which was less and less frequently these days.

"Barely remember me bloody birthday," he said to himself, looking at the date on his watch.

"Sorry, sir—did you say something?"

Harry shook his chops and grinned back at the young bartender—or *mixologist*, the term that apparently he preferred.

"Talking to myself again, son. It comes with age."

He used that smoke screen often to avoid answering unwanted questions, either that or his drinking, or, if he really needed to, both combined.

His old mate James Parsons had sent him an email a couple of weeks ago saying he was heading back to Belize via DFW and would pop in for a night.

Of course, typical Parsons staying in some fancy hotel like the Adolphus, but to be honest, Harry hadn't pushed too hard to stay at his own house, now empty and far past its former glory.

Harry's passage to where he was today had been a long one.

An investment banker with Barings in London, he'd take long lunches at the Jugged Hare, the Old Crow, or the Viaduct, with copious amounts of London Pride and Chateau Palmer, and oysters to hold down the alcohol intake. Three-hour lunches, half-cut, and walk out with million-pound deals.

"Those were the days."

He sat shaking his head, looking into his cocktail. He squinted back at the mirror and glared at his red nose and cheeks, evidence of his eating and drinking habits over the years.

He had pulled his old city chalk stripe out of the closet and donned an old regimental tie for his old mate.

He recalled the conversation in the Hamburg bar all those years ago with the two young 2 Para men. He remembered their recollection of their apparent sighting of the *Ella Sophia* laid in her closet of a grave at the bottom of the Caribbean Sea. Harry had read about her fabled history and never discovered treasure and riches. If the legend were true, then somebody would be set to make a lot of money on her find. Problem is that the two paratroopers had failed to log the exact coordinates of her resting place, and now, years later, she remained a mystery.

James had mentioned his Hamburg conversation in his note. Harry was intrigued at the coincidence and the timing.

He looked at his Breitling again: 1:36 p.m. Parsons was late—unlike him, but maybe his flight was delayed. Harry pulled out his phone to check the flight schedules. BA flight 193 had already landed. *He must be on his way.*

He continued tapping his foot on the barstool next to him, and as he looked up, he saw the familiar figure striding toward him, smiling, holding his hand out, looking him up and down.

"Blimey, old boy, you shouldn't have dressed up for me," Parsons said and grinned.

"Least I could do, *old boy*"—the quick-footed banter of two old friends.

A handshake, a slap on each other's back, and a hug, and then Parsons sat beside him at the bar. "What's your poison?" he asked, looking down at the Dark 'n' Stormy.

They settled in with their cocktails as the bartender laid out the place mats and silverware and handed them both white card menus, which they examined in silence.

Parsons looked up at the attentive mixologist and recited the menu word for word. "The Australian filet, pomme puree, rapini, with the sauce bordelaise—rare, please."

Harry looked up. "Make that two. And how about the Royal Osetra to share?"

The young bartender nodded.

"And let's get a portion of the Castelvetrano olives to kick us off!" Parsons said.

"Splendid idea. Just like the good old days." Harry silently grimaced.

They tentatively stuck into their conversation; they had a lot to catch up on.

"Sorry about Christine," Parsons said.

Harry just looked down at his drink.

"How are the boys?"

Silence.

"How's business?"

"Never mind me—what the hell is going on with you and this crazy cruise in the Caribbean?"

As they made their way through the olives and the caviar with an accompanying glass of Taittinger, the steaks arrived, along with a decanted bottle of Chateau Palmer 1985, one of Harry's last from his all-but-depleted wine cellar.

Through mouthfuls of the Australian grass-fed beef, Parsons went on to tell his old friend about N. Waring, Jemol Litions, Litions Industries, and the SS *Indigo*.

"So, what's with the *Ella Sophia*?"

Harry volunteered his recollections of the conversation in Hamburg, and Parsons nodded attentively throughout, smiling at his old friend Harry, putting it to one side and thinking of it as a side excursion to the bigger event.

By five o'clock, they were both done. Parsons needed rest before his next hop south, and Harry needed to give his liver a rest. They said goodbye in the lobby, shook hands, slapped each other's back, hugged, and then turned on a sixpence, Parsons to his room and Harry in his black car back home to Highland Park.

"Farewell, my friend." Harry meant it.

II.
The Florida Coast

The young girl sat on the fishing boat with her rod and net dangling over the edge into the clear blue water below. She had grown up by the beach, and at the tender age of twelve, she was both extremely independent and by now a competent navigator.

That day, she had stolen her father's boat. He was a traveling salesman and wasn't at home most of the time. Her mother worked as a waitress in the local beach bar. She and her two sisters lived free lives, the only condition that they attended school and reported progressive grades. Angela had a mix of As and Bs and kept out of the wrath, with her sisters earning Bs and Cs. She was OK with that. In fact, to an extent, she engineered it, taking the most from Sally and Sarah and not giving them very much in return. That kept her ahead, and she had learned the art of superior positioning even from an early age.

Her father's boat was a sixteen-foot Avenger with an Evinrude propeller engine—a simple aluminum-hulled boat, easy to handle and ideal for cutting around the shore.

Recently, there had been a lot of noise in the press around a treasure hunt offshore. She was interested in fishing, but she thought about getting close to the salvage site to take a peek. The story of long-lost treasure fascinated her.

Even at this early age, she was attuned to being in the right place at the right time, and this experience did nothing but affirm the merits of that philosophy.

Nuestra Senora de Atocha was the rear-guard ship of the 1622 treasure fleet, which left Havana several weeks late, causing them to run into the jaws of a hurricane on September 6 that same year. Eight ships of the twenty-eight-ship fleet were lost, wrecked on the reefs between the Dry Tortugas and present-day Key West. Only five people survived from the *Atocha* and were saved by another vessel. The wreck itself was scattered after another hurricane hit the site exactly one month later, so the Spanish were never able to salvage what was allegedly one of the richest galleons ever to sail the seas.

She anchored the boat at a safe distance from the now famous *Northwind* and cast her line. She brought her boogie box and was listening to her tunes—"Maggie May," "Imagine," and "Stairway to Heaven"—basking on the deck of the Avenger, soaking up the sun.

When she awoke from a nap, something was wrong. She sat up and looked over at the salvage vessel, obviously in trouble, sinking, its hull pointing in an unnatural angle. She could see people jumping from the boat. She watched and stared, paralyzed, not knowing what to do.

As she stood there, stunned by the quickly disappearing boat, she noticed some items floating toward her in the water in ziplock bags. She fished the first out of the water, a golden snake clasp bracelet; then another, what looked like an ancient gold coin; and then more and more, and more, a total of over fifty items all told. She used her net to scoop them up into the boat, and as the booty dried up, the distant figures in the water did too.

For a moment, she glanced at the stowage where the life vests were housed and thought—thought of her father and the trouble she would be in for borrowing his boat. She looked down at her newly found treasure. She paused, checked, and turned the Avenger back toward the shore.

She allowed herself just one look back at the capsized ship and put to one side the people bobbing up and down in the water.

"They'll be fine," she said as she cranked up the Evinrude to full throttle and headed home.

The next evening, she watched the local news announce that the captain's wife and son and a crew member had all drowned that day. It was hard to take, hard to live with, but the riches she had gathered made it a whole lot easier.

She never told anyone about the incident, and she intended to keep it that way. Forever. Over the years, she had sold a couple of the coins and rings, but she kept the snake bracelet for a rainy day.

III.
The Grand Dining Room

That evening, dinner was a somber affair, but Zach was determined to make the best of it. He realized that the apparent suicide of Father Perkins had gotten everyone down. He also understood that everyone naturally wanted to know why they were aboard the ship and what would happen next.

"Right, gang. Let's get to know each other a little better," he said. "Start with me?"

He looked around for approval and saw at least some appetite from Lady Helen and Sal. Chalmers and Jacobs looked OK with the idea, the two military men were po-faced, and the rest looked down at their plates as if they could be invisible.

He theatrically cleared his throat. "OK, well, how about I kick off, then?

"Well, hello. I'm Zach Carter, originally from Sonoma County, Northern California. I studied at the CSU Maritime Academy, Vallejo, California. I'm a qualified maritime engineer, having grown up on my father's day-trip boat out of Sausalito, and I'm proud and delighted to be on the SS *Indigo*." He gestured to the ship around them.

"I am also delighted at the opportunity to meet with all of you," he added, once more sweeping his hand around him, this time indicating his audience and resting on Lady Helen Bailey. Zach sensed a blush he was afraid that all would see. Lady Helen just smiled back knowingly. He quickly cleared his throat. The audience was starting to warm up, but boy, was it hard work, he thought.

"I've spent a lot of time in these waters and on the islands from Trinidad and Tobago in the south, the Grenadines, Saint Kitts, Nevis, across to the Dominican Republic, Haiti, up to Cuba, and up as far as the Bahamas."

He conveniently omitted his time in Virgin Gorda—a very private memory and one that he preferred to forget. He was, however, gaining traction, as all the passengers were now engaged, heads up, and listening.

"I am also a member of the Antigua and Barbuda Rum and Tot Club, thanks to my father, and Lord Nelson's great-great-great-granddaughter is my godmother!"

There was a muffled round of applause. Zach saw that the audience didn't have a clue about the important role Lord Horatio Nelson played in these waters in the mid-seventeenth century.

Given the apparent interest, Zach went on to tell one of his old tales of how Nelson was stationed in English Harbour, Antigua, and was commanded to enforce the Navigation Act that forbade trade with nations other than the crown territories.

"This is where, according to legend, he married Fanny Nisbet, the daughter of a wealthy plantation owner, on the tiny island of Nevis, close by."

Now even Simpson and Sharp were fully engaged.

"Before leaving to return to Old Blighty, Nelson had to divorce poor old Fanny, as good old Horatio was already married to Lady Hamilton back in London!"

"Wait, Nelson was already married?" Lady Helen asked.

Zach nodded with a knowing grin.

"Bloody hell, Nelson was a chauvinist," Sheldon said.

"A *bigamist*, I think you mean, Sheldon," Jacobs said with a sarcastic smile and another point scored in his game of one-upmanship.

"Well, technically, he was a polygamist as well." Even Dr. Brown was engaged in the conversation.

The rest broke into a soft round of applause.

"Very good, Zach," Jacobs said. "Very good indeed."

The mood in the Grand Dining Room had lifted. Mission accomplished.

Both Chalmers and Jacobs were eager for their turns to tell the group how important they were.

Jacobs pushed himself to the front of the queue, typical of his type A personality. During his career, he had trampled over many in favor of his own progress. He was used to that. Second nature by now. He cleared his throat.

"Stuart Jacobs, chairman of the San Francisco Chamber of Commerce; former global sales director for IBM; CEO of French software company Xperient, who I sold to Getners for eight hundred million. I have an apartment in San Francisco, a house in St. Francis Wood, and a farmhouse in the Tuscany. I am also a musician, and when I was younger"—he smiled broadly and tapped his belly—"a lot younger, I appeared on the TV show *Opportunity Knocks.*"

Sheldon was the only one who looked like he was genuinely impressed, like a little kid. "We have a celebrity in our midst," he said and looked around. "I used to watch that all the time. Hughie Green, the man himself."

Still receiving only blank looks, Sheldon turned his gaze to his Old Speckled Hen in front of him.

Angela Chalmers was next.

She went through her résumé like she was at an interview for the CEO role that she had been waiting for for so long. She latched on to Jacob's property résumé, the locations, and the accumulated assets—that's the sort of accumulation she wanted for herself. As she talked, she referenced only me, myself, and I.

Lady Helen enthusiastically talked about her world travels, and the audience seemed genuinely interested. Especially Sheldon, who was letching and flirting like a schoolboy. At five feet nine, slim, with blonde hair and green eyes, she was a good-looker, according to Sheldon, and had a magnetic personality that was hard not to like, even for Dr. Brown, who went next.

Dr. Bronwyn Brown was a woman of few words. She went over her career with the NHS and her current role at St. Mary's and stated that she was an avid reader and collector.

"A collector of what?" asked Zach, in good spirits.

"Never you mind, Mr. Carter" was her only response, followed by an awkward silence and pause in the momentum.

Sal, the Australian, broke the silence and waxed lyrical about how all things Australian were better than anywhere else in the world—apparently the coal, the sheep, the weather, the beaches, the health care system, the food, the beer, and the people, among other things.

"Shame about the cricket," Sheldon teased, drawing a cheeky smile from Salmond.

Parsons gave a matter-of-fact thirty-second introduction. Then the two military men told the audience nothing about themselves, apart from how they liked rugby, football, boxing, and an occasional Cuban cigar, in that order.

They wound up the dinner and retired for the evening.

IV.
The Dauntless Suite

Sir James Parsons sat in his cabin, its name a reference to the *Indigo*'s own following her acquisition by the US Navy back in January 1942: the USS *Dauntless*.

She'd had an interesting life—originally from the Great Lakes Engineering Works, commissioned by Horace Dodge, founder of the Dodge Brothers, which became the Detroit automotive giant Dodge. In 1926, she caught fire and sank in New York, to be recovered and restored. She suffered further damage in 1940, when she ran aground in the Great Lakes, needing repairs. Then she served for the US Navy as the flagship for Admiral Ernest King, commander in chief of the US Fleet and chief of naval operations.

After World War II, Dodge's wife, Anna, purchased her back from the navy and restored her to civilian life and service. Then the rest is history, with the ship eventually falling into the hands of Litions Industries, with a no-expense-spared refurbishment back to her former glories and beyond.

The decks and the passenger areas had been upgraded with the finest furnishings, fixtures, and fittings, the engine room totally gutted and upgraded. From the galley to the staff quarters—and then there were the carefully curated and crafted luxury cabins and suites. The Dauntless Suite was the largest, with its own lounge area and study off the king-size bedroom.

Parsons sat at the antique Georgian desk, inlaid with red leather, with its matching Chippendale chair in the classic English rococo, neoclassical style from the mid-nineteenth century. It was an original—Parsons had done his homework on that too. He pondered the events of the past few days and those to come.

He looked at his papers on the desk in front of him—the dossier of passengers, the photographs of Bland and Perkins crossed out. Who was next? He tapped his forefinger on the photograph of Chalmers, thinking.

He also had the papers on the history of the *Indigo*. The various old photos, including of his troop on jungle training; his friend Harry in his chalk stripe suit and famous red braces outside the Ritz in London after a very memorable long late lunch; Emily and the boys in happier times; his eldest son, William, at his graduation from the Royal Military Academy Sandhurst, proud in his newly awarded Royal Engineers colors. Parsons paused to look at the photograph of Shelly and her newborn, a little girl, over thirty-five years ago. He passed by the oncology report once again, but it served as a reminder for him to take his daily dose of pills, also on the desk before him.

He'd often wondered how he had got here, as so many did at this time of life. More to look back at than look forward to—the sense of anxiety that the worst was yet to come and the good times behind you. He knew that was the case for him, and that's why he was here, on the SS *Indigo*, in the middle of the Caribbean Sea.

He pulled out his leather-bound journal from the lap drawer and reached for his Alfred Hitchcock–design Montblanc and turned to the last page he had left off.

He looked out the window over the ocean with the pen in his hand. He remembered how twenty years ago, in Monte

Carlo, with Emily, he had won big at the Café de Paris and used the proceeds of his winnings to buy the cherished pen set. He could feel the quality and the memories in his hands. A recollection of days gone by, happier days.

He didn't know quite why he had ended up with so many skeletons, no less so than the daughter he had never met. He knew she was on his trail, and he also knew she was close. It wasn't that he was fearful of her, nor should she be of him, but the longer he went without making contact, the more the anxiousness grew. She was well within her rights to hate him, and he often wondered whether she did. He was also fully aware of the consequences of her potential claim on his inheritance.

The danger of a career-changing scandal at that time was too much to consider, as was at the time the prospect of breaking up the marriage and the lives of their two sons.

He had loved her mother, as he knew that she did him, but it was just far too complicated, and life was sometimes that way.

He turned to financial matters. He had the stock sale pro formas in front of him, waiting to be executed. The main stocks were simpler, in a buy-and-sell market of common stock. He had to be careful not to flood the market but at the same time not to drip-feed too slowly to give the signal that their largest investor was bowing out.

The gold and diamond mines were less of a headache for him. Some of his big bets were still too young and volatile, so that was less of a risk. The real issue for Parsons was the divesting and separation from his other investments, global players, nontraditional investments—that's where the issues would occur. He would need to handle that very carefully indeed and even be willing to forfeit them for the safety of his future family.

He sent an encrypted message to his *friend,* signaling for them to speak in the next twenty-four hours. Over the years, they had built a distant respect for each other. They had both done very well for each other during their business relationship.

The man didn't trust anyone, and certainly Parsons didn't trust him.

Parsons turned to his journal, put pen to paper, and started to recount the day's events, the theme tune still playing in his head on repeat.

"... Relax. I'll need some information first. Just the basic facts. Can you show me where it hurts? ..."

V.
The Marilyn Monroe Suite

The next morning was silent. The sea was calm, the sun was up, and the waves lapped gently against the bow. Zach woke up from his dreams—his nightmares—remembering Virgin Gorda all too vividly.

It's true that's where he had met the Branson babes, where he met Eva, but his secret was that's also where he got involved with the Castida Cartel. They'd approached him one morning, not too dissimilar to this, a perfect Caribbean sunrise, the wind flapping around his clapboard house, with their unrefusable demands for him to help them smuggle their drugs, launder their money, or the *Lady of the Bay* and his father would be no longer.

He recalled the regrettable transaction, against his free will, and his contempt for these people, especially their leader, Esteban. He regretted that he'd ever met him, in his high-rolling suits of white linen, designer watches, and his Guccis worn with no socks—even Zach had sufficient self-respect not to do that.

As he came to from his sleep, with the silk curtains blowing in the breeze, the sound of the ocean, the smell of the sea seeping through, Zach could hear in the distance— well, not too far away—the rat-a-tat-tat on one of the thick mahogany guest suites and the distinctive holler of Captain Igor Bromovich.

He looked at his watch. He'd slept in. It had been the combination of the sea air, the journey here, and the majestic *Indigo* and his beautiful cabin, fueled probably by too many lonesome tequila-shot nightcaps and too much weed. It was almost noon.

"Madam, it's Captain Bromovich. Are you there?" Zach could hear the bellow down the hall.

"Madam, can you please let us know you can hear us?" Silence.

"We want to know you're safe."

Zach sat up in bed and rubbed his eyes. Then he took a quick stretch and pulled on his pants and T-shirt before padding to the bathroom, where he splashed his face with cold water and wet his hair. He took a quick look in the mirror and then headed for the door to see what all the commotion was about. He hurried down the hall to join the others outside the Marilyn Monroe Suite—Bromovich in his bright white uniform, a little less starched than it was when Zach had first seen it; Kayla; and the two military men.

"Mrs. Chalmers, last call! We're going to break the lock and come in," Bromovich said.

Zach had noticed how the more stressed the captain became, the more he would revert to his sometimes thick Baltic state Eastern Bloc accent.

Kayla had a worried look on her face. Apparently she'd been trying to service the room since earlier that morning.

Not a stir from inside.

Bromovich and the two military men closed in—*like a Para Reg door-to-door-type routine*, Zach thought as the image passed through his mind.

Bromovich reached down, slid the brass master key into the lock, slowly turned it, and started to open the door, but the security latch on the inside was engaged.

A slight sulfur-like whiff came from the room.

Bromovich turned to Zach. "Can you smell that?"

Zach shrugged and shook his head. After last night's tipples and spliffs, Zach's senses were in no state to respond otherwise. He looked at the others—similar responses from them.

Bromovich described it. It was all so slight that it could have been sweaty socks. But Angela Chalmers was not one of those who even wore socks, never mind sweaty ones.

With the door ajar and the internal lock still engaged, Bromovich bellowed, "Ms. Chalmers, are you in there? Can you hear me?"

Still silence.

It was a fine balance, whether to disturb the guests, but especially after recent events, the passengers' safety was of paramount importance.

Zach shouted into the room, "Ms. Chalmers, if we don't hear from you in the next thirty seconds, we're obliged to force access to your quarters to ensure your safety."

Still silence, and this time, Zach whiffed a sulfur-type smell as Bromovich had suggested.

On that, Zach stepped in front of the others, grabbed the wrench recovered from the engine room from Bromovich's hand, and proceeded to jimmy the door open. He pulled on the wrench, and they could hear the cracking and splintering of the wood as the latch pulled away from the casing and, eventually, they were in.

They fell into the Marilyn Monroe Suite—Zach in front, Bromovich, Simpson, and Sharp behind, almost falling over one another.

Zach stood observing the scene in front of him.

Curtains still closed, and even at this time of day, their effectiveness of blacking out the light was testament to the level of detail and expense behind the *Indigo*'s design.

The bedside light was still on. Angela Chalmers, the Floridan implant to Texas, was seemingly peacefully tucked up in bed, eyes closed.

"Ms. Chalmers?" Zach shook her arm. "Ms. Chalmers." A little harder.

No movement.

He grabbed her hand—icy cold. "She's dead."

There was no need to check her pulse. She was as cold as ice, and Zach figured she probably had been dead for at least eight hours.

Notwithstanding, Sharp stepped up, checked for a pulse, or breathing, and then slowly nodded. "She's gone."

During the diagnosis, Kayla had opened the blinds and cracked the window to let the fresh air in. She then went to the room controls and turned the air-conditioning fan on to maximum to get rid of the stale, dank odor lingering in the air.

Angela Chalmers, pronounced dead, was tucked up neatly in her bed, with no sign of any struggle—her door latched from within, and not a window wide enough to enable access—peacefully laid down with a book on her chest, the Machiavellian musings of *CEO for a Day: How to Engineer Your Way to the Top.*

9

I.

The Smoking Salon

SHELDON WAS SUMMONED TO THE smoking salon. Simpson and Sharp sat down on the matching red leather chesterfield chairs, Sheldon and Jacobs on the sofa, with Zach in close attendance and Bromovich looking on.

"You were the last to see her alive, old boy," Zach said. "We simply need to understand what happened and gather any insights we can."

Sheldon looked hurt, almost wounded by the comment. "Listen—I don't know what this is all about, but I can tell you it's absolutely nothing to do with me." He looked around the room for some support or empathy but didn't see any.

"We just want to know what happened last night at the bar. When did you last see Ms. Chalmers? What was the conversation, her mood?"

"I tell yer—I've no bloody clue what yer all on about or what the hell this is all about."

Bromovich looked at Sheldon in the eyes and delivered the weight of the circumstances. "We believe that you were the last person to see Ms. Chalmers alive."

The room went quiet as the statement settled in. Sheldon, eyes cast down at his boots, slowly rose his head and looked around at his audience, and his audience carefully returned his gaze. His eyes were reddening. A look of fear. "She's dead?"

"Yep. We found her this afternoon. Dead," Zach said.

"When was the last time you saw her, Sheldon?" Jacobs asked.

"Tell us about the bar last night. What did you talk about? What was her mood?"

"What happened, Sheldon?"

Like a little boy accused of stealing candy, Sheldon was red-faced, holding back tears of frustration, shaking, angry. "Look, I don't know what you fuckers are suggesting, but it was certainly nothing to do with me. I swear on my life. I swear on Catherine's life." He put his head in his hands. "What the bloody hell happened?"

Zach went on to explain the circumstances of them finding her in the Marilyn Monroe Suite.

"So, were you with Ms. Chalmers at the bar or not?" Sharp asked.

Sheldon looked around once again for support. "Yes, of course I was. You all know that I have been open about all that. But I was not in her room at any time." Sheldon looked genuinely scared. He was cornered.

"When was the last time you saw her?"

Sheldon was clearly under pressure. It was obvious that he was the odd man out, and he looked like a man who understood the seriousness of the situation.

"Look, we hung out for a couple of drinks—she was telling me about her job, her life, her husband and kids. She was telling me about her aspirations for the future, her fears from the past, and how, like me, she had an eye on setting up a winery somewhere. We talked about how I might be able to help her. That's all."

"I bet you did," Sharp said.

Sheldon showed his annoyance but immediately stepped down, as the situation he was in was tough for anyone, never mind the clear athleticism and experienced-soldier characters of Sharp and Simpson before him.

"Then what?" Zach said.

From when he was a kid, Zach had seen a lot of *Columbo*, his father's favorite detective show, and the famous manner of the mac-wearing, cigar-smoking detective, complete with a smelly old car and a smelly old dog. Just as the title character appeared to have completed his line of questioning, he'd go back in and catch the interviewee off guard—and the line "Just one more question," delivered with a smile, was always the killer blow.

Sheldon said, stuttering, "Nothing. That was it. At around midnight, we left the bar, both went to our accommodations, and we said good night in the hallway. We went our separate ways, saying good night as we headed to our cabins. That's it!"

He looked around and pleaded once again with his audience, in the corner, acting not like a conqueror but like a victim. He was visibly shaking, eyes wide and wild. He looked nervous and completely out of his depth.

Zach took the moment and gave rationale and logic to the situation.

"Look, the door was latched from the inside—there's no way that anyone else but Ms. Chalmers could have done that. If we're looking for a killer, it's not of the human type. There must be some other logical explanation."

Sheldon deflated like a balloon released of air. He was off the hook, out of the spotlight. "I swear on Catherine's life this was nothing to do with me."

It turned out that Catherine was his wife of thirty years, and he would rarely if ever talk about her or reference her unless he really needed to, and this was one of those times.

"Don't look at me. I don't like the look of that cook, that Perry lad. Maybe it was him. I was tucked up in my cabin. It wasn't me. You have to believe me."

"Gentlemen," Bromovich said, "Zach has a point. Just because he was the last person to see her doesn't mean that he was responsible. Besides, seeing her earlier, she looked like she was pretty peaceful, tucked up in bed, reading, and with the inside security latch in place."

The penny dropped. *This may have been natural causes after all*, Zach thought.

Simpson and Sharp stood up together and, without apology, without a word, headed up to the top deck.

"I told you, Zach—nothing to do with me. Maybe she just up and died on us. Shit happens, you know."

Zach shrugged in agreement.

"Anyway, who do them arrogant bastards think they are?" Sheldon pointed after Simpson and Sharp, knowing they were no longer in earshot.

II.
Bradford, England, Years Earlier

Christmas Eve, Little Horton. Vic Sheldon walked into the two-up, two-down redbrick-built tenement house on Rothesay Terrace straight from the Black Horse after too many pints of Tetley's.

It was Christmas Eve, the fire was blazing, and the family dinner was *boiling* on the stove. The roast joint was ready two hours ago, the roast potatoes were now like bullets, and the peas had turned an unappetizing yellow with a long-faded hint of green.

This was a repeat of almost every Sunday of the year. This Sunday was the day before Christmas 1972.

Mary Sheldon stood at the back door with a Rothmans dangling from the corner of her mouth. The two boys were playing pirates in the backyard, Tony getting the better of his younger brother and hitting him over the head with the toy saber, part of a pirates set they had as a hand-me-down from their clan of older cousins.

"You're fucking late again, Vic Sheldon!" Mary shouted as she heard her husband stumble through the front door.

"And you fucking stink of ale. I thought you said you were going to be back by two?" She turned and looked at the clock. It was nearly four. "I thought kick-out was at three. Where the fuck av yer been?"

Sheldon Sr. just glared at her and waved the boys in from the yard, young Andrew Sheldon's head showing the signs of new bruising. Vic stood them in front of the open fire and flashed a shiny penny in front of them both.

"Right, lads. First one to draw blood wins the penny and gets first presents to open in the morning."

They knew the drill. The boys raised their fists, and before the old man could even kick off the bout, Tony was laying into Andrew, haymaking, punching him in the face indiscriminately, without hesitation or a moment for the younger boy to take a breath. The blood splattered from Andrew's nose and splashed on the tiles around the hearth.

"And Anthony is the winner," Vic declared, patting the older boy on the back so he nearly fell over, then giving a backhander to Andrew to add to his pain.

"You need to get a grip, son, and start winning yer battles" were his words of fatherly advice.

Andrew ran to the kitchen sink, grabbed a tea towel, and ran the tap of cold water.

With another cigarette in her mouth, Mary brought out the plates of food with piping-hot gravy and threw them on the dining table.

"Happy fucking Christmas," she growled. "Yer bunch of bastards." And she meant it.

III.
Staff Quarters

Perry and Kayla were winding down. It had been a long few days since their arrival in Belize, and they were both scratching their heads over the incident-packed first three days of the journey.

"What the hell is going on, Perry?" Kayla asked in her shrill tone.

Perry sat there at the kitchenette table with a can of Heineken in his hand and a cigarette hanging out of the corner of his mouth, his chef's jacket open at the chest and his blue-check chef's pants unbuttoned.

"I have no fucking idea, Kayla," he said and glared at her. "Frankly, I'm not even sure I care. If they pay us, and we get the hell off this ship in one piece, I'm not sure I really give a fuck."

Kyla glared back in silence, tapping her hand on the table and shaking her leg beneath. Finally, she said, "Yeh, you said that about the truck too, Perry."

"For fuck's sake, you're not still on about that, are yer."

"Well, they all died. They didn't have to die—the children, Perry?"

It was a sensitive subject for both of them, to say the least.

"Look, we've been through this," Perry said. "It wasn't our fault. It would have happened anyway without us. They were going to do it anyway."

"Yeh, but if it wasn't for us making the connections, it might never have happened to them." She had tears rolling down her face.

"They would have done it anyway. They were desperate. If it wasn't us, then it would have been the Russians, or the Albanians—that would have been even worse for them."

Kayla glared at Perry, remembering the scenes on the local news, twenty-eight souls lost, thirteen of them children, cramped in the back of a box van, suffocated.

"You fucking heartless bastard." She picked up the ashtray and threw it at him with all her might, and it glanced off his head.

"You little fucking bitch!" He jumped across the table and grabbed her throat, strangling her with his bare hands as she slowly slipped into unconsciousness. He released her before she passed totally out, as she collapsed into a chair.

"You fucking bastard. Touch me one more time, and I'm gonna fucking turn you in!" she said.

"You do that, and it'll be the end of both of us, you stupid fucking bitch."

"I don't fucking care, Perry. How can you live with yourself?"

She sat there tapping and shaking her leg, her right eye bright red with blood—she'd burst a blood vessel and picked up a black eye in the altercation. Her conscience wasn't at ease as it apparently was with Perry. In fact, she was tormented by the memory.

"All for a grand!" she said. "How the fuck do you sleep at night, Perry?"

Perry lit another cigarette and poured Kayla another four-finger glass of vodka, with a splash of the Rose's lime cordial, just the way Dr. Brown and the old women back home liked it.

"I don't like these fucking people," Kayla declared.

"You don't have to. We're not here to like them; we're here to feed them and collect our ten grand a week. Besides, three of them are dead already."

"Fuck off. You're such a fucking wanker."

Kayla tugged his hand and pulled him off to the bedroom. The altercation had made her horny. That was their relationship. She went down on him, pulled down his chef's pants, and straddled him on the bed.

"You fucking bastard, Perry," she said as she rode up and down, back and forth. "You fucking bastard."

Ship's Log (Special Report)

SS *Indigo*
Captain Igor Bromovich
Klaipeda Naval Academy

Transmission: July 18, 2003: 10:05 p.m. CST

Incident: July 18, 2003: 12:05 p.m. CST

Earlier today, the body of passenger Mrs. Angela Chalmers was found unresponsive in her cabin.

The door to the Marilyn Monroe Suite was locked, and the internal safety bolt was engaged. She was found in her bed seemingly peaceful, with no signs of anything untoward. The bedside reading light was on, and an open book lay on her chest. She was formally pronounced dead at 12:15 p.m. local time.

1. Mrs. Angela Barr Chalmers, US citizen, passport number 479212543.

Although there was no conclusion as to what caused her death, there was no evidence to suggest foul play.

This is the second passenger we have lost in as many days, and a third was murdered ashore. We will continue with the itinerary as planned unless instructed otherwise.

Captain Igor Bromovich

<END>

10

I.
Nidderdale, England

SHELLY SAT UPRIGHT IN BED. She'd had a bad twenty-four hours. The pain was getting worse daily. She tried to concentrate on *Countdown*, but the drugs made it hard for her—the letters and numbers kept getting jumbled in her head. She turned off the television out of frustration.

She stared out of the window of St. Mary's across the green fields overlooking the dales. She used to be good at the game and had been an avid fan of the Richard Whiteley–Carol Vorderman tag team, showing their flair with consonants and vowels and numbers and solving the often-impossible puzzles before them.

She had once applied to be on the show, but that didn't work out. Yet another of her list of regrets—too many to remember, too painful to forget, especially now that she could see the end far clearer than she could the beginning.

As a young girl growing up in the dales, she had hoped that this day wouldn't come peppered with regrets. She looked back at her life now and realized how wrong she had been. She wondered whether it was even possible for anyone not to have a number of regrets—or secrets. She knew she had a whole closet full of the latter, including at first the existence of, then the identity of, her youngest daughter's real father.

They had continued their fling for many years—she had kept that secret too. Clandestine meetings to suit, always orchestrated to make sure it was behind the curtain and never to be seen, by anyone, never mind the children.

She had often agonized over why, but she knew why: He was married with kids of his own, and she had her other children, two boys and another two girls. She was a lowly girl from Nidderdale, and he was a highflier. Theirs was a meeting of souls and of bodies, and although it was difficult for most to understand, the two of them did understand, and that's just how it was.

She rested easy at that thought. She wished him the very best. In that moment, she realized that she loved him like no other. He was also her secret—and one that she would take to her grave.

Shelly looked out the window and could see the sheep in the fields with their spring lambs. It was really a wonderful time of the year to see the green and the daffodils and the burst of life promising that summer was on its way.

She thought of an old tune from her past.

"... OK. Just a little pinprick. There'll be no more, arrggh, but you may feel a little sick ..."

She saw his face in front of her. This was goodbye, and although they were destined never to be together, they always were and always had been.

It was Shelly's favorite time of year, with winter over, new life, and the promises of a warmer, brighter future. She was ever an optimist, but it was now time to go. She lay there peacefully, calm, and content that she was ready to move on.

The doctor arrived to do the deed. Shelly just smiled and nodded, and that was the end of that. And of Shelly Bailey.

II.

The rear deck was a hive of activity. Simpson, Sharp, Lady Helen, and Sal were going on a Jet Ski safari and snorkeling expedition. With the *Indigo* anchored just off the reef a couple of hundred yards away and the Jet Skis ready and waiting in the water, the four were all set.

Zach was excited. This was the closest he would be to Lady Helen since they left St. George's Caye, and he was working on the knot in his stomach and the stammer in his chops. He was mindful that he was hired help, but that didn't stop him from throwing her a smile and a wink. She smiled back. He could feel the flush coming on, and he quickly turned away to get on with preparing the equipment.

Sheldon was on the back of *Indigo* to watch as they set off. Zach spotted Jacobs and Parsons joining him as he sat on his Jet Ski and waited for the others to climb down to the remaining two. Soon they were all fired up and ready to go.

"Aww, come on," Lady Helen said to Sal. "I want to drive."

Most found it hard to say no to her, especially Sal. He conceded, and she mounted the craft and took the reins. Simpson and Sharp were getting ready on theirs, with Zach keeping a watchful eye.

"Race yer!" Lady Helen hollered across to the two military men as she pulled all in on the throttle, spun 180 degrees, and careered off across the bright blue ocean, heading to and parallel to the reef.

Zach kept a safe distance behind the Simpson-and-Sharp ride, lagging behind Sal and Lady Helen, who were way in the lead, crashing on the tops of the choppy Caribbean outside the protection of the coral enclave behind.

"Woo-hoo!" Zach could hear her scream, Sal joining in the chorus as the pair seemed content on challenging the world before them.

Zach looked on feeling a tinge of jealousy. "How did that gormless bastard land such a catch?" he muttered.

He watched as Helen Bailey, riding up, standing up, the wind in her hair, burned down the reef. There was no chance of any of them catching up with her after her surprise start. Eventually, she pulled up, and the others joined her moments later.

"What kept you boys?" She winked and flashed her big infectious smile.

III.

Zach was a qualified divemaster and once an accomplished free diver. He had dropped a buoy at the preferred spot on the reef as a reference point for them. They tied the Jet Skis up to the buoy, and Helen, Sal, Simpson, and Sharp jumped in the water. Zach stayed on the surface, straddling his Jet Ski.

While he was in Virgin Gorda and arranging a dive trip off Necker Island, one of his dive party had died as a result of pulmonary barotrauma—ascending from too deep, too quickly. The tour company's insurance covered the claim. At the tribunal, he was found not guilty of professional negligence, and retained his credentials, but that was the last dive he had been on.

Despite that, these were all experienced divers—they didn't need him. And besides that, in these waters, three Jet Skis can quickly get nobbled and disappear.

That's how Zach rationalized the situation as he watched the four in the water do their thing. Particularly, he kept his eye on Lady Helen Bailey, toyed with the idea of jumping in to join her, then as quickly changed his mind.

He thought of his father, and of the *Lady of the Bay* and the Ford Bronco, the two of them riding home together and his father's stories of long-lost treasure as well as his lifetime of adventures trying to find it in various parts of the world. Of course, the *Ella Sophia* was one of those legends, and he remembered the tale well.

As he bobbed up and down on the ocean surface, he thought about Eva too. He wondered whether he'd ever find the right one. Although he'd done so much in his life so far, equally he'd achieved very little to speak of—no woman, no real career, a near-disastrous encounter with the cartel, hopping from one bar to the next, listening to people and their stories. One door closes, and another one opens. A lifelong circle of revolving doors.

He pulled out his pouch, grabbed a prerolled spliff, and lit up.

IV.

Parsons, Jacobs, and Sheldon stood together, shoulder to shoulder, on the fantail of the *Indigo* as they watched on toward the reef, the three Jet Skis and the snorkel party.

"That looks like fun," Sheldon said.

Neither Jacobs nor Parsons seemed sure whether he was being serious.

"Did you dive in the service, old boy?" Jacobs asked.

Parsons nodded. "A little bit, a long time ago. You?"

Jacobs nodded, not wanting to be outdone by Sir James. Then he said, "Funny goings-on with that Chalmers woman."

Sheldon cringed at the mention.

"Bromovich mentioned in his report that he smelled an odor like sulfur when he opened the door."

They all nodded and grimaced at the same time, and Sheldon's eyes lit up as if he had discovered something.

"What is it, Sheldon? You look like you've had a eureka moment."

"The sulfur."

"What about the sulfur, old boy?"

"First off, Jacobs, don't call me an old boy. Secondly, when I was at Bradford Plumbing College, we learned some stuff, including death caused by exposure to toxins."

"Oh, yes?"

Parsons and Jacobs looked at each other.

"What about it?" Jacobs asked.

"Well, as I remember, the toxin is airborne and first numbs your sense of taste and smell after the initial whiff of sulfur. Then that turns off your alarm mechanisms, and continued exposure can result in death."

"And so could a million other things," Parsons said. "What's that got to do with Chalmers?"

"She's directly above the septic tank."

"How do you know that?" Parsons asked.

"Because I'm a plumber!"

"No, you idiot, how do you know where the septic tank is?" Jacobs asked.

"Because I am a *plumber*! That's what plumbers do, just like you probably know about all the financials, investments, and assets of this dodgy fucker Litions."

Sheldon looked over and realized these two men knew more than he did about their mysterious absent host.

"You haven't a fucking clue, do yer?" He pointed at the two silver tops. "Two eureka moments in one day. Try to match that, Arcimboldo!" He stuck two fingers up to the cloudless sky.

"Archimedes, you fucking idiot," Jacobs retorted.

Sheldon clenched his fists but quickly decided to back down. Getting accused of one murder in a twenty-four-hour period was enough, never mind two, even for Andrew Sheldon.

He let it pass but kept the thought with him about the sulfur.

V.
San Francisco

Austin Davies, originating from Anglesey, North Wales, had been an officer in the Welsh Guards, comically known in the British forces as the Foreign Legion.

He'd served more than twenty-five years for queen and country and was at heart a soldier and a devoted, dedicated subject to Elizabeth II, the Queen.

After his final posting in California as liaison officer to the US Army, he and his wife settled in San Francisco and called it home. They both then became involved with the local chamber of commerce, hosting soirees and persuading British expats to join, then over time corporate sponsors, and organized the first Annual Christmas Luncheon, now legendary in the city.

Austin was a proud man. He had earned the right to be. He had engaged in every major conflict since he joined back in 1947, just after the war. He had joined as others were finishing their time. It was a great but difficult time for the forces, and he was proud to be there at that time. There were plenty of battle-hardened and rightful heroes who as a young subaltern he learned so much from—they had so much to offer. Austin had been like a sponge, keen to learn all that he could from those around him and their experiences.

That's the way he had been throughout his military career and beyond. Always learning, always observing human behaviors, and he had learned sufficiently that not much was beyond him.

Just turned eighty years old, he had seen almost everything, and as he sat in his wingback chair, in his once-termed *swanky* apartment in Pacific Heights, he pored over the photographic history of his career and life.

Major Billy, the goat, the mascot of the Welsh Guards, on parade at the Queen's Birthday Parade. On active duty in Germany during the Cold War. In Northern Ireland during the Troubles, Aden, and the Falkland Islands campaign. He paused at the photograph of his time in the jungles of Belize as training officer, and there was Parsons, Harry, Mac and Mac, Tom, Blue, Vince, Red, and the rest of the crew. He reminded himself that these were among the best of his times.

He had an immense sense of pride for his achievements, and a deliberate resistance to any regrets—at the end of the day, you can only do what you believe is right in the moment. Colonel Austin Davies had learned that from the battlefield. It's simply no use torturing yourself over *shoulda, coulda, woulda*—a phrase he had learned from his American experiences.

It's not that he felt malice toward the usurpers who had effected his departure from the chamber. He understood by now how humans behave. He was just sad and disappointed how long-term loyalties could be discarded for gain in the moment.

He knew enough about human nature to understand that was the case, but somehow, as with many of his military brethren, he had hoped to emulate the same levels of loyalty in civilian life as in the military—a hope he had long since abandoned.

Since then, the reality of the situation was that he had lost purpose, and a man without purpose and hope has nothing.

He sat in his wingback chair, trembling and weak. He was ready to say goodbye. He had no more strength left. He was drained and depleted by the disloyalty, the treachery, the sad way that human beings treat fellow human beings.

He felt it coming like an earthquake deep inside his chest. He closed his eyes, visualized the sharp pain, and after a few moments went to sleep for the last time, clutching his memories of which he was so very proud.

VI.
On the Top Deck

Simpson and Sharp were more engaged over that evening's dinner. Even Dr. Brown cracked a joke about the locally caught seafood on the menu: a smorgasbord of red snapper, a grouper, and a barracuda, along with a couple of lobsters, crab, and some more exotic fish to boot.

Perry had taken the day's haul not knowing what half the species were and went online to work out how best to cook them. He knew for the most part, but there were a couple of fish he didn't know, and he also knew that especially in this part of the world, there were a lot of animals on land and sea that could be fatal if not treated with respect.

There was laughter at the dinner table on the top deck as the evening drew in, plenty of wine and champagne and, in the case of Sheldon, Old Speckled Hen—and for Dr. Brown, who offered a smile or two over the course of the meal, vodka and lime.

Zach thought it a bizarre scene sat at a table set for twelve and now with only nine guests. Given the frivolity, he wondered whether any of the others even noticed, never mind cared.

For the observant, and Simpson and Sharp were observant, Jacobs began struggling. He loosened and undid the top button of his linen granddad shirt, was sweating more than usual, and started drinking water like it had gone out of fashion, his hand shaking as he put the glass to his mouth. He looked around at his fellow guests, not talking, holding his throat, and then fell off his chair and collapsed on the deck. Sixty seconds from start to fall.

"Anaphylactic shock," Dr. Brown said and knelt next to Jacobs. "His airways have closed, and he's having a heart attack. Where's the ship's doctor? Is there an EpiPen anywhere?"

Jacobs was now white as a sheet, motionless, with white froth coming from his mouth. Dr. Brown commenced CPR with Jacobs's body jolting up and down and from the sheer violence of her motion, ribs cracking audibly, which made Zach almost puke as the gathering of guests checked themselves and one another for any signs of seafood poisoning.

When Bromovich arrived, Jacobs was already pronounced dead. The remaining eight retired to the Indigo Bar.

"Mine's a double Grey Goose, neat," Dr. Brown growled at Kayla behind the bar.

II

I.
The Indigo Bar

"WHAT THE HELL'S GOING ON around here?" demanded Sheldon, visibly shaking with a combination of both rage and fear.

The rest of the group just sat there nursing their drinks, not really knowing how to respond.

Parsons took the lead in the room full of silence, Sheldon looking around nervously at each of his fellow passengers, one by one, with wild eyes wide open.

"Look, old boy, it's very unfortunate, it's true, but all these incidents have been happenstance, acts of God, accidents or otherwise," he stated with an air of certainty, trying to convince the room.

Lady Helen Bailey noted the use of the word *happenstance*—an unusual word, often used by her own mother. For a moment, she locked her eyes on Parsons, before adding her own twopenneth.

"Yes, Mr. Sheldon, Sir James is right. There's nothing to be fearful of here. We know that Perkins was suicide, Chalmers passed away in her sleep, and tonight Jacobs had a reaction to the shellfish, most likely."

She looked around the room, nodding her assurance. Parsons was nodding with her, and so was Sal, nodding like a dog on the back shelf of a family saloon. Sal agreed with almost everything and anything that came out of Lady Helen's mouth.

"Shit happens," Sal said.

Even Dr. Bronwyn Brown piped up, spirited by her limeless vodka. "Yes, they're right. This is just an unfortunate coincidence. Sheldon, I really think you are overthinking this. What do you think this is, *Murder on the Orient Express?*"

At that, the entire room turned their heads, not previously having thought about that possibility.

Lady Helen found herself looking at Sir James. Was this just *happenstance*, or something else? She recalled her faintest memories of the stranger in the big car all those years ago. The high roller, big businessman, financier, investor, the father she never knew of.

"So, what about Bland, then?" Sheldon said, recklessly accusing anyone who was listening.

This was really a true test of the man underneath and the substance of his character. Everyone in the room looked at one another.

"What?"

"What happened to Bland?"

A smile sprung to Sheldon's face. He liked it when he was in control, when he knew information that others didn't. He suddenly regained confidence and addressed his fellow passengers. "You didn't know?" he teased. "They didn't tell you?"

The response from the audience was obviously a no, and he went on to explain with accentuated detail, filling in the gaps where he didn't know.

Simpson said, with Sharp's obvious support, "Forgive me for asking, but what the hell has our gummy Australian rent-boy enthusiast got to do with what's happened in the last few days? He wasn't even on this bloody ship!"

Guests nodded in agreement until Sal spoke his thoughts.

"But yeh, mate, he was on the original passenger list."

His words just lingered in the air.

Visualizing Bland, nailed to a door, facedown, all the bacteria, crabs, fish, and critters devouring his body in short order, prompted Lady Helen to order another round.

She'd often have plenty of nightmares of her own stepmother as she crashed to the ground, smashing her bones on the hard rock below. Little Annie in her pretty flowery dress emerging from the slurry pool covered in barnacles and seaweed just standing and staring. Of the mother and her two children burning to a crisp that terrible night.

She was now seeing the image of Bland in her mind. She ran to the bathroom, the feeling of nausea rising quickly. She hoped it was the images in her head and not the seafood.

II.

With three bodies now in the ship's morgue, there were nine more slots. Bromovich found it a little strange. *What ship with a maximum of fifty passengers and crew combined would have been designed with a ship's morgue that would accommodate a potential quarter of the overall payload?*

It seemed a little weird to him, and he also noted that the extension was part of the comprehensive refit the *Indigo* went through recently.

He walked to the rear deck, leaned on the railing, and lit up one of his cherished Don Rafael cheroots, looking out over the ocean, deep in thought.

He heard soft footsteps behind him and immediately recognized the cheery "How the devil are you, old boy?" coming from the ever-smiling and ever-cheery Zach. He had a bottle of Liddesdale whisky in his hand and two whisky glasses, and he poured them both a nip while Bromovich offered one of his cheroots.

They stood in silence, sipping their whisky and puffing on their cigars, as the Caribbean night sky closed in around them, the sound of the lapping against the hull and, from deep in the *Indigo*, Sheldon on another of his rants.

"So, is Litions aware of the events of the past few days?" Zach asked.

Bromovich took a deep puff of his cigar. "I think so," he replied, uncertain.

"You think so? Are you not in contact with him?"

Bromovich shook his head. "I have sent the reports out."

"Any response?"

The silence spoke for itself.

"Is he in Grand Cayman?"

"That was the plan."

Zach looked puzzled.

Sheldon's ranting in the distance was cut short as they heard a loud crash and a bang to the fore of the ship. They turned and paced at speed to where the sound came from, throwing their cheroots overboard on the way.

When they arrived at the foredeck, Simpson and Sharp were already there. Simpson was knelt, peering into the fore hatch, shaking his head.

"What the hell happened?" Zach asked.

Sharp just pointed down the hatch and into the darkness.

Zach could see the lifeless body of Dr. Bronwyn Brown contorted in such a way that it was obvious the prognosis wasn't good.

Bromovich scaled the ladder and within a couple of minutes confirmed that she was dead. "Likely broken neck," he said.

"What the hell happened?" Zach repeated.

The military men shook their heads.

Lady Helen, Sal, and Parsons came rushing up, Parsons in his paisley-pattern pajamas and burgundy silk night-robe.

Sheldon appeared and took in the scene. "Another one bites the dust."

The rest of the passengers just stared at him.

He looked down at his builder's boots having put his foot in it once again.

Ship's Log (Special Report)

SS *Indigo*
Captain Igor Bromovich
Klaipeda Naval Academy

Transmission: July 20, 2003: 11:23 p.m. CST

Incident: July 20, 2003: 9:05 p.m. CST

It is with much regret that I must report another passenger loss this evening. We found the body of Dr. Bronwyn Brown at the bottom of the fore hatch with a broken neck, pronounced dead at the scene.

It appears accidental and that she fell down the hatch in the darkness of the night. I cannot explain, however, what the hatch was doing open, as I checked the decks at sunset this evening.

2. Ms. Bronwyn Alexander Brown, British, passport number 382149777.

The other passengers are growing in their concern for their safety.

Captain Igor Bromovich

<END>

III.
The Vettriano Suite

Zach went to check on Lady Helen and tapped gently on the dark mahogany door. He could hear shuffling inside.

"Who is it?" she called.

Zach could feel that knot in his stomach again and let out what came out as a squeal. "It's Zach—Zach Carter." He cleared his throat to get his pipes back in working condition. "Just thought I would check in to see if you're all right, Lady Helen."

There was a pause, and then he could hear the unlocking of the dead lock and the click over of the latch before the door opened.

It had been two hours since she'd left the bar, and as Zach looked at her, it was obvious that she'd fully recovered. Wearing a turquoise caftan with, from what Zach could see, very little underneath, and with her hair wet, combed straight, and her face, this close, quite clearly in no need of makeup, Lady Helen Bailey was a natural beauty—and for a moment, it paralyzed Zach. He cleared his throat again.

"Just checking in, Ms.—I mean m'lady." He shook his head. "I mean Lady Helen."

She was smiling up at him. It felt as though she were looking right through him, as if he were naked. He was embarrassed and sure he was flushing, probably bright red, but he hoped his lifelong tan was enough to hide it.

"Would you like to come in and share a nightcap and some of that weed of yours?" she asked.

That was it; he completely lost it. He had no idea where to look, which direction to go in. He was caught in the headlights, paralyzed, just like a jackrabbit, and he felt like one too. She took his hand and led him into the depths of the Vettriano Suite. She had the lights on low, the shower was still steaming, and "Moon Safari" by Air played on the Bose sound system. She waved him to the black leather sofa and poured him two fingers of Diplomático Ambassador and sat next to him. Zach's heart was racing, and his knots were taut.

"Well, then?" she offered.

He cleared his throat, with "Sexy Boy" now playing on the album to make the moment even more intense. "Well, what?" he said and managed a smile.

"I thought we were going to have a bit of fun."

He felt like crawling under a rock, or under her bed, or just bolting out the door. She was smiling at him, her beautiful green eyes twinkling in the soft lighting, her blonde hair like gold.

She laughed. "I thought we were going to share a spliff?"

Air started pumping out "All I Need." Zach was relieved. He pulled out his tobacco pouch and papers, his fingers shaking, and started to roll a joint.

Lady Helen was looking at him intently, and after a few moments of Zach's fumbling around, she grabbed the papers, laid one flat on the coffee table in front of them, and rubbed and distributed the tobacco evenly. When she finished, she looked up at him, prompting him for the key ingredient, to which Zach obliged. She ground it so it was soft enough to sprinkle over the tobacco, and then she rolled the paper and licked along the length of it. She rolled it adeptly between her fingers and smiled. Then she lit the end and took a deep inhale.

She was still smiling and looking Zach straight in the eyes, right through him, when he took a sip of the Diplomático. He thought he was about to melt.

After a couple of drags, she passed the joint back to Zach. She was still staring at him when she asked, straight to the point, "Why do you get so nervous, Zach Carter?"

Zach didn't know where to look, waiting for the weed to kick in. After a couple of deep inhales, he let out a burst of nervous laughter, and so did she, although hers wasn't nervousness, he guessed. There wasn't a nervous bone in this woman's body, he thought.

She started the conversation. They shared, laughed, and rolled another spliff—this time Zach, and he rolled a Zach special. Lady Helen moved the Diplomático bottle to the coffee table and poured two more.

They finished the next spliff, and she laid her head on his chest. Then she undid his zipper, pulled her caftan over her head, revealing her tanned body and pert breasts, and climbed on top.

Zach realized there and then that Lady Helen Bailey was a woman who got exactly what she wanted and when she wanted it.

It was one in the morning by the time she had slipped off to bed, and Zach slipped out the door, gently closing it behind him, and headed outside to look at the ocean and the stars to gather his thoughts.

He rolled another joint, shaking his head. "What the fuck just happened?"

12

I.
The Grand Dining Room

THE NEXT MORNING OVER BREAKFAST, Sheldon was continuing to lead the inquisition. It was clear that he was probably the most affected by the situation. He had a look of fear and paranoia about him, eyeing each of his fellow passengers as a potential suspect—and a threat.

His invitation was right, that there may well be trouble ahead, but he hadn't suspected anything like this to be possible. A couple of potential investors getting physical, or a cantankerous passenger throwing their weight around, even some drunken altercations—he could have probably handled any of those, but this wasn't anywhere near what he was expecting. Not that he really knew what he was letting himself in for or what he should have expected. The invitation didn't say.

"So, who the bloody hell has met Litions?" Sheldon demanded between mouthfuls of toast and Marmite, a delicacy he always brought with him wherever he was.

Parsons was looking down his half-moon spectacles from the head of the table, eyeing Sheldon with copious amounts of contempt.

"He's one of the most secretive men on the planet," Sal said.

"Not sure even his own mother has ever met him," Simpson said and smirked, prompting Sharp to let out a laugh, and Lady Helen a giggle.

"What?" Sheldon looked around angrily. "This isn't a bloody joke. If you haven't met the man, then why the hell did you come on this jaunt in the first place?"

"Probably the same reason that you did," Parsons replied.

Sheldon wasn't used to being challenged, but he knew Parsons was right.

In his world, he held all the aces, and he could pretty much say or do what he wanted, when he wanted—if one of his hairdresser tenants didn't like it, then he would just push up the rent and force them out. On one occasion, he had an elderly woman, a sitting tenant, in a property he was converting into upscale apartments. She refused to leave, so he just took out the stairs, eventually forcing her to surrender, and he scooped her and her belongings up in a cherry picker and sent her on her way.

Sheldon's bark was far worse than his bite, however. He had built his reputation by picking on the weak and vulnerable.

At school, he had stood on the sidelines watching rugby. He tried proper boxing once with proper gloves, but given what he had been through as a kid and the beatings from his own brother and father, it was too much for him and just brought back bad memories. His father had tried to persuade him to join the army, but he failed the selection, miserably.

The reality is that he was intimidated by people with a greater intellect, and that, on the *Indigo*, that was the case with all the passengers—namely, the real men who obviously Simpson and Sharp were.

He took a big swig of his specially brewed builder's tea and stormed out of the dining room and onto the promenade deck.

II.
The Churchill Suite

The two military men were in Simpson's cabin, a picture of the great man above the bed, with the words "Never, Never, *Never* Give Up." The room was adorned in what apparently were Churchill originals: there was one of a seascape under a stormy sky; another, *Daybreak at Cassis*; *Racecourse, Nice*; and a scene similar to one both of these men had encountered during their tours in the Middle East and North Africa, *Tower of the Koutoubia Mosque*.

Both Simpson and Sharp had joined the Parachute Regiment straight from high school and their respective council estates—seventeen, eleven stone wet through—but their enthusiasm made up for their greenness.

They were in the same selection platoon, and during basic training, their first encounter wasn't a pleasant one: milling in the gymnasium, both showing the grit and determination required to be airborne and both refusing to give up. Simpson secured a black eye, Sharp a broken nose, and plenty of blood between them splattered about the audience. They had been best friends ever since, and that was a long time ago. A very long time ago.

After passing out, they served on active duty with 2 Para in all sorts of places, including in Northern Ireland, where they had seen some of their worst days.

Both young men found themselves in a sticky situation, ending in the two being trapped at the end of a Belfast housing estate. Under fire, they let loose with their semiautomatic SLRs and let rip. Unfortunately, out of the seven bodies recovered later that day, only one was an adult, barely eighteen, the rest adolescents, including two eleven-year-old girls.

It was less about what they had done and more that the authorities needed to be seen at least doing something about the situation to avoid even further uproar. Therefore, there had been a full inquiry into the incident and the deaths of the children.

They both provided their statements and made intense appearances before the court-martial, with them stating their case.

"All we knew, sir, was that we were under fire and our lives were in danger. We had no idea the age of the combatants. They were completely hidden from view, firing from the roofs, from widows, from half-open doors."

The panel listened intently to them and other witnesses, including experts who had made arguments based on ballistics as well as a mockup of the street, the houses, the location of the two soldiers, and where the bodies of the victims were found.

After a weeklong trial of arguments and representations, including from the local Sinn Féin representative, both soldiers were exonerated but marked for life as targets of the Provisional Irish Republican Army.

They were immediately pulled from patrolling the streets of Northern Ireland, or even setting foot on the territory ever again, at least in uniform.

They both tried to put it behind them as best they could. The Falklands War took care of that.

Early on May 27, 1982, Simpson and Sharp were with the regiment at Goose Green, held by the Argentinian Twelfth Infantry Regiment. Five hundred of the British Army's best and almost double that from Argentina. The battle waged during the night and into the next day. The 2 Para and their fellow British troops won the battle but not without the loss of seventeen fellow soldiers.

It was a seminal moment of the conflict and one that enabled the breakout of the San Carlos beachhead. Simpson and Sharp were among the more enthusiastic, dispatching their Argentinian adversaries without regret or remorse.

After that, they went to Belize, jungle training, and then off to Hereford for selection, which was their route back to Northern Ireland—this time in civilian clothing. Together, they were part of several operations, dispatching their enemy wholesale, including in their roles in the Loughgall massacre.

They'd also served in the Gulf War together as spotters behind enemy lines.

While in Belize, they'd gone on one of many dives together in search of shipwrecks and treasure. They would hire a boat, just the two of them and their scuba gear, and search the ocean floor—no plan, no charts, no maps, and little clue. Apart from the marine wildlife, most of their dives had come up as big fat blanks.

That's until, one trip, they somehow stumbled on the *Ella Sophia* buried deep in her concealed resting place. Running out of air, they surfaced, headed back to land, and then spent the next two weeks trying to find the same spot again, to no avail.

"Fucking schoolboy error" is how they described their regret and the ever-present image of the *Ella Sophia* in their minds. "The one that got away!" was their toast.

On one such salvager's expedition, they were in the Baltic searching for a mystery German submarine apparently full of gold as it was running away at the end of the war.

They weren't sure whether Bromovich had recognized them, but they certainly remembered Bromovich, as he hadn't changed that much since their extraction from Russia.

Simpson and Sharp were reminiscing. "Pull up a sandbag" was their familiar phrase as they sat together, side by side, and they both raised a glass.

Their thoughts moved from the past to conversation about the moment at hand.

"Thing is that these have all been natural causes, suicides, or accidents, right?" Sharp said, trying to make sense of it all. "Who the hell is this Litions guy, anyway?"

Simpson shrugged and shook his head.

"Can you reach out to de la Billière to find anything on him?" Sharp asked, pushing the point.

Again, Simpson shook his head. "I tried already. He's on some safari in some remote part of Africa. I looked him up. He seems legit, or at least his investments do, for the most part."

"What do you mean?" Sharp asked.

"Well, he's placed some interesting bets in his time. There've been a couple of investigations into insider trading and insider information over the years."

"Where does he live?" Sharp asked.

"He's domiciled somewhere in Russia, with the protection of Putin."

"But he's Algerian, right?"

"Apparently," Simpson said. "But he got involved in some of the oligarch deals early on."

"The ones where they bought the oil fields?"

"Yep, that would the one and the same.

"This was an unprecedented time at the breakdown of the Soviet Union. They were bust and needed to sell off assets, including the oil fields. A small group of businessmen were called in to raise funding, where the international oil firms dared not go. Investment bonds were set against the oil field assets to buy them from the state and make themselves billionaires overnight.

"Jemol Litions was one of those men, thanks to Vladimir Putin, as well as his rainmaker, Dmitri Dankov.

"The big international firms like BP, Shell, Total, Chevron, and Exxon wouldn't go in. Neither would the traditional banks, but thanks to people and institutions like Litions, they did—and made a very handsome profit."

"We've been in the wrong job, mate." Sharp passed Simpson another bottle of Heineken.

"Tell me about it."

They clinked their green bottles together.

"Cheers, brother!"

III.
The Dauntless Suite

Parsons knew that timing was everything. He sat at his desk in the study like a grand master contemplating his next moves.

He had already instructed his stock sales, and they would be live at the opening bell in New York in the morning. The triggers had already been set, and there was already significant interest and advance holds on his stocks.

That hadn't surprised him. The likes of Microsoft, Apple, Google, Nike, Starbucks, and more were in high demand. Even the likes of Tesla and Salesforce, although fledglings and more volatile, had a lot of speculative investor interest.

He also had a portfolio of second-tier, less-high-profile investments, including the likes of Ford, Hilton, Compass, and IBM. These would likely get sold under the radar, but some of the others may not be so fortunate—not that he really cared, as long as he liquidated his positions safely.

Over the years, he had been careful to accumulate stocks on the NYSE, and that helped him in this moment. He didn't want to send unnecessary signals to multiple financial markets in different time zones.

This gave him the buffer he needed and the time to speak to his friend about the other less structured investments in his portfolio.

His alias had happened by accident. Shortly after leaving the army, he got involved in an investment opportunity with his friend Dmitri Dankov in Algeria, the gas fields. And at the time, it significantly helped to grease the deal if you weren't American, for sure, or British—and if you were Algerian, then *bingo*. So that's what he did to seal the deal.

Jemol Litions was his best friend's son's name jumbled up, and a great front. He created the persona of Algerian origin, growing up in Paris, and over time, deal after deal, Litions Industries was born as a result. And the momentum quickly became impossible to stop.

The legend of the secretive industrialist and soon billionaire was born.

He looked at the time: it was 11:30 a.m. local, therefore 7:30 p.m. in Moscow.

He grabbed his satellite phone, paused for a few moments, and then pressed frequent caller 1 and pushed the oversize phone to his ear.

The familiar sound of the clicking through exchanges, covering his whereabouts and encrypting the call for security, and then the Russian ring tone confirmed they were connected.

Parsons could imagine his contact in one of his casinos, in one of their brothels, in some dark operations somewhere in the empire, the Russian Empire.

After five rings, the recipient picked up. "Da?"

"It's me."

"Tovarishch, kak dela druzhishche?" *How're you doing, my friend?* The man from Moscow then reverted to English. "What's going on?"

"I wanted to talk about your—about our exit plan?"

"What exit plan, my friend?" His words were slow and deliberate and perhaps a little menacing for a novice in this game.

"I'm liquidating my assets."

"Yes, I saw that."

Parsons knew that his actions were visible, but this was validation that his contact in Moscow had always kept a close eye.

"I need to ensure a soft landing."

"What were you thinking?"

Parsons knew the value of his investments—so did Dankov. They also both knew the risks and the exposure.

"I'll take fifty percent of current value. Just need the funds to be in my account by end of day tomorrow."

The man on the other end knew this was a good deal—it was a good deal—but he also knew there was a weakness here. Parsons was prepared for that. During the pause, Parsons could just imagine the man in Moscow diverted by things going on around him, sitting in one of his many lap-dancing bars surrounded by girls, big cigar in his mouth, drinking the most expensive Russian vodka, while negotiating. That was the kind of guy Dankov was. Parsons had been dealing with him for over two decades.

"I think you take thirty-three percent; I need to speak to other people to get agreement?"

Parsons knew that wasn't true. Dmitri Dankov had full executive powers in his organization and related powers that be.

"Listen—pay the money into my First World Bank account by the end of day tomorrow, and we're all good?"

Parsons knew that paying the funds into their own investment bank would be an easier pill to swallow.

"I will check with my friends, but I think you're being very reasonable. Let me get back to you."

They both knew each other well enough to know that the deal was done.

"Spasibo, moy drug." *Thanks, my friend.*

Parsons was about to hang up, but the Russian asked one last thing.

"Everything all right, my friend? We've been through a lot. Do you need help?"

"I'm good, Dmitri. Thank you for asking."

Parsons pressed the End button and hung up the phone. That was better than expected; however, he also knew that it was a good deal for both of them.

He sat back in the Chippendale chair, took his dose of pills to kill the pain, and sat there looking at the ocean, thinking about his next moves.

"… There is no pain—you are receding. A distant ship, smoke on the horizon. You are only coming through in waves. Your lips move, but I can't hear what you're saying …"

IV.
The Grand Dining Room

The remaining seven sat for dinner in silence. Simpson and Sharp, Lady Helen and Sal. Sheldon, Parsons, and Zach. Bromovich was in the pilothouse, Perry in the galley. Kayla uncorked the Chablis with a pop and poured the wine for everyone—apart from Sheldon, happy with his can of Old Speckled Hen with the widget in the bottom that poured it thick and creamy.

The table remained silent as Kayla passed out the goat cheese tartlet with grapefruit and beets. The group tucked in, and the only noise was the lap of the ocean and the clinking of silverware on the fine porcelain.

Eventually, it was Sheldon who broke the silence, looking around the table with his now maniac and paranoid eyes.

"Why are we taking our time? Why don't we just steam on and get to dry land, Grand Cayman? Eh? Eh?" he said, taunting anyone to respond.

Eventually, Parsons said, "Perhaps Litions isn't ready for us yet."

"Well, if he leaves it too long, there might not be any of us left."

"I think you read too much into Dr. Brown's Agatha Christie comment, Sheldon," Parsons said tersely.

It was very clear by now that Parsons didn't like Sheldon at all. In fact, neither did the rest of the passengers, captain, or crew of the *Indigo*.

"Well, that's maybe why she's fucking dead, Parsons," Sheldon said angrily, inadvertently spitting across the table.

They ate their first course in silence. Shortly afterward, Lady Helen attempted to change the tone.

"Are the boys excited about our dive trip in the morning?" She beamed at Simpson, Sharp, and Zach.

She and Zach smiled at each other under cover of the conversation, both knowing their little secret.

"Damn right," Zach said enthusiastically, not just for the dive trip but in the hope that they might have a repeat performance. This time he would be better prepared.

"Apart from the 5:00 a.m. start," Simpson added with a touch of sarcasm.

"Thought you military boys would be used to early rises," Lady Helen said and smiled.

The men at the table got the quip. Zach looked at Lady Helen, and Sal shot a look at Zach. Did he know? Zach could feel the familiar knot in his stomach.

Something had been bothering Zach. With all these people dying around them, there seemed little empathy to the situation. Yes, Sheldon was fraught with paranoia, but none of the others seemed to be fazed about it at all. It was as though they were all above it all, oblivious. It reminded him of the entitled Silicon Valleyers who would come to the Bounty Hunter, with their air of self-righteousness—many would call it arrogance—and the sense that they had a right of passage and were somehow superior to all around them.

Back in Marin County, Mill Valley was a haven for these types, the ones who had graduated from engineering and made it out of San Jose or San Francisco, paper millionaires now with children. It had the air of the town where everyone believes they're related to Jesus Christ himself somewhere along the line.

He looked around the table, at the two military men; at Sal; at Parsons, who he just couldn't quite weigh up; and at Lady Helen Bailey.

The night in the Vettriano Suite was still very fresh in his memory. The intense look on her face as she pleasured herself—and the talk of the deaths happening around them seemed to spur her on even further. And as they talked, during sex, about the situation at hand and the prospects of further deaths, she had climaxed as though it was some sort of dirty talk that had got her there.

It wasn't that it wasn't enjoyable. Zach was now smitten, swallowed up, consumed, but it was something darker, deeper, more worrying that disturbed him, but he put that behind the curtain of how beautiful she was. Maybe this is the one after all, he thought, but he didn't see her in a clapboard house with its white picket fence in Sonoma and 2.2 kids somehow. Lady Helen Bailey wasn't that type of woman.

The next morning, led by Zach as the guide and qualified divemaster, Lady Helen, Sal, Simpson, and Sharp were going to the site of a legendary old shipwreck that had met its peril on a reef outcrop and plunged to the ocean floor. The legend included the obligatory hidden treasure that was allegedly on board the Spanish ship before its demise.

Earlier that day, Zach had been busy on the rear deck refilling the air tanks and carefully preparing all the dive equipment—the suits, fins, masks, BCDs, weight belts—and checking the regulators and the dive computers. Each was clearly marked with the name of each diver—Simpson, Sharp, Lady Helen, or Sal. It was all checked and ready to go. It was going to be an early, predawn start, with the group heading out at 5:00 a.m.

"Given all that's been going on, you all really think you should be going on a bloody diving jaunt?" Sheldon said.

The whole table just ignored him.

He pushed his plate to one side. "Fucking fancy shite," he said and leaned back in his chair. He stared at the others, one at a time, gripping on to his pint of beer, his knuckles white.

The filet mignon, Wellington style, arrived at the table with its duxelles stuffing, wrapped in filo, served with a delicate béarnaise and a bundle of spring vegetables—a special request from Zach and one of his favorites.

Zach was fond of his traditions, and this was one of them. As the plates arrived, he looked around the table to gauge the delight of his audience.

"Chateau Neuf, anyone?" He stood up and stood in as sommelier for the course.

"Bon appétit!" he said, and the six clinked their glasses and tucked in.

"To sunken treasure!"

Apart from Sheldon, they all raised their glasses.

"To sunken treasure!"

V.

After the main course, Sheldon slipped out and went for a walk around the ship. He went to find Bromovich to see whether he could get anything out of him. He found the captain in his usual spot at that time of the evening as he puffed on his cheroot, overlooking the ocean with a bottle of vodka next to him and a sipping glass in hand.

Bromovich looked over as Sheldon approached and stood at the ship's railing beside him.

"Vodka, Mr. Sheldon?"

Apart from beer, Sheldon wasn't a big drinker. He looked suspiciously at Bromovich and at the bottle of vodka, then rolled his eyes. "Bugger it. Why not?"

Bromovich grabbed a glass and poured a two-finger serving and handed it to Sheldon. "Štai Purvas Tavo Akyje."

Bromovich moved to clink glasses, and Sheldon reluctantly obliged.

"And cheers to you too, Captain." He watched Bromovich swallow the contents of the glass and followed suit.

Bromovich poured two more, this time for sipping purposes. They shared a moment in silence.

"What's your assessment of the situation, Captain?"

"What situation is that, Mr. Sheldon?"

The Yorkshireman couldn't hide his frustration. "What's wrong with you people? Can't you see we're in a bloody situation? There are dead people in the morgue, for Christ's sake!"

Bromovich let the anger pass over. "I see nothing, Mr. Sheldon. All I see is a series of unfortunate circumstances. I don't see anything untoward. What is it you are seeing that no one else is? I think you're reading too much into all this."

"Why don't we just hightail it to Grand Cayman and stop fannying around?"

"All in due course, my friend, all in due course. I have my orders."

"From whom, exactly? Litions? Does he know what's going on?"

"Mr. Sheldon, there's nothing going on. You've been watching too many films."

Upon that, Sheldon turned and went to retire to his cabin. "Good night, Captain."

"Good night, Mr. Sheldon."

VI.
The Promenade Deck

Simpson and Sharp sat shoulder to shoulder, overlooking the ocean glimmering in the full moon. It was a silence shared by brothers, a comfortable silence. They could almost hear each other's thoughts; they both knew where they were.

They had been just young boys at the time. It was an impossible situation. Surrounded by the enemy, all eager to see the red bloodstains to match the berets of their uniforms. Their own age didn't matter to them, no matter what age they were. The hatred disguised rational thoughts.

The two men had gone over it many times together and in their own thoughts.

At the end of the day, they were doing their job—*weren't they?* It was both unfortunate and very sad that the kids died, but at the end of the day, they shouldn't have been there, and they certainly shouldn't have been involved in the gang of junior IRA wannabes firing on two highly trained Parachute Regiment soldiers, right?

The incident was very public and turned very political, and Simpson and Sharp were under the spotlight.

You see, they needed someone to blame. The Troubles were a political hot potato, and the British government didn't want to be seen putting an unnecessary wrong foot forward. This was a size 10 boot in the political balance, and someone had to carry the can.

They stuck by each other like the brothers-in-arms they were, prepared to do whatever they could for each other in the most desperate of circumstances. The regiment was also supportive, despite the political connotations, and so were their families, regarding what little they told about the incident. You see, however high profile the situation had been in Northern Ireland, the mainland got only snippets of the news, and for many it felt like a selective storytelling. The reality was that people were being killed every day, from both sides of the fence, yet this wasn't common news.

It was also this selective reporting of reality that continued fueling the funding of the Provisional Irish Republican Army by those far removed. It was a deliberate ploy to hoodwink the Irish Americans, believing the propaganda, into thinking they were funding a *struggle* as opposed to a group of murderous terrorists and gangsters. The reality was that it had nothing to do with the Catholics and the Protestants,

England and Ireland—it was so much more complicated than that.

"Those who say they understand Northern Ireland don't truly understand Northern Ireland."

Simpson just nodded and held his glass up for a toast.

Trapped at the end of a cobblestone street, with a row of tenement houses on each side and a barrier wall at the end built to keep the Catholics away from the Protestants, Simpson and Sharp had been completely exposed to anyone who wanted to take a potshot at them, and on that rainy Belfast afternoon, there seemed to be plenty of takers as they came under heavy fire from all directions—from the house windows on each side, the rooftops, and the occasional alleyway.

Sharp let out an involuntary shiver.

"Cold, mate?"

"Fucking freezing," Sharp replied.

They wasted no time in their well-rehearsed banter.

Simpson topped up their whisky glasses from his regimental hip flask. "Do you think we'll find her tomorrow after all these years?"

"Fuck knows, mate. We'll see."

"And what if we do? Then what?"

"This time we plot the fucking coordinates," Sharp said and glared.

"Hey, we've been through this—it wasn't my fucking fault."

Sharp paused for a long moment. "There's something just not right here."

"No shit, Sherlock!"

"I've never quite come across a more motley group of people than on this ship."

Simpson nodded; it was hard to disagree.

"And the mysterious letter from Litions. What was that all about? Why the hell would we, did we, accept this gig?"

Simpson shrugged. "I guess the money helped."

"Thing is, there's no obvious or immediate threat. Each one has a plausible reason."

"Or we have an enemy we cannot see."

The pair returned to silence at that prospect.

"Come on. Let's get back inside, where it's a little warmer."

"We've got an early start."

13

I.
The Rear Deck

ZACH STARTED THE BRIEFING. HE was in his element. This is exactly what he loved to do—surprise and delight his audience, give them the best experiences possible. Lady Helen, Sal, Sharp, and Simpson were his direct audience, the others watching on, with Perry and Kayla belowdecks. The whole ship had risen early for this big day.

"The *Ella Sophia* departed from Chetumal on May 8, 1774, heading to Cádiz, Spain. She joined an eight-ship fleet for protection in the Gulf of Honduras just north of Roatán. After twenty-four hours, the fleet accumulated, giving sufficient time for the pirates to surround their rendezvous point."

Because Zach had been doing this sort of thing since he was a kid, he knew when he had his audience and when he didn't. This morning, it was plain to see that his audience members were mesmerized. Even Parsons seemed impressed by Zach's abilities to draw the audience and recollect facts. Zach had done his homework and knew the Caribbean better than most. He'd made that his business as he'd charted the waters many times in his previous life, often under cover of darkness, and always off the beaten path; away from the cruise ships, tourists, and fishing boats, and out of sight.

"Having gathered their fleet," Zach continued, "Captain Andreas Jose Barbarella ordered them to commence their passage to Spain, in short order and a tight defensive formation. He knew how dangerous these waters were, not only the reefs and the hurricanes but the treasure hunters too."

They were really going on a treasure hunt, and even Simpson and Sharp were excited at the prospect.

"Among the fleet, the accumulated cargo of gold and jewels was immeasurable in the context of wealth today, but according to legend, the *Ella Sophia* had the largest haul of all and, to this day, has never been found following her demise thanks to the pirate ship *Ubique*, Latin for *everywhere*.

"Today, my friends, we're going to follow in the footsteps of many others before us to discover the hidden treasures of the *Ella Sophia*."

Simpson and Sharp exchanged a knowing glance. It had been nearly twenty years since, and all these years later, they often questioned if they had actually found her all those years earlier or in fact dreamed it.

Sheldon broke the moment, looking around the audience with his wild eyes, frantic. "What is wrong with you people? Don't you realize we have a situation here?"

By now, if any of them had any respect for the uncouth Yorkshireman, it had completely evaporated by now. Sheldon no longer had a listenership. Everyone just ignored him.

"Bloody hell, mate, how do you know all this stuff?" Sal asked.

Zach beamed. "Many a day out at sea to learn more about what goes on at sea."

He then climbed down to the tender and shepherded the four on board. Lady Helen and Sal, Simpson and Sharp. The mood was sleepy but excited—after all, it was five in the morning. Zach had been up since four o'clock preparing, including brewing a large flask of Royal Navy tea, complete with plenty of milk and plenty of Pusser's Navy Rum. *That will wake them up,* Zach had thought to himself, weighing up the dangers of alcohol, fun, and diving.

Zach offered his gentlemanly hand as they climbed down to the tender. Only Lady Helen took it, and as she did, Zach's heart skipped a beat, and she smiled and brushed by him as she climbed aboard. They were all experienced divers, and probably collectively more experienced than him, but that didn't stop Zach from continually trying to play host.

"Welcome aboard, crew. Today we're going to find the long-illusive treasure of the *Ella Sophia!*"

Zach considered his audience with a bright-eyed, manic sort of look that he'd modeled from his favorite book as a kid, *Charlie and the Chocolate Factory.* Deep down, Zach aspired to be like Willy Wonka: a little nonconformist, mysterious, but lots of fun—he liked nothing more than to entertain.

As they cruised away from the *Indigo*, he continued to explain more about the fate of the *Ella Sophia* and how, according to records of the time, she had left port laden with gold and riches to take them back to the motherland, Spain. That was until she encountered the pirates flying under the Jolly Roger, the Spaniards' nemesis at that time, suspected to be acting on the encouragement of King George III himself.

"This, my friends, is what you call a real pirate's treasure hunt!"

With that, he cranked up the engine of the tender, and they sped into the Caribbean Sea, the crashing of the waves and the bounce of the tender on the crests of the white tops eliminating any further opportunity for anyone to hold a conversation.

With Zach piloting the boat from the rear, the four sat in twos, Lady Helen Bailey and Sal on one side, the two military men on the other, all looking forward in their shades, tight mouthed, with the wind in their hair.

II.
The Cook's Quarters

On the bridge, Bromovich watched on from his vantage point, seeing the tiny tender disappear. He hoped that they would have fun and find treasure and that there would be no more accidents associated with his captaincy of the SS *Indigo*. He'd already had enough of those.

He turned to his task of investigating Kayla's black eye. Bromovich headed belowdecks to their quarters and knocked heavily on the door.

"What the hell, Captain—what time is it?" Perry said as he answered the door in his shorts, a lit Marlboro Red already hanging from the corner of his mouth.

Bromovich looked him up and down through the crack in the door. "How's Kayla?" he asked, straight to the point.

Perry left the door ajar and looked around the small cabin. "She ain't here," he said, puzzled. "She ain't here. Where the hell is she? What time is it again?" He looked at his watch, trying to focus on the hands on the dial.

"Where is she?"

"I don't know," Perry said. "I don't even know what day it is at this time in the morning."

His eyes were bright red and looked itchy—perhaps some sort of allergies, too much alcohol, been up all night, or a combination of all three.

"Perry, I need to come in," Bromovich said, staring with his mahogany eyes and Eastern European dispassion.

Perry paused for a moment and let him in.

Bromovich pushed through the door and looked around the cabin: clothes strewn everywhere, empty cans of beer, half-finished bottles of vodka, an ashtray piled high with cigarette butts, and remnants of half-finished meals. Apart from Perry, there was no sign of anyone else, no Kayla.

"How did you manage to create such a pigsty in such a short space of time?"

Perry glared at him. "Making breakfast, lunch, and dinner, drinks, canapés, and generally being slaves on this boat with no time whatsoever—that's how, Captain!"

Bromovich glared back. "I need to find Kayla," he said matter-of-factly.

He walked the short distance from the cook's quarters to the galley and popped his head into the break room. No sign of Kayla. The kitchen was in dark silence. There had been no à la carte breakfast today, as, with the five, including Zach, on the scuba dive, a help-yourself cereal bar, toast, juice, and coffee were sufficient.

"Kayla?" Bromovich bellowed, with no response.

Perry scurried behind him in his boxer shorts, the Marlboro still hanging out the corner of his mouth.

"When did you last see her?" Bromovich asked. "And lose the cigarette."

Flustered, Perry grabbed the cigarette, looked around as if lost about what to do with it, and stubbed it out in the handwashing sink.

Bromovich glared at him again.

"I don't know." Perry looked down as if to find the answer. "Around ten, I think," he said, scratching his head.

"And where did you see her last, *Perry?*"

"She stormed out of the cabin—I just left her to it."

Bromovich continued his glare of contempt.

"That was Kayla," Perry said and shrugged. "She's always doing that kind of thing," he said.

In the galley, side by side were the walk-in fridge and freezer, with a padlock on the latter.

"Is this usually locked, Perry?"

Perry shook his head, with a worried frown.

"Where's the key?"

Perry scampered to the office, pulled out a big bunch of keys, and handed them to Bromovich with the right key selected for the walk-in freezer. "Here you go, Captain."

After fumbling with the keys for what seemed like an age, Bromovich gently turned the key in the lock, and the bracket popped out, allowing him to disengage from the handle lock and pull open the door. As the cool fog billowed out into the humidity, he pressed the switch next to the fast-freeze button, which was on, and turned on the light.

Bromovich stood clear a few moments and peered into the freezer, with Perry right behind him.

The freezer was by no means full—a small payload compared with the capacity of the *Indigo*, and the menu lent itself to fresh, not frozen. But as with any ship of the oceans, it was prudent to stock up with reserves, just in case.

The icy air started to dissipate, and slowly, the full contents of the walk-in became apparent.

As Perry let out a sharp gasp, Bromovich saw the image emerging at the back: there was the hostess, Kayla, hung on the rack, a belt around her neck as a noose. Her skin pale and frozen, with purple-blue lips, and eyes wide open, staring at them, she was still in the uniform she'd been wearing the last time Bromovich had seen her alive. Despite the blueness of her frozen corpse, the black eye was still visible.

Bromovich turned to Perry and just glared again.

Perry stood there, now shivering, shaking his head, looking to the captain with some level of disbelief and confusion.

"What the hell, Perry?"

The cook was speechless.

Bromovich ordered Perry to get some clothes on, and Perry scampered off to follow his instruction.

Bromovich's heart sank—another body, another death. This captaincy was quickly turning from a dream into a nightmare. The difference between Kayla's death and the others' is that this was clearly murder; there was no way that Kayla, all five feet nothing of her, could have managed to string herself up in the way that he'd found her.

At the back of his mind, he was worried that Perry may not return—but there was nowhere for him to go, he rationalized. He waded inside to lift the weight of the body and loosen the belt, and by the time he had carried her to the entrance, Perry had returned, still looking as worried but at least now with some clothes on and no cigarette.

"I'm going to need a full statement from you, Perry."

The cook nodded obediently.

"Now help me with her body and take her to the morgue."

There was no point in even trying to look for vital signs. Kayla was quite clearly dead, and frozen solid. On fast-freeze Bromovich estimated that she'd been in there at least four hours, probably longer.

The two manhandled the body and laid her to rest in the ship's morgue, with Perry's already bright red eyes brimming with tears. Kayla's frozen corpse added to the growing inventory.

III.
On the Tender

Zach sat in the tender. The diving party had been down for forty minutes already, and he was expecting them back up at any moment.

He sat on the boat bobbing up and down with the gentle waves, soaking up the morning sun and the tranquility of his surroundings. He loved the ocean. This was where he was meant to be, especially in the Caribbean.

That morning's preparations had included his knocking up a Bloody Mary. He sipped gently as he considered the question he was sure all the other passengers had considered: What the hell was actually going on here?

In his mind, he had been going through the passenger list, and even by the Bounty Hunter's standards, they were the most eclectic mix of people he thought he'd ever seen—and that was saying something.

He reflected on the blatant ambivalence of most of the passengers to the deaths. He pondered Litions and who the hell this mystery man was and whether he was ever going to make an appearance. He remembered the No Name Bar in Amsterdam where he'd met Willy Mitchell and the genesis of being here. He remembered the darker days of navigating these oceans, running cocaine and worse from one island to another, from one drop to another. He'd been in too deep. He'd got out of that, just, and now he was back in the same waters feeling as much peril as he had before.

He thought of himself, of how now he was riding the boat instead of being the water. It wasn't his fault; he had no control over the spontaneous actions. He'd done all the right things, taught the right lessons, the safety, the dangers in ascending too quickly. It was the high profile of his guests that turned it into as big a deal as it was. But as he looked out onto the waters, he still had a deep regret. After all, losing a life wasn't something to take lightly in any circumstances—especially on his watch.

He had sat there for the past forty minutes mulling these things over without very many answers at all and with lots of head shaking. Just him, the boat, the ocean, and his extra-strength Bloody Mary with extra Tabasco and black pepper, just how he liked it.

He took another sip, and his thoughts turned to Lady Helen Bailey. There was something in their interaction in the Vettriano Suite that really disturbed him. Although he enjoyed the sex, of course, she seemed to enjoy it more, and although Zach would have liked to have taken full credit for that, he knew he couldn't. Although, deep down, he knew all along, but saying it out loud would bring the shock of the reality home.

"She was getting off on all the death around her!"

He stared blank-faced across the ocean to the horizon, a look that he had heard of in the past; the look of a sniper who had seen too much action, too many deaths; the look of shock. It was called the *thousand-yard stare*.

IV.
The Wreck of the *Ella Sophia*

Lady Helen Bailey kicked off in her usual self-confident style, leading the way with Simpson and Sharp close on each side and Sal right behind her as they dived into the depths toward the area where the legend of the *Ella Sophia* lay.

She looked over each shoulder and shot a wink to the two military men—both confident and clearly capable. She guessed that this wasn't their first rodeo. She also sensed an air of excitement in them both, which she thought was a little out of character, but she had let the thought go as quickly as it came.

Helen Bailey liked to be in the lead. She considered herself to be smart. She was confident and had little self-doubt, and for good reason—she'd done more than most, taken more risks. *Maybe even more than these two old Paras*, she thought. Who else had been through what she'd been through?

Diving was one of those things that she did to push herself. It wasn't as though she liked it—in fact quite the opposite—but that's what pushed her to do it more, to stand up to her fears, become accomplished, and enjoy the thrill of living in fear and danger.

She reveled in the whole sense of being in an environment so alien to what the human form was accustomed to. The reliance on the tank on one's back, the equipment, and the ocean life, beautiful and sometimes dangerous.

Every time she dived, she would see little Annie, in her pretty little floral dress up at the farm. They had been friends as children. Annie had a loving father who was at the dinner table each evening, helped her with her schoolwork, and stayed out of the pub. Annie was always perfectly dressed, a sweet little girl, and although Helen and her mother had tried that, Helen was really a tomboy at heart. Although Helen certainly was no dunce at school, Annie was the top of the class and went to church every Sunday without fail, and in the choir to boot.

Helen was no Annie, and she knew that.

As Helen sat on the edge of the slurry pool that day, all her emotions were at play as she pushed Annie and watched her drown in the thick, dark, smelly sludge. She imagined how the girl's lungs filled up with the toxic treacle, and, over time, she had lost the connection between herself and the hand that pushed her.

Happenstance had been a big part of her life, and that recall reminded her of Parsons's strange selection and use of the word. Annie's face was replaced by his in her mind as she continued to descend—something vaguely familiar. The way he looked at her was different, for most men had that look in their eye with her, but not Parsons. With him, it was a mixed look: one of anxiety yet confidence, weakness yet power, vulnerability yet superiority. And when she saw him stare down Sheldon the other day, she saw something else. She had been trying to put her finger on it since.

She found her time below the ocean therapeutic. A place for no words, only thoughts. A place where even her thoughts were safe from any intruding eye. Strangely, despite her hidden fears of the depths, she found comfort in the watery silence, with just the sound of her heart beating, her chest breathing, and the bubbles surrounding her.

"... When I was a child, I caught a fleeting glimpse out of the corner of my eye. I turned to look, but it was gone. I cannot put my finger on it now. The child is grown; the dream is gone ..."

They got to the ocean floor, and Sharp and Simpson were facing each other, gesticulating around a rock—maybe a Para thing, she thought. Sal was chasing a turtle between the coral. She let them all do their own thing as she set out to do hers, making her way down a crevice-like tunnel into the giant wall of coral.

The ornate tunnel surrounded her now on all sides, but it was broad enough for her to comfortably navigate without too much fear of snagging her air lines, although she did occasionally hear the clinking of the coral against the tanks on her back.

She swam onward and downward, keeping an eye on her depth gauge, her compass for position, and the air in her tanks, as well as the occasional coral reef shoal swimming before her.

It was in these moments in the deep blue that she found herself among all her demons and her memories. She could see the mother and the children swimming toward her with their bodies burned and crisp, Annie with her pretty flowery dress covered in barnacles and seaweed. She could see her mother on her deathbed at St. Mary's, her stepfather in his coffin at the funeral, and her stepmother with her battered face and smashed bones. She could see the long and distant image of her real father—his big fancy car, his suit, his money—as he dropped her mother back home.

It was at these depths that Helen saw everything.

The tunnel started to open up, and the golden sand on the floor reappeared, with shards of light coming down from far above. She turned the corner and into what seemed like a magical opening, and in the middle, there she lay right before her, with the brass plaque to her fore: *Ella Sophia*. She took a double gulp of air at the intense shock and beauty of what lay before her.

She swam around the ship, resting there on the sand, barely a ten-foot perimeter around her before the vast walls of rock and coral rose above her. The ornately carved figure on the stern, a beautiful young woman dressed in blue and white, and the detail of her rose-tinted lips and cheeks were still visible despite her years of rest. The sun shimmered down on her perfectly preserved form at the bottom of the ocean.

Helen looked up above her and saw how this deep canyon led up to the surface and the clear blue waters above. "No wonder no one's ever found you, you beautiful girl." She raised her hand to her mouth as if to kiss her and then placed her hand lovingly on the beautiful carving and closed her eyes.

"Well, bloody hell, wait till the boys see this."

She'd learned that time went by on steroids down below, and as she made her way back through the coral tunnel, back up the crevice, to where she had last seen Sal, Simpson, and Sharp, she hoped they were still there.

As she released out of the tunnel, she saw Sal first. He was floating facedown, harpoon right though his mask at the front and the barb sticking out the back of his head, oozing deep purple blood, already attracting the attention of the ocean life.

The other phenomena she realized about diving was that things all happened in slow motion, and in this moment, things were even slower than usual. She looked at Sal and felt a pang of guilt at the relief. Since the incident in Australia, she'd almost felt beholden—that their dark secret would get out for others to know, that he held her to ransom with the knowledge, that it was his fault they had got so drunk and high, and that it was Sal's fault the mother and children died, not hers.

She wrestled her thoughts, and although he was quite obviously dead, she checked his pulse for the inevitable answer. Then she decoupled his weight belt with the quick release buckle, and he slowly started his last ascent.

Simpson was still sitting on the floor, no movement. She swam over and tapped on his face mask. His eyes were wide open and milky, and he wasn't breathing. Again she checked for a pulse. Nothing. She pulled his weight belt. "What the fuck?"

Despite the slow motion, this was also happening too quickly. *What the hell happened?* she thought, trying to weigh up the situation and make sense of it.

She found Sharp. He had got himself snagged on a big outcrop of coral like an altar at the church, still holding the harpoon gun, finger still on the trigger, same wide-open milky-white eyes. No pulse. Three dead. She pulled his belt.

She could taste the puke in her regulator, and it made her even sicker. Her mind was whirling, disorientated, and she felt the need and the fear of passing out. Although a gradual and purposeful ascent was what this depth of water called for and respected, she unbuckled her weight belt and rose from the depths, just looking at the sun shining through the sea above her. She slipped into unconsciousness as she rose through the water to the surface.

V.

Zach was brought back to the moment. He started to see signs of life from the ocean below. Bubbles popping at the surface indicated at least one of his divers would be emerging.

Lady Helen Bailey shot high into the air, waving her arms around in clearly some state of panic. He leaned over, grabbed the harness of her BCD, and hauled her aboard the tender. She pulled back the breathing apparatus and goggles, and Zach could smell the sweet, sickly odor of the puke. He could see the fear in her now bright red eyes, and he knew there was something wrong, and very wrong at that.

Then one body rose to the surface, then another, and then the third, all facedown and lifeless.

"What the bloody hell has happened!" Zach said.

Lady Helen blabbered and blubbered, not making any sense.

"Lady Helen, what the hell happened?"

She sat at the bottom of the tender, head shaking, body shaking, hands shaking.

"Lady Helen, what the hell?"

She was clearly in a state of shock.

"The barb was sticking right out the back of his head," she said and blubbered some more, shaking uncontrollably, sobbing, eyes bright red. "The sharks and the barracudas were circling. Simpson, Sharp, both dead, milky-eyed. Just floating, motionless, dead."

Zach reached for his backpack, grabbed his water bottle, and passed it to her. Then he helped her take in some water and calm down her breathing. She was hyperventilating and in danger of passing out.

"I got to Sal. He was dead. Released his weight belt."

"Yes, dear," he said, prompting her to continue as he helped her remove her air tanks.

"Then I got over to Simpson first. I tried to wake him. His eyes were wide open, but he wasn't breathing, so I released his belt too. Same with Sharp. They were all three dead." She stared at Zach with a look of pure fear and terror.

She lay back in the bottom of the boat and curled up into a fetal position, rocking to and fro. Zach positioned his backpack under her head and pulled out a blanket and placed it over her.

He grabbed the boat hook attached to the inside of the tender and went about pulling the three bodies from the water, one by one, and hauling them over the edge and into the boat.

He cranked up the engine and turned the tender back in the direction of the *Indigo*. Zach just stared forward in disbelief. Three of his four-person dive party were dead.

"For fuck's sake!"

VI.
Back on the *Indigo*

It was noon, and Bromovich was in the pilothouse looking through his binoculars at the approaching tender: Zach steering the craft; what looked like Lady Helen sat on the bench, looking out to the ocean; and three lifeless bodies seemingly still in their dive suits in the bottom of the tender.

"What the hell has happened now?" he said to himself.

Any more bodies, despite how accidental, was either some sort of curse or something else. Bromovich didn't believe in the former, and he also didn't believe in coincidences. He dashed down to the fantail to meet the tender.

Zach's face was as white as a sheet and Lady Helen Bailey's even whiter.

"What the hell is going on?" Bromovich asked.

Lady Helen was fumbling to string a sentence together. Zach spoke for her, reciting the tragedy they had just encountered. Parsons and Sheldon heard the panic and joined them on the rear deck.

"What the hell is going on here?" Sheldon shrilled.

Parsons just shook his head and observed under his half-moon spectacles without saying a word.

Zach escorted Lady Helen to her cabin while Bromovich and Sheldon transferred the three new bodies to the morgue.

VII.
The Vettriano Suite

Lady Helen Bailey woke with a start; sat upright in her bed, sweat dripping from her brow; and looked around anxiously in the darkness of her cabin, the images on the walls coming to life like the ghosts haunting her dreams. She'd always had dreams, vivid dreams, ever since she was a child. They had gotten worse recently, especially after the incident in Australia and even more so lately as she had gotten closer to finding out who her real father was.

She looked at her bedside clock: 4:30 a.m. This was a regular time for her to be awake—always the same time, like it was haunting her, the same time she and Sal had woken in the midst of the fire.

She could hear the children screaming as they burned in the house, she and Sal helpless. Even if they could do something, they were too stoned to even try, although the scene and the screams were enough to leave the scars.

She grabbed a bottle of water from the fridge, took a deep swig, and popped a handful of pills, her hands shaking, and she then lay back on the bed.

Annie was also constantly in her dreams. Lady Helen had always struggled with the question as she saw little Annie, just eight years old at the time, teetering on the edge of the slurry pool at the farm, Was her pointed finger enough to send her over the edge? She didn't mean to, but by the time Annie plunged into the thick dark treacle, it was too late, and there was no turning back.

She had grabbed a pitchfork and tried to hold it out for Annie to grab, but it was all too quick and all too late. Annie was unable to swim, especially in the thick slurry and with her little lungs quickly filling up with the toxic slime. In seconds, it was over.

There were many ghosts that haunted Helen Bailey, never mind who her real father was, and maybe in him she would find the clues of who she was today and what she had become.

She kept seeing the harpoon shot through Sal's head, into his face and out the other side. The billow of blood in the water attracting the gathering of marine life. The looks in Simpson's and Sharp's eyes as she cut their belts. She wondered who had killed the men. Logic said it could only have been Zach, but that didn't make sense. And if it had been Zach, why hadn't he killed her too?

This whole trip was just a complete nightmare, adding to the many nightmares she already had.

And who the hell is Litions? was the question ringing around her mind. Why her? Why had he invited her?

Maybe it was all happenstance—she caught herself using that word, her mother's word, and played back an image of Parsons using the same word, fitting the bill of her long-absent and never-seen-before father.

She was getting close, very close, and she didn't know how to feel about that.

She had a lot of hatred built up for this invisible man who had never been a part of her life, a secret her own mother had taken to her grave.

Ship's Log (Special Report)

SS *Indigo*
Captain Igor Bromovich
Klaipeda Naval Academy

Transmission: July 21, 2003: 8:26 p.m. CST

Incident: July 21, 2003

Today we had three more. The following passengers returned from a scuba diving excursion and were pronounced dead upon their return to SS *Indigo*.

1. Mr. Anthony James Sharp, British, passport number 419974212.
2. Mr. Keith Alan Simpson, British, passport number 557632901.
3. Mr. James Atlas Salmond, Australian, passport number MO 921787.

Although the ship no longer has a trained medical doctor on board, it seems that Simpson and Sharp likely suffered some sort of polluted air poisoning.

Mr. Salmond had been shot through the head with a speargun.

We have a growing number of bodies in the ship's morgue. It is a worrying time for the remaining passengers, to say the least.

We will now be heading directly to George Town.

I look forward to meeting and a full debriefing when we arrive.

Captain Igor Bromovich

<END>

14

I.
London, England

IT HAD BEEN OVER SIX weeks since he had last made the commute to the office, and this morning he knew why. If it wasn't the rain and misery of the winter, it was the humidity of the summer.

As the tube train pulled into Charing Cross, he squeezed his way through the sweaty crowd of tourists and commuters and released himself from the sardine can on the way to the fresher air and on to Trafalgar Square unnoticed.

He didn't quite understand his habit of wearing a suit to the city, but today he wore the dark blue suit he had proudly purchased from Anderson & Sheppard thirty years earlier. Back then, he was a young operative of the Serious Fraud Office, at the beginning of his career, young, bright, and full of hope and optimism.

How things had changed but the suit had not.

Today he wore his Guards Club tie; his three-quarter-length herringbone coat; and his comfortable walking shoes that somehow seemed at odds with his other, more formal attire. At the office, he had a range of Church's to choose from.

He tipped his hat at Lord Nelson before walking down Spring Gardens and into the Trafalgar Hotel for his morning coffee and bacon sandwich. He grabbed a copy of the *Financial Times* and sat in his usual spot at the window overlooking the Canadian embassy and the entrance to the SFO he had departed long ago.

Although he had made the same trip probably hundreds of times, no one knew him. Apart from the concierge at the Trafalgar, who gave him a knowing smile—it was about his only connection.

He was an ordinary man in a big wide world, and although, for many reasons, including his line of business, he yearned for something more, maybe that day had long passed him by.

After breakfast, he headed back out and turned left on to Cockspur Street, toward the memorabilia shop next door, the Crest of London, with its British flags, mugs, and tea towels, the Union Jack branded everywhere, everything made in China. The Chinese shop owner, Mrs. Chang, sort of politely nodded her knowledge of his presence. He didn't understand the concept at all.

He passed by the entryway to his office, number 20. Not much of an entrance, just a battered old wooden door—no signs, no glamor, just the number 20. In brass and cushioned between a Thai restaurant and an all-you-can-see London bus tour.

One thing that he had concluded, and had solved the puzzle to, was that he disliked the new London Town, a lot.

He turned the key in the lock, let himself in, and headed up the rickety stairs to the second floor, where his office was on the right at the top.

He checked his safety lock. The otherwise invisible horse's hair was still attached and therefore told him there'd been no uninvited guests since he last left.

He cracked the door open, flicked on the lights, and illuminated his long-familiar den of business—quiet, silent, and dark.

There was a receptionless desk and a back office, which was his. He creaked the door and stepped to the back of the room to his closet and collection of city shoes. He removed his walking shoes and halted midway through his change to deal with the highly annoying beeping from the fax machine—out of paper.

"For fuck's sake," he said to himself quietly and in his sweaty bright red socks stepped over to the machine in question, cranked it open, and replaced the roll of paper. "Who uses these machines nowadays anyway? For fuck's sake!"

From his ambitious beginnings, he struggled every day to work out how he had got to this line of business. He didn't even really know what that meant. Fixing things, doing other people's dirty work, in the shadows, but this one was the strangest of all.

He went back to the cupboard behind his desk and pulled out his favorite brogues. As he laced them up, the fax machine was in full swing, spitting out page after page after page.

He finished tying his laces and strolled over to the fax, waited for it to stop printing, and scooped up the papers and placed them on his dusty desk.

Hearing the kettle whistle, he grabbed his mug and a spoonful of instant coffee, and then he poured over the boiling water, added a splash of long-life milk, and sat down at his desk.

He carefully read the faxes one by one, in date order, and as he considered the situation far away in the Caribbean, he literally scratched his head to try to make sense of the unfolding events.

"Why the hell are they faxing me?"

He already knew the answer. What the hell had he got himself into?

He had no idea who Jemol Litions, or Litions Industries, was. At the time, he didn't care. He just responded to, and accepted the terms of the proposal he had received in a letter six months ago. He didn't know who or why, and frankly he didn't care—that was the line of business he was in.

He sipped his coffee and grimaced. He hated the combination of cheap instant coffee and long-life milk. In fact, he hated this office—the musty smell, the dust, the emptiness, in fact everything about it. He hated the fact that no one knew him; he was just a faceless man with his suits and old leather briefcase and nothing to say. He hated the fact that although once he had been a wannabee, thirty years later, he was now a bona fide nobody.

He stared at the stream of messages from Captain Bromovich, held his head in his hands, pressing his fingertips against his temples, and looked at his watch: 11:00 a.m.

"Fuck it—let's go for a beer."

And on that, he put the papers in his briefcase, shut his office door, stepped back out to Cockspur Street, turned right, and headed to the Admiralty for a pint or two of ale and maybe a whisky chaser or two.

"What the fuck?" he muttered to himself as he walked through the front door of the pub. Then he ordered a pint of London Pride and a whisky chaser.

He sat at the bench seat at the back of the bar and went through the faxes again.

Three hours later, he stumbled toward Charing Cross and his miserable commute back home.

"For fuck's sake!"

II.
The 1921 Suite

Zach had not seen Sheldon in the past few hours, and after a stroll around the decks, he headed to the 1921 Suite. The ship was now eerie as he walked past the other suites, now mainly empty, the morgue now full of passengers. He was now convinced that a killer was aboard, but he could not for the life of him figure out how the killer could knock off three passengers underwater and not be seen. Frankly, the entire situation scared the hell out of him. He got to the door of the suite, and it was open. Alarm bells immediately went off in Zach's head.

"Not another one," he said and made a sign of the cross as he walked in.

Sheldon was sitting motionless at his desk, a syringe and a needle in his right hand, his left sleeve rolled up, a rubber tourniquet strapped around just above his elbow. Of course, Zach was familiar with the concept of shooting up, but for all Sheldon's obnoxiousness, he never had him down for a druggy, as evidenced by the lack of any other needle marks on his arm.

He felt for a pulse, but he already knew by touch that Sheldon's chilled temperature meant that he had been dead a few hours. He called for the captain, and they moved an ninth body to the ship's morgue. Only three slots remaining.

Bromovich motioned for Zach to follow him, and so he did, to the captain's cabin.

III.
The Captain's Cabin

Bromovich opened the door, and Zach followed him in. Bromovich walked to his desk, opened the bottom draw, and pulled out a bottle of vodka and a revolver.

For a second, Zach looked at the Lithuanian with clear concern on his face.

Bromovich beamed as if reading his mind. "No, no, young Zach. Don't worry—it's not me."

Zach was relieved; he somehow knew the statement to be true.

Bromovich poured two glasses, headed to the toilet, and left the revolver on the desk. Zach looked around the cabin—much more utilitarian than his Liddesdale Suite, but charming nevertheless. The room was neat and regimented, with bed made and Bromovich's personal belongings meticulously in place: the family photo on his desk, his journal and pen neatly laid out, his night-robe and padded jacket hung up behind the door—not a thing out of place.

The sign of a true captain, Zach thought, then heard the toilet flush and the sound of Bromovich washing his hands.

He came out of the bathroom, sat at the desk, grabbed his glass, and took a swig. "What the hell do you make of all this, Mr. Carter?" he asked, deliberately formal.

"I was hoping you could tell me."

Bromovich looked at him blankly.

"Have you heard from Litions?"

Again, nothing from Bromovich, apart from a slow shake of his head.

"Nothing?"

"Nyet."

Zach knew the Russian response for no.

"What the hell is going on?" he asked, now more serious than ever.

Bromovich shook his head in his hands. "I don't know, Zach, and more to the point, I have no idea what to do about it."

"This is now well beyond a joke."

"Yep, and a fucking sick joke at that."

"If we do have a murderer on board, and if it's not me, and it isn't you, then that leaves three other possible suspects: Parsons, Perry, and Lady Helen herself."

Bromovich lit up a cigar, and Zach rolled a spliff. Bromovich persuaded him to have a cigar instead.

"We want you quick-witted, young Zach, not on another planet."

It was a fair point, but before they managed to enjoy either, their conversation was disrupted as they heard a man's voice boom, "Man overboard!"

The two froze, looking at each other, and in synchrony stood up and ran out of the door to the direction of the call.

"What the hell now?"

Zach and Bromovich ran to the rear of the ship, where the tender was. They could see a body floating facedown donned in the instantly recognizable shell suit. Zach assumed it was the cook. Without thinking twice, they both jumped in the tender and sped away from the *Indigo* to his recovery.

There was a strong breeze down on the water, and that was pushing the body farther from the ship and impeding the tender's headway at the same time.

Battling against the wind, they eventually caught up with the body, and with Zach at the engine, Bromovich stood up with the boat hook, trying to grab on to pull the body closer. With the shell suit ballooning and slippery when wet, there wasn't too much to grab on to, and the salty water on the skin made it as slippery as catching a baby seal.

Eventually, after a struggle and grappling, Bromovich managed to pull the body close enough for Zach to help and manhandle the body into the tender.

They turned him over. It was Perry—white and turning purple.

After five minutes' attempted resuscitation, Bromovich gave up and looked at Zach. "He's dead."

They both sat down in the boat just looking at each other. No words could express how they were feeling.

What the hell was this? What the hell was going on? Had they woken up in some murder-mystery screenplay?

It was Bromovich who first noticed, and he stood up and just pointed.

The *Indigo* had pulled her anchor and was steaming away from them.

"What the hell?" Zach shouted above the wind, scrambling to the engine of the tender that had now cut out.

Zach grabbed the starting handle and frantically pulled. On the first time, it spluttered to life, then died. He tried again—nothing. He pumped the petrol twice and tried again, and it spluttered and died.

"What the hell is going on?"

He traced the fuel line, and seeing that it was full of air, he hand-pumped again. Nothing. He leaned over to check the tank: empty. There was a pool of purply petrol residue in the water below them.

"The bloody tank's leaked empty! The fuel line has been cut!"

The two of them sat in the tender with Perry's body as they watch the *Indigo* sail off into the distance at a rate of knots.

"What the hell?"

IV.
The Smoking Salon

Parsons summoned Lady Helen to the smoking salon. They were the last remaining passengers of the *Indigo*. They both knew that. In that moment, they realized that this encounter had been a long time coming. Long before the *Indigo*—a lifetime of mysteries, of shame, abandonment, and betrayal.

She'd prepared herself as best she could. She had over the course of the past few days put two and two, plus two, together and come up with 5.999. In the Vettriano Suite, she put on her little black dress and grabbed her clutch bag, and then she marched to the smoking salon. There was no way that after all these years she would show any form of weakness in this moment. This was the moment she had been waiting for all her life, her mum's life. This was their moment.

She could hear the engines on full throttle rumbling far below, the ship shuddering at the sheer power. She wondered for a second who was driving this thing but quickly worked out that this was as much Parsons's moment as it was hers— just the two of them, finally. *The final showdown*, she thought.

She slowed as she neared the entrance to the salon. Pulled out the mirror in her clutch, looked at herself, fluffed her hair, pouted, and then walked boldly toward the door. In that moment, she was less scared and more angry, less frightened and more sad at the tragedy of it all. She flashed back to the dock at St. George's, the string quartet playing Brahms, the push and the pull, the tension. She saw Sal with the harpoon through his brain, and the two military men, all dead. The roll call of passengers, all dead. Even she believed to a point that it was all unfortunate coincidences.

She paused at the door. She thought once more of her mother, Shelly Bailey, and how she had failed her. She wasn't there for her mother in her final moment as she had always promised she would.

She shook her head one last time, lifted her chin, and marched into the smoking salon.

Parsons was sitting on one of the chesterfield wingback chairs in front of the open fire. Although the night was breezy, especially with their increased knots, the curtains were flying in the breeze. It wasn't that the room needed the warmth—she knew it was all about effect.

Across from Parsons was an empty chair facing him as well as a chessboard—seemingly set up in the middle of a game—a bottle of Macallan, and two glasses. He waved to Lady Helen to sit down opposite him.

Parsons immediately noticed the pearls around her neck, the same ones he had bought for her mother all those years ago on a trip to London, from one of the small boutique jewelers on Sloane Square.

"Would you like ice?" he asked as she slowly made her way around and sat opposite him, her eyes never leaving his and vice versa.

At this point, he was bereft of feelings—they had departed his soul a long time ago—but after all, this was his own flesh and blood, and in many ways, he was so proud of her.

"You fucker" was her opening statement as he poured two glasses of the Macallan.

She stared at him, her eyes drilling into his soul. "What the fuck?"

He'd spent a lifetime of playing it calm in high-level, high-tension meetings with executives, corporations, countries, and even presidents, but this was different. This was his own daughter.

He sat in his chair holding his whisky, with Helen Bailey holding hers. She was watching closely, he assumed, waiting for him to drink first—which he obliged. She quickly followed.

"So, why?" she asked. "Just tell me why."

"Why *what*?"

"Well, first, why all this bullshit?" she said and waved her hand around, indicating the *Indigo*.

He paused for a second, took a sip of his whisky, looked into the fire, and chose to answer another question.

"I loved your mother."

The tears started to well up in Helen's eyes.

"It was just the wrong time, the wrong place. We had no choice."

"Fuck off—she died of a broken heart, alone in her tiny little cottage, in her tiny little village. But you know what? She was happy despite you, you heartless fucker!"

"I've been watching you."

"Oh, so what's that supposed to mean? You were never there for Mum, for me. Am I now supposed to feel grateful?" She looked at him with anger in her eyes, shaking, and took another sip of the whisky.

"How do you think that you've never been held to account, Helen?"

She just sat there staring at him, angry, murderous.

"First there was the *accident* with Annie when you were just a child. Your mother told me about the strangled cat that you blamed on your next-door neighbor Walter. Then there was the incident at Brimham Rocks, the bed-and-breakfast in Australia, and the other incidents that have followed you around like the plague, Helen."

She stared at him, red-eyed, seething. She reached into her clutch bag and pulled out the micro Colt Mustang. At only five inches in length, carrying six rounds, plus one in the chamber, and weighing less than a pound, it had been easy to conceal on her beloved Triumph and had been with her on her worldwide travels. She pulled it out and at point-blank range pointed it in the direction of Parsons's head.

Parsons just sat there and laughed.

Helen Bailey sat there red-faced, embarrassed, and angry. She pulled the trigger, and they both heard the hollow sound of the firing pin hitting the empty chamber.

They sat in silence as Parsons topped up their whisky and ice.

"Is that what you used to dispatch the monk in Thailand?" he teased.

She just ignored him, throwing the useless weapon onto the table before them, knocking over a handful of pawns and the white queen.

"OK," she said. "What the fuck do you want from me?"

They both sat in silence, not quite knowing whether it was a question.

"Did you come to kill me tonight, Helen?"

She held her head in one hand and the glass of whisky in the other, tears rolling down her face. "Why Litions? Why the disguise all these years? Why didn't you ever tell me? Why did you stop Mum from telling me?" Her eyes were brimming with tears, uncontrollable emotions.

Parsons looked at her from across the table. "Life is complicated, Helen Bailey."

"You fucker." She drilled her eyes into him, tears rolling down her cheeks. "Where the hell are we going?"

"Grand Cayman. And by the time we arrive, young lady, you will be a very wealthy woman indeed."

"I don't need your fucking money."

He went on to explain the situation—the sizable wealth that he had amassed during his career; his diagnosis of a rare, genetic, and terminal cancer; even the circumstances around the creation of Jemol Litions.

"But what about Mum? Why didn't you ..."

"I loved your mother like no other," he said, looking her straight in the eye.

"But why these people?" Again she pointed around the *Indigo*, and, more specifically, in the direction of the ship's morgue.

The last words she heard before she passed out were "They had all trod the path and the journey to hell."

She faded away into a deep and distant sleep.

PART 2

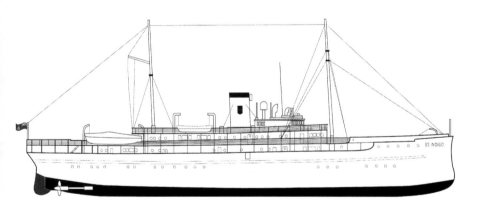

15

I HAD ALWAYS WONDERED HOW the Caribbean cruise had gone, but frankly, that summer, with the entry of the Baltic states to the EU, both RekruitUK and I were busier than ever. The money from Litions had sure helped with working capital, and we were placing workers in hotels, restaurants, with facilities services companies, janitorial firms, hospitals, you name it—anywhere they needed unskilled or semiskilled labor, we were there. The ironic thing was that many of the placements in mind-numbing jobs were lawyers, accountants, and professionals just looking to earn some money for their families back home.

Now that we had a team in place, I was heading down to Australia to explore a similar deal there and take a bit of downtime during my stay to visit some old haunts.

I.
The Tiffin Room, Raffles, Singapore

I was heading back down to Australia, and to break up the ridiculously long trip, I called into Singapore. It was lunchtime at my favorite, the Tiffin Room, in the old Raffles Hotel, adorned with its varieties of tiffin boxes and its delightful curry lunch buffet.

It was a piece of living history—the old white wooden building, the Tiffin Room with its ceiling fans and waiters adorned in white starched tunics and turbans. The array of tiffins, from the ordinary to the ornate, where workers, fisherman, and expeditioners would store their lunches, with different compartments for the different courses.

I had always wondered if anyone did ever use the most ornate, solid gold, or if it was just for display—which I suspected it was then. If so, why would anyone go to the expense of doing so? It was another of life's great mysteries.

I picked up a newspaper at the hotel reception and was leafing through it as the waiter made my chapatis, table side. And then, on page 8, I saw the picture of the beached SS *Indigo* and the headline "Ghost Ship Crashes into the Ritz."

I lost focus on everything at that moment and frantically read the story.

> Luxury steamship SS *Indigo* made an unexpected stop last week as it crashed onto the beach of luxury getaway the Ritz-Carlton, Grand Cayman.
> Guests at the resort and witnesses noticed the ship steaming toward them at a rate of knots before

it came crashing onto the beach, disturbing the tranquility of the cabanas and suntan oil.

But that's not all the story. Local police boarded the vessel and found nine bodies in the ship's morgue, the body of Sir James Parsons on board. Explorer and adventurer Lady Helen Bailey was found unconscious but alive and was taken to the George Town hospital, where she is in stable condition.

The ship had cruised from St. George's Caye, Belize City, just a few days previous with twelve passengers, two crew, and Lithuanian captain Igor Bromovich.

George Town police captain Joseph James said of the incident, "We're looking into this as a potential murder scene. In my years in the force, I have never quite seen anything like this, and we will be applying all our resources to get to the bottom of this most unusual incident."

The captain, Bromovich, and passenger Zach Carter from California were rescued some two hundred miles away as they were found floating in the *Indigo*'s tender with a twelfth body, that of ship's cook, a Perry Kirkham from Rainham, Kent, England.

Holidayers at the Ritz-Carlton described the moment that the *Indigo* came ashore: "We were just having our first prelunch cocktail of the day down by the beach bar, and there was all this commotion and the ship accelerating to the shoreline. We thought it would turn, but it kept on going, crashing right on to the beach."

"What a mystery," said another. "It's like something straight out of an Agatha Christie novel."

The ship was rescued and taken under police guard to George Town harbor, where a full investigation is underway.

My chapatis were ready, but the story was just too compelling despite the aromas from the curry buffet around me.

The story went on:

> Sir James Parsons was chairman of Watershed Investments, and just two days prior to the incident, the *Financial Times* reported a breaking story of how the veteran investor had become linked with Litions Industries and the illusive and secretive billionaire Jemol Litions.
>
> As Litions seemingly was liquidating his portfolio, alerting the investment world, transactions of funds were linked back to Watershed Investments and to Sir James Parsons.

And a twist in the tale:

> Marine engineer Zach Carter, who qualified at the US Maritime Academy, was arrested by the Grand Cayman police on arrival in George Town due to an outstanding warrant issued for his part in drug running for the Castida Cartel in years past. Carter is set to appear before the Right Honorable Judge Marvin Milassi later this month for sentencing.

I made my way to the buffet and helped myself to the Indian delights before me, then sat down and ordered a Singapore Sling. Why the hell not?

I recalled the meeting with young Zach back in the No Name Bar in Amsterdam. I knew that there was something about him from the day I met him. I hoped that Judge Milassi would be lenient on him.

I took a big swig of my extraordinarily expensive Singapore Sling and looked out the window at the bustling city around this colonial oasis, reflecting on what was an incredibly unusual set of events.

The mystery of what happened on the SS *Indigo* remained. The Grand Cayman police could find no evidence other than a series of accidents, suicides, and misadventures, but nothing that pointed out to more than a hint of foul play. But if it was murder, who the hell was it?

The only survivors were the captain, Bromovich, and Zach Carter, both of whom I had placed on the request of my contact Waring, but it clearly couldn't have been them, as they were stranded in a tender two hundred miles away when Sir James Parsons met his demise. Turned out that Bromovich went back home and never went back to sea. After a six-month stint in the local prison, Zach returned to Sonoma County and was running his father's tourist boat in Sausalito. I would take a trip and go see him. I felt a sense of responsibility for them both.

Helen Bailey was considered the prime suspect for a while as the sole survivor on the ship. It turned out that she had also been poisoned, but not with the same dosage level that killed Parsons. She had also benefited handsomely from Parsons's death.

She came clean about Parsons being her real father, and after DNA tests, that was proven. Although suspicions remained, there simply wasn't any evidence to implicate her as the culprit.

That said, they didn't know what evidence they were looking for.

Paul Bland—he was killed, and he didn't even set sail on the *Indigo*. Left floating, facedown, hands and feet nailed to a door, no chance of survival but symbolic nevertheless. Was this a coincidence? One of twelve coincidences?

Perkins was a clear suicide; Chalmers, natural causes; Jacobs, anaphylactic shock the most likely cause; Brown, an accident that happens too often on ships at sea, especially for a novice sailor like Bronwyn Brown; Salmond, Simpson, and Sharp, a diving incident; Perry Kirkham, drowned; Sheldon, an overdose.

Salmond could have been murder, as could have been the stewardess, Kayla, but there simply was no evidence to go from, no eyewitnesses, no nothing—just their bodies and a postmortem and no suspects left to point a finger at.

I took a look at the transactions on the days leading up to Sir James Parsons's passing—multiple billions in trading, selling stocks, liquidating assets, a significant sum invested on his behalf to an account with the First World Bank with links to the Russian state and Russian mob.

Then there were the large donations to charities for the victims of pedophilia and elder abuse. Other large deposits to a St. Mary's Hospice.

A £10 million deposit to Austin Davies's widow, Elizabeth. He had wired another £3 million to Igor Bromovich and another £1 million to a business headquartered at 20 Cockspur Street, London.

He had also purchased Sheldon's property portfolio for a handsome sum and then immediately released the titles back to the former tenants. They now owned their own hairdressing shops.

Fifty million pounds was wired to Harry Bloomington, a resident of Highland Park, in the Dallas area, and an old friend of Sir James.

Then the balance of the funds was put in a trust for his wife, his two sons, and Lady Helen Bailey. He had made each of them a multibillionaire with the transaction.

In the spirit of following the money, I decided to look into some of these to see what I could dig up and headed to Dallas first.

II.
4500 Belclaire Avenue,
Highland Park, Dallas, Texas

Harry was sitting in his study of the five-thousand-square-foot home in a leafy and very clearly well-off area of the city, fifteen minutes from the city center. I parked on the driveway in front of the property, which looked like an implanted chateau from France rather than what I had imagined from watching *Dallas* and the Southfork Ranch when I was a kid.

I got to the front door and patiently rang the doorbell. I could hear the chimes inside, and a few moments later, a Hispanic lady answered the door.

"Sí, Señor?"

I explained my appointment with Mr. Bloomington, and she ushered me inside.

It was very clear that Harry was doing all right for himself. Then again, he was £50 million better off thanks to his old friend Sir James Parsons.

The maid escorted me to the study, and there sat Harry, just how I'd imagined him, maybe just a little older. Through my research, I had learned that he was a legend of the square mile and famous for his chalk stripes and red braces, both of which he was wearing today for our meeting.

He ushered me to sit down, and I obliged, into a red leather chesterfield wingback chair, which immediately reminded me of the *Indigo*. As I settled in, I looked around the room and saw the group photograph in pride of place, a group of soldiers posing for a team photo somewhere in the jungle.

He caught the direction of my eye and cleared his throat. "For what do I owe the pleasure, young man?" He made the point of looking at his watch, a shiny Patek Philippe, I guessed at a distance—a pretty packet, too, in line with the opulence and style of the house around me.

After around an hour, the meeting was fruitless. Apart from his retelling old stories of long late lunches in various cities around the world, when we got to the lunch at the Adolphus, his memory conveniently lapsed, and he referred to his mature years, saying that he'd drunk too much in his lifetime to remember everything.

"Not like Sir James," he said and smiled. "Now that man could remember everything." He winked at me, and I left.

Next stop: Sausalito, California.

III.
Cavallo Point, Sausalito, California

It had been an easy flight from Fort Worth to SFO. The hotel had arranged for a town car to pick me up outside T2 arrivals. I looked out the window as we headed north toward San Francisco and watched the familiar sights pass by as we trundled through the traffic on Nineteenth Avenue past the Golden Gate Park and Presidio and onto the bridge.

The sky was clear blue, Alcatraz was sitting pretty in the middle of the bay, and the San Francisco streets were shining gold, as they often do on days like these.

Past the bridge, we dropped down into Cavallo Point, the former Marines barracks now a luxury hotel, nestled under the Golden Gate Bridge and a spitting distance from Sausalito.

I checked in at reception, in what used to be the officers' mess, overlooking the grass in the middle of the former barracks, which I assumed was once the parade grounds—although, from my own experiences, I couldn't imagine square bashing on grass.

My room was in the main building, overlooking the bay under the shadow of the bridge. This place had a sense of calmness. *What were they worried about?* I thought. *Did they really think the Japanese would have attempted a land invasion back then?* I'd been reading up and was surprised how many US troops had occupied this area during World War II, and all the armaments around to protect the bay.

I checked my watch: 4:30 p.m. I had a quick shower, put a fresh set of clothes on, and took the courtesy town car into Sausalito.

The car pulled up at the head of the marina, and I immediately spotted the *Lady of the Bay* and recognized Zach as he finished up for the day, padlocked the pilothouse, and gated up the boardwalk. I got out to greet him.

"You know mysterious strangers in black limos scare the hell out me, right?" he said and greeted me with his big smile, mustache still intact.

We actually barely knew each other, but we gave each other a bear hug like a pair of old friends.

To be fair, while he was in Northward Prison, I'd managed to get messages to him, some supplies and a couple of treats smuggled. When he got out, we had kept in touch by email, and I knew that since his dad died, he'd taken over the family business.

We jumped in the car and minutes later pulled up outside Salito's—according to its big blue sign, a Crab House & Prime Rib restaurant. I was hungry.

After we'd ordered a couple of pints of the local Fort Point brew, I dived right in.

"So, what the hell do you think happened out there?"

He related the story from his perspective—told me about him and Lady Helen Bailey, their night together, then how he and Bromovich were in the tender with the *Indigo* steaming into the distance.

"At that point, I really didn't know what to think," he said and shook his head. "And then there was the whole Lady

Helen thing. It was like she was, you know"—he hesitated—"turned on by it all."

It was my turn to shake my head. I stayed silent and just listened. I felt like I was in a therapy session, not having supper with an old pal.

"Then, of course, I got to the dock, and they were fucking waiting for me." He looked me in the eye and smiled. "I was only young back then."

"You got away with it lightly, my friend," I said and smiled back.

"Are you fucking kidding? Grand Cayman may be a paradise on earth, but I can tell you: Northward ain't no paradise."

He acknowledged my generous gifts and ingenuity.

"She's in India now," he said and looked at me, and I sensed that Lady Helen was more of a thing than he was letting on.

"I heard. I was thinking about going to see her."

His eyes lit up, and then quickly he looked away, clutching the wedding ring on his finger.

We were sat at the square bar at the far end, with a picture-postcard view of the water—the boats moored, the sail boats having fun in the late-afternoon sun. He pulled out a photograph of a clapboard house with a woman and two toddlers, and with his finger, he pointed. "That's Molly, Thomas, and Milly." He looked at me and smiled.

"Good on yer, Zach Carter. You finally tied the knot."

I realized how long it had been since I first met him and then read the story of *Indigo*, and how, busy with work, I hadn't had the opportunity to catch up till now.

We bid our farewells as he climbed in what I assumed was his dad's old Ford Bronco, window down.

"Say hello to Lady Helen from me."

I winked back. "Of course, Mr. Zach Carter. Until next time."

IV.
20 Cockspur Street, Trafalgar Square, London

I had decided to stay at the Trafalgar Hotel for many reasons—I was a lifetime Hilton member from my many travels, and it was just around the corner from 20 Cockspur Street.

After breakfast, I turned out of the hotel and took a left, passed by the Best of British tourist shop full of tat, and next door found the wooden door with the brass number 20 on it. I rang the bell and stood there waiting, looking up and around, trying to make something of this unmemorable building before me. No sign of life. I knocked firmly but hard. No answer. It was nine in the morning, and I figured that, as it was a place of business, someone should be around at this time of day.

I went next door to the British shop, and the Oriental lady behind the counter greeted me with barely a smile.

I showed her the address and asked whether she knew a Mr. Neil Waring, and given the blank look on her face, she evidently did not, or at least she wasn't willing to share. I was dressed in my usual: Polo shirt, Polo jeans, Eddie Bauer boots, and North Face padded jacket. It's not like I looked like a detective or anything—but maybe if I had, I might have gotten a better response.

I turned to the front door and saw a young lady struggling with her umbrella and bag and trying to open the door next door. I rushed to her help.

"Can I help you, miss?"

She seemed appreciative, and when I asked her whether she knew Waring, she clammed up, said her *thank yous*, and closed the door. I could hear her shuffling up the steep stairs behind. I tried knocking again and rang the doorbell but heard only silence from within.

Undeterred, I walked to Piccadilly and to St. James's Church, the final resting place of Sir James. Only a billionaire could get a burial place in a church that had long since stopped burying people. Parson's ashes had been cast behind a stone plinth inside with the simple inscription "Sir James Parsons, 1940–2003, 'The road to hell is paved with good intentions.'"

I had long since been fascinated by this phrase, and I thought it so apt for Parsons, if he was indeed the killer.

The exact origins of the proverb are unknown, and its form has evolved over time. This modern version of the saying was first published in 1855 in *A Handbook of Proverbs* by Henry G. Bohn. But earlier versions of the saying appeared in a newspaper in 1831, and as early as 1670 in *A Collection of English Proverbs* by John Ray.

In Franco Zeffirelli's 1968 adaptation of *Romeo and Juliet*, the character Mercutio says, "The best intentions pave the way to hell," with even earlier references going as far back as the year 1150.

A common meaning of the phrase is that wrongdoings or evil actions are often undertaken with good intentions, or that good intentions, when acted on, may have unintended consequences.

I thought long and hard about this as I took a cab to Canary Wharf and the headquarters of the First World Bank. I had managed to secure an appointment with one of their investment managers.

Another blank. The woman apparently knew nothing of Litions Industries, or the hefty deposit that I alleged had been made into related accounts with the First World Bank. It was clear that she either didn't know or just wasn't saying, hiding behind the standard "I'm sorry, Mr. Mitchell; we can't divulge such private and protected information."

My plea that it was seventeen years ago fell on deaf ears.

I decided to go for lunch and headed into Soho. I was an out-of-town member of the Union Club on Greek Street, and once past the big red front door and credential check, I was out of the hustle and bustle and back in the familiar territory of this quaint, eclectic private members' club.

After the incident in Grand Cayman, SS *Indigo* was retired—not forcefully, but out of circumstances. She had incurred limited and repairable damage on the beaching, but the fact of the matter was that no buyers were willing to put an investment into an overly appointed old steamship, especially against the backdrop of the now legendary story of her fatal last journey.

She sat rotting in the George Town harbor behind the barbed wire fencing protecting the port authorities' assets. She was now an unclaimed asset of the authorities, but an asset is only an asset if you can find someone to pay the claimed value.

I had agonized for years over this puzzle. Bromovich and Zach were out of the picture for several reasons, not least that they had been stranded themselves and left out of the final scene.

As some thought, it could logically have been a series of unfortunate events, and that was the SS *Indigo* curse theory, but somehow I didn't quite wear that. The final scene in the play was the answer, I was sure, and if it was murder, then it was either Parsons or his daughter. Or both.

I did some research into Helen Bailey's past and discovered the story of the little girl drowning in the slurry pit, only eight years old. Her stepmother apparently slipping, the rumor that Helen was with her. The bed-and-breakfast in the outback of Australia. These all prompted valid questions but nothing conclusive.

Could she have murdered her own real father, having eventually found out the truth after own mother had passed away? Possibly, but at the time of the second autopsy, there were no longer any remaining strains of poisoning in his body. The first hasty tests had been discounted as void by the courts.

In my mind, if there was a killer, it had to be Parsons.

He knew he had only weeks left with a rare, hereditary cancer of the brain. He made all the transactions and gifts just days before he died. He was the last man standing, literally, and through my research, he had at least second- or third-degree connections to all the passengers on the list.

"It had to be him." I was convinced.

But I still wasn't quite sure about how the diving murders, or accidents, had occurred. Perhaps the entire case involved a combination of coincidences mixed with a murder plot. I found the whole thing puzzling, to say the least.

After my chicken salad and a couple of glasses of Chablis, I decided to head back to the hotel. It was an early start to get to Heathrow for my flight to Bombay and on to Goa in the morning.

Passing by the Admiralty, I thought I would pop in for a pint before heading to my room.

It was five o'clock on a Tuesday evening, a workday, and the place was packed. With the pub's limited sitting room, businesspeople crowded around the bar noisy with chatter and postwork discussions. Mates meeting mates before their commute home, colleagues and colleagues, team socials and bonding. I made my way to the very back of the bar and found a quiet corner standing at the bar, away from the main throng and the deafening noise.

I patiently waited my turn and ordered a pint of London Pride.

As I took my first sip, I looked around at my fellow drinkers and noticed the woman I had seen that morning with her bag and umbrella, sat down at one of the few seats tucked away in a corner by the back door at a pub table with two stools—her recognizable bag and umbrella on the second. She had a half pint glass in front of her, and she was busy texting on her phone.

"Do you mind if I join you?"

She looked up and immediately appeared nervous.

"It's OK," I said. "I don't bite. I am an author, that's all. My name is Willy." I held out my hand. "Willy Mitchell."

Her eyes widened. Perhaps she had heard of me, even read some of my books.

I shook her hand, sat opposite her on the vacant stool, and took a sip of my beer at the same time she did. Over the top of my glass, I observed that she was attractive in a not-so-obvious way. She fell into my category of someone you would have no qualms taking home to meet Mother.

We put our glasses down on the table simultaneously like a pair of synchronized drinkers.

"Hello, Willy. My name is Sally. Nice to meet you." She smiled. "I read *Gipsy Moth*." She smiled again, and I felt like I blushed but pretended nothing of it.

"Why are you looking for Waring?" she asked.

I explained.

"He doesn't exist, you know. He never did."

"How so?" I was taking the view that sometimes less is more in situations like this.

She went on to explain how she had been the occasional on-demand secretary for the agency, and as he didn't go to the office frequently, she would go in now and again to check on things.

"Agency? What did they do?"

She struggled to explain, to articulate what they did— seemed like almost anything that others didn't want to do: serve papers on once friends or family members, provide investigations and reports on nefarious affairs, investigate potential frauds, and act as an often-anonymous office for communications and correspondence.

"So, who was Neil Waring?"

She laughed. "Don't you get it? N-W-A-R-I-N-G."

The penny dropped. *Shit, why didn't I see that before?*

"If he didn't exist, who was running the show?" I paused for a moment, seeing her glass empty and mine almost. "Can I buy you another drink?"

"Sure."

I headed to the bar and the throng. My spot on the corner was no longer available, and I was in a rush to get back, so I headed right for the mosh pit in the middle and squeezed myself in. By the time I had ordered, paid, and gotten back to the table, I must have been less than two minutes. Sally was gone, and so was her bag and umbrella.

"Shit."

I stepped out the back door to see whether I could spot her, but in the warren that was Spring Gardens, she could have cut through toward the Admiralty Arch, left toward the Mall, or right back into Trafalgar Square.

"Shit, shit, and *shit.*" *A schoolboy error.*

V.
British Airways Flagship Lounge, Heathrow, London

I was booked in first class on BA flight 139 departing at 10:15 a.m. and heading to Bombay, arriving at 11:55 p.m. local time. I had a hotel booked near the airport for a few hours' rest and then onward to Goa on a 10:15 a.m. with

Vistara Airlines, arriving at Dabolim Airport an hour and a half later.

I was making the most of my flagship experience and had helped myself to a full English, a freshly squeezed orange juice, and a latte. I was sat down at a dining table reading the *Times*. There was plenty more comfortable seating in the lounge, but a full English deserves the respect it has earned and is a sit-down meal, not a sit-on-the-sofa-watching-television kind of deal.

Coincidentally, there was an article about Lord Lucan and his disappearance from London in the middle of the night after the family's nanny had been viciously slaughtered in the family home. Apart from one sighting of him heading toward the ferries on the south coast of England, the theory was that he had escaped to Goa all those years ago and lived a secret life of an all but hermit and recluse on the west-coast Indian state.

The article went on to explain that back in 1974, when he went missing, Goa was as good a place to hide as anywhere else. The British peer suspected of murder apparently lay low in a largely uninhabited part of the coastal region.

Over the years, according to eyewitness recollections, every once in a while, large luxury yachts would turn up looking to visit him, Lucky Jim. There was a picture of the front of the book *Dead Lucky*, by authors William Hall and Duncan MacLaughlin, and a photo of an old man with long white hair and beard alleging to be that of the one and only Lord "Lucky Jim" Lucan.

"So that's why people go to Goa." I took a sip of my latte. "To disappear."

Maybe it was no wonder that's where Lady Helen Bailey had chosen to hole up.

VI.
Dabolim Airport, Goa, India

I had somewhat grown immune to the trials and tribulations of travel and long-haul flights, although flying first-class always helped. On boarding the flight in London, I settled myself down in my cocoon and set about catching up on emails, and then I continued with my mission, and painstaking research into the mystery of the *Indigo* I had somehow got embroiled in all those years ago.

A couple of hours into the flight, lunch arrived, and I sat upright and noshed on the delicacies served at thirty thousand feet cruising altitude. Smoked salmon and crème fraîche, and a glass of Dom Perignon, followed by filet of beef rossini with dauphinoise potatoes and baby carrots Chantilly, with a glass of French malbec. Then a platter of artisanal British cheeses—no dessert for me today.

I settled down to watch *Trainspotting 2*, a reminder of my Scottish roots.

After a tedious and incredibly humid stopover in Bombay, the Vistara flight to Dabolim Airport was easy and uneventful. Outside the airport, my driver, Reyansh, was ready for me with a cardboard sign: "Welcome to Goa, Mr. William Mitchell." It had been a while since anyone had used my Sunday name.

Reyansh grabbed my bag and loaded it into the back of the yellow-and-black Standard Pennant Saloon. On my travels, I had always found it an interesting personality stamp of any country, what the taxis of choice are and how they vary from country to country. With a fleet of these outside the airport, this was or at least had been the taxi of choice in Goa.

Reyansh and I, me in the passenger seat, set off on our hour-and-three-quarter boneshaker ride south to Cola beach, close to Canacona village, in the south of Goa.

I wanted to sit in the front. This was my first time to India, and I wanted to take in all the sights.

VII.
Palaayan Villa, Cola Beach, Goa, India

Built on top of a cliff, Palaayan Villa stood above the isolated beach overlooking the Arabian Sea and the sprinkling of dwellings farther down the coast. It was a secluded spot and somewhere you had to be looking for or stumble across by accident. It wasn't the kind of place you would call a destination.

The double gates of the entrance at the rear of the property opened up as Reyansh spoke in Hindi to the hidden security guard, with only the cameras each side and above giving away their presence.

As we drove in, the well-kept grounds were distinctly different from what I had witnessed on the journey down.

"This is truly an escape, Mr. Mitchell," Reyansh said, referring to the Hindi translation of the villa's name.

"Indeed. It seems to be that way," I replied, keenly looking out the window at these new surroundings, not quite sure what I was going to find.

A man in a starched white tunic and turban was there to meet me at the double front doors. Solid wood, they looked truly ancient and were a foot thick and what must have been twelve feet high, with inscriptions in what I assumed was in Devanagari script, one of many derived from the original and ancient Brahmi system of writing.

Without a word, just a series of welcoming gestures, the man ushered me through. I could immediately see that there was no expense spared in the construction of this residence—too grand to simply call it a house or a home. A symphony of marble and more ancient woods and carvings, and although it was midafternoon, lanterns sparkled and caught the eye. Music played softly, that of flutes and hand drums, and the aromas of essential oils floated in the air.

"Wow, quite a retreat." It was hard not to be impressed.

A friendly lady, looked like a nurse, padded softly toward me and bowed, clasping her hands together.

"Welcome to Palaayan," she almost whispered in what I recognized as a soft northern British accent.

"Why, thank you."

It sounded dumb, but I didn't quite know what else to say at this point.

"Please—this way."

I followed her down a long balustrade corridor overlooking the ocean and the beach. She paused and pointed to another ornate and what looked like ancient door.

"This is your room, Mr. Mitchell," she said and opened the door.

"Wow," I said as I stepped in. "This is beautiful. Thank you."

It wasn't that I was here for a hotel stay or a romantic weekend for one. I was here to see Lady Helen Bailey. The nurse seemed to read my mind.

"Lady Helen is a little unwell this afternoon. She will see you in the morning. In the meantime, please make yourself at home, and if there is anything you need, please ring this bell." She pointed to a sort of cowbell that could be pulled via rope chord just inside the suite.

She noticed my cell phone in my hand—I had been trying to get online while arriving in the taxi.

"I am sorry, Mr. Mitchell; we don't have a signal here at Cola beach. Nor do we have television, but we do have plenty of opportunities for spiritual healing." She pointed at the cowbell again.

She quickly showed me around the room and then bowed, hands clasped.

"Remember, Mr. Mitchell, if there's anything you need at all, please let me know." Then she backed out of the door and softly closed it behind her.

What was I expecting? I wasn't sure—it was a good question. Bailey would be in her early fifties by now, and she was a billionaire at least twice over, so why would I expect anything less than this place?

I looked around the room in awe of the simple yet sophisticated, the modern yet ancient, the no-expense-spared impression you get when you walk in a place that you just know is quite special. This place was one of those places, and I was dumbstruck at the beauty of it.

I grabbed a change of clothes from my bag, along with my washbag, and headed to the bathroom for a shave and a shower and to get out of my sweaty and now well-travelled clothes.

Afterward, relaxed in a T-shirt and some sweats, I explored the room barefoot and found the drinks cabinet, including a bottle of Plymouth Gin, Schweppes, lemons, and a miniature ice machine.

"Bingo."

It immediately reminded me of the flowery character Zach and one of his many old sayings, "It's always six o'clock somewhere in the world."

I looked at my watch. It was close enough here local time.

I poured myself a generous measure, rang the cowbell, and went to sit on the balcony overlooking the sea and the sun closing in for the evening.

Two young ladies padded their way softly toward me and bowed. One was carrying a stack of newly laundered, fresh white towels and a bamboo satchel over her shoulder. The other said softly, "Yes, Mr. Mitchell—how can we help you?"

I cleared my throat nervously. "Well, I was wondering what the arrangements for dinner were?"

She went through the available menu, a combination of local delicacies that included the offer of a tasting menu. Why not?

"Sounds fantastic."

"Now, Mr. Mitchell, we give you a nice, relaxing massage."

Before I knew it, I was ushered onto the daybed on the balcony, and the pair went through their routine, with essential oils and a double massage, soft music in the background, and their singing a hypnotic lullaby.

I woke up with a start and looked at my watch. It was now eight thirty, and my tasting menu was arriving. I sat in my robe at the table while the feast was laid out before me, plus a bottle of Chablis to wash it all down with.

"I think I have just discovered heaven."

The next morning, I awoke to the sounds of flutes and sitars gently playing. The sun was fresh in the sky, and a light breeze was blowing the linen curtains, the sound of the ocean lapping the beach behind.

The same thought ran through my mind as the last one I remembered before I fell asleep: *Yes, I think this could be heaven.* I had never had a better night's sleep in my entire life. I had this strange feeling like I was a baby cocooned in my crib. I had this sense of extreme safety, of peacefulness. It was a heady sensation. I could smell the constant waft of aromas kissing the air. It was like I was high. And then, for a moment, I realized that I might just be that.

Whatever it was, it felt good.

The Yorkshire nurse came to collect me after breakfast, and I followed her as she walked me back toward the center of the house.

"She's a little better this morning. She has agreed to see you, but you have to remember—she hasn't been well, since, you know ..."

I nodded my understanding.

She went on to explain how Lady Helen Bailey had suffered significant posttraumatic stress disorder after "the incident," accompanied by severe bouts of anxiety and depression, even several suicide attempts. Apparently, after her last attempt of hanging herself, she'd had a stroke and had barely spoken since.

She guided me to what appeared like a large grand lounge, with white linen sofas; hanging tapestries floating in the gentle breeze; a grand piano in the corner; and Lady Helen Bailey, laid in her white robe, who attempted a smile when she saw me.

I smiled back but realized that the smile was a permanent fixture on her face.

Lady Helen Bailey was clearly not in a good place. She had aged more than I expected, looking like she was in her midseventies rather than midfifties. She looked dangerously thin, and she rocked her whole body slightly backward and forward.

I realized that there was nothing I wanted to ask that I could or was willing to.

She silently gestured me toward her, and I sat on the coffee table in front of her. She looked at me with her green eyes and held out for my hand. We held hands together for what seemed an age, her looking up to me. Her eyes were smiling—I'm sure.

"We found her, you know," she said.

I didn't know how to respond. I paused for a moment, trying to think what she was referring to. I smiled with all the kindness I could. "Who?"

She stared blankly into the distance, as if seeing some sort of mirage before her. "She was beautiful, you know."

I didn't interject for fear of disrupting the moment.

"So regal and peaceful the way she lay there, in her secret hiding place, away from harm, and prying eyes. Safe from people to take advantage of her, abuse her, share her stories, reveal her secrets."

Her grip on my hand had tightened to the point it was actually beginning to hurt.

"Rape her."

Whoever she was referring to, she was clearly paralleling her own life and experiences with the characterization.

"Who did you find, Lady Helen?"

She looked up to me and smiled, her green eyes focusing on mine. Even in her frail state, I could see why Zach had fallen for her. She had this mystique and beauty about her—deep, complex, intriguing. "Just like a great glass of cab" is how Zach had described her, and in that moment, I agreed with his explanation and understood.

She let out a big, white-toothed, full-on smile. "The lady *Ella Sophia*. We found her."

I recalled the story of the dive, in search of what was considered by many the mythological shipwreck. I nodded and smiled back, not quite knowing if she had or if that, too, was a parallel reality.

I thought about pushing the point of the exact location, thinking about all the fame and riches if such a find were discovered.

She summoned me toward her, and I leaned down. And as she whispered in my ear, the chills permeated my body, even as they do as I write this on the page: "The road to hell is paved with good intentions."

Later that day, I left to return home, with the story of the SS *Indigo* still rattling around in my head.

FURTHER NOTES

The mysterious Mr. N. Waring was indeed nonexistent, but the lessee of 20 Cockspur Street, a Mr. Terrance Armitage from Epping, Essex, was also wired a sum of £1 million. Shortly after the transfer or funds, he was involved in an unfortunate traffic accident while crossing the road close to his home. A black S-Class Mercedes-Benz registered to the First World Bank was confirmed to be the car, but the driver of the vehicle was never identified.

Before I left Palaayan Villa in Goa, I did verify that the nursing staff were piping "relaxants" and my senses of feeling high were not just paranoia. That said, although never having been into drugs of any kind, I found it kind of nice.

There have been various explanations and conspiracy theories regarding what happened on the SS *Indigo*, from it all somehow being the work of the Church of Scientology, or the Russians, to it being some elaborate plot of multiple personal vendettas.

I have come to the conclusion that the truth is that maybe no one will ever truly know. But this is the result and summary of my research of each of the characters and the once Princess of the Seas herself, the SS *Indigo*.

Lady Helen Bailey

There was a lot more to Lady Helen Bailey than caught the eye. Not only was there the incident about her stepmother's untimely death and fall from the rocks at Brimham, and the marijuana-fueled fire in Australia that resulted in the death of the mother and her two children. There were other incidents in her background, including the tragic death of her childhood friend, who fell into a slurry tank on her father's farm when Helen was only eight years old.

It seemed that Lady Helen Bailey was surrounded by tragedy from a very early age.

There was a further hidden secret, the revelation that her real father was not the one she knew but an unknown wealthy businessman whom her mother had had a recurring fling with over the years. From her papers, it was clear that Helen was on the trail and getting closer to the identity of her real father.

Shortly after my visit to Cola beach, Lady Helen Bailey had a massive stroke. She didn't recover, and she died. She was buried in the gardens of her villa, Palaayan, Hindi for *escape*.

Harry Bloomington

Harry's downturn in fortunes reversed thanks to the generous deposit in his bank account just prior to the death of his old friend Sir James Parsons. He resurrected his fortunes, remodeled his home to former glories, and unfortunately contracted COVID-19 and passed away at home.

Captain Igor Bromovich

One of only three survivors, Bromovich returned to his family in Lithuania and, despite the events on the SS *Indigo*, was cleared of any wrongdoing. However, he did come under some criticism for accepting the instructions to undercrew the *Indigo*, but that didn't stop him from taking up the captaincy of a Baltic cruise ship. And in the seventeen years since, he's had an unblemished record.

With the proceeds from Sir James Parsons, he purchased a plot of land just outside Vilnius and built his dream home by a lake. He sent all his children to university and purchased a holiday home close to Trakai Castle.

Dr. Bronwyn Brown

Shortly after the demise of the *Indigo*, an inquiry opened into Dr. Bronwyn Brown. It turned out that her real name was in fact Elizabeth Manning. She had never completed medical school in Johannesburg as she had claimed, having been disqualified for administering prescription drugs to a vulnerable patient and self-subscribing opioids.

Secondly, upon reviewing Brown's patient records, investigators revealed that in her ten years at St. Mary's and of the nearly two hundred patients in her care over that time, of those who died, more than forty had cut Brown into their wills.

Brown's assets upon her death were summed up at more than $10 million and came under dispute by a class action of the deceased relatives against St. Mary's and Bronwyn Brown's (a.k.a. Elizabeth Manning's) estate.

The plaintiffs won, and even her gold sovereigns were auctioned off to settle the suit.

Paul Bland

It turned out that Bland was a serial philanderer of the worst type. He would prey on innocent and often vulnerable young men—mostly boys. If he had still been alive at the time, Bland could have been the cause in his own right of the Me Too movement.

After Bland's death, and with no one to leave his estate to, several of his past conquests came out of the woodwork to claim against his AUD$1 million in savings and to share the proceeds of the sale of his Darlinghurst town house and den of iniquity.

Zach Carter

Zach, one of only three survivors from the SS *Indigo*, after his stint in Northward Prison went back to Northern California to Sonoma. After his father passed away—prostate cancer—he had enough money to buy the No Name Bar in Sausalito for nostalgia's sake. He took over his dad's motor yacht, the *Lady of the Bay*, and was sailing tourists around the bay and then going for food and libations at his bar afterward. At night, the No Name, just like the one in Amsterdam, sprang to life with the local crowd of artists, musicians, and serious drinkers.

He married a Sonoma girl, Molly, and had two children. They bought a clapboard house with a white picket fence in Sonoma, and he still drove his dad's old Ford Bronco.

Angela Chalmers

Chalmers's list of enemies was long, but had her crimes against her fellow colleagues and business associates been serious enough to call for her murder? There were various stories where she had screwed someone over or had been the architect of someone's downfall, all in the name of progressing the outcome for Angela Chalmers. She had won the nickname Memyi for a reason.

Stuart Jacobs

Jacobs's autopsy agreed with the in-the-moment diagnosis of anaphylactic shock, probably caused by an acute reaction to the fish he had consumed on the *Indigo*.

Jacobs had also apparently spent a career screwing people over. There was little activity after his death other than the empty church that greeted him back to Mother Nature and a long list of very distant well-wishers.

Sir James Parsons

Parsons's postmortem revealed that he had died from a heart attack, likely induced by what was described as an "unidentified substance." It was also revealed from his medical records that he had been diagnosed with a rare genetic terminal brain cancer in early 2003.

Before his death, he distributed his amassed fortune to his wife; his two sons; his daughter, Lady Helen Bailey; and numerous other personal and charitable causes and beneficiaries.

Quentin Perkins

The news of Perkins's involvement with an international pedophile ring broke at the same time as the announcement of his death. The ring was linked to several high-profile celebrities, politicians, and dignitaries. The boy found dead at his London home was concluded as a case of manslaughter, and several senior London Metropolitan Police officers had lost their careers as a result, including the police constable, who silently resigned.

Perkins's home and assets were sold off to settle a long string of claims from his victims, who on average received $1 million each for the trauma that they went through at his hand.

James "Sal" Salmond
Salmond's body was shipped back to Australia and his body buried in a small wood of eucalyptus trees on the family farm. After the inquiry into his death, Sal's parents sent an undisclosed check for AUD$5 million to a retired miner now living in Adelaide with only faded pictures on the mantelpiece to remember his wife and their two children.

Andrew Sheldon
Sheldon's body was flown back to Leeds Bradford Airport and transported to Bradford, where he was buried. With only a handful of attendees at Sheldon's funeral, his tenants stayed away and were quietly celebrating. An unknown beneficiary had written to them shortly after his death assigning the deeds of their properties over to them.

Apart from the cash in the bank and the family home, Sheldon's property empire had all been assigned back to the tenants, and Sheldon was gone for good.

Keith Simpson
On leaving the army, Simpson had fallen into Scotland Yard and a fraternity of ex–military men within. Although he'd never been called out directly, there had been several investigations into Simpson and his colleagues for covering up crimes, accepting bribes, and

even fraternizing with London's world of organized crime.

Tony Sharp
Apart from the Northern Ireland incident, by the nature of Sharp's livelihood, there had been a few. "Comes with the territory," one of the Parachute Regiment officers said during one of the interviews on the matter.

A man with an outstanding military career, he had a few blemishes, but none that the Special Air Service was going to own up to, admit, or even disclose.

And that just left the cook and the stewardess, Perry and Kayla.

At the nursing home where Kayla worked, there had been several suspicious incidents of otherwise healthy residents passing away suddenly. There was plenty of suspicion, but there were no investigations; the extent of the materiality of these crimes was the pounds in their purses and the pittance of their weekly state pensions.

Apparently, no one was interested in these low-level crimes.

Or were they? It seems that someone might have been.

The events on SS *Indigo* will always be a mystery to many, including me.

The criterion for the invitations is still largely unknown. Some of the passengers had links to Parsons's past—some directly, some indirectly, some by association, and some who appeared more random but carried the traits he had grown to despise.

Consider not only that his brain cancer was a factor in taking the course that he did but also how such diseases can warp the mind and turn seemingly rational minds into otherwise.

The SS *Indigo* came into my life in an unrelated off chance, but the story will now remain with me for the rest of my days.

I hope that you have enjoyed the mystery and the intrigue as much as I have telling this previously untold story.

SS INDIGO

**Provided by Zach Carter as Part of
His Prejoining Homework**

The *Indigo* is a beauty for sure: 250 feet in length, a 25-foot beam, and her brilliant white hull with the simple inscription SS *Indigo* emblazoned on her bow. She stands proud with her fore flag flying the Stars and Stripes and her two masts full of sheets, ready to sail. The big single chimney rises above her four decks, revealing her underlying power of steam. There's a bunting of flags from the stem to the stern, her lifeboats and tenders dangling from her sides with the promise of adventure in these warm, friendly Caribbean seas.

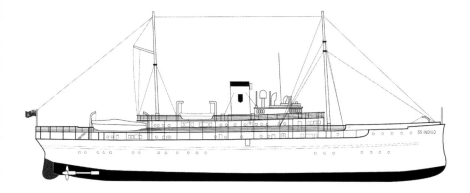

Aboard adorned with teak and brass, the plans below polish like glass. The entrance through the main deck reveals the opportunity for cocktails and convivial meals.

Along with her toys, from paddleboards to Jet Skis and boats, it's obvious that her top deck is ready for toasts.

With her dining table on top deck set for twelve, and the views all around a sight to behold, the luxury cabins and amenities aboard are something that even the most seasoned traveler must applaud.

⚓ **Launched:** 1921
⚓ **Builder:** Great Lakes Engineering Works
⚓ **Passengers:** 26
⚓ **Crew:** 24–30
⚓ **Tonnage:** 1,961 (gross)
⚓ **Length:** 257.8 ft
⚓ **Beam:** 35.5 ft
⚓ **Draft:** 14.6 ft
⚓ **Power:** Steam
⚓ **Propulsion:** Propeller
⚓ **Speed:** 12 knots

The Accommodations

Dining Room
A formal affair, with mahogany panels placed everywhere. The plush cushioned seating and the gourmet eating make for a formal dinner occasion.

The Indigo Bar
With its U-bend wrapping around, it's a perfect place to drink cocktails with friends and have conversation.

The Indigo Lounge
Comfortable furnishings, with the option of playing chess, checkers, backgammon, or a game of cards. With its own private library, it's a great place to relax away from the noise.

Music Lounge
With its baby grand and its views so fine, it's the perfect place to unwind. Listen to Elton, Chopin, or Mozart. The experience is tempting, as is the exquisite art.

Smoking Salon
Furnished with red leather chesterfield-style sofas and wingback chairs, surrounded by mahogany furniture and oak paneling, the smoking salon is the perfect retreat to have a quiet conversation and enjoy a tipple and a cigar.

The Cabins (and allocation)

- ⚓ Horace Dodge (Jacobs)
- ⚓ Churchill (Simpson)
- ⚓ Marilyn Monroe (Chalmers)
- ⚓ 1921 (Sheldon)
- ⚓ Vettriano (Bailey)
- ⚓ MacArthur (Sharp)
- ⚓ Oscar Wilde (Perkins)
- ⚓ Marie Curie (Brown)
- ⚓ Delphine (Bland)
- ⚓ Monaco (Salmond)
- ⚓ Dauntless (Parsons)
- ⚓ Liddesdale (Zach)

ABOUT THE AUTHOR

Willy Mitchell was born in Glasgow, Scotland. He spent a lot of time in bars in his youth and into adulthood. He's always appreciated the stories, some waned by time past, some imaginary, and some true.

A shipyard worker, he headed down from Scotland to Yorkshire with his family to work in the steel mills. Now retired, he lives in California and has turned to writing some of the tales he's listened to over the years, bringing those stories to life.

Operation Argus

Operation Argus is a fast-paced, thoughtful, personal, and insightful story that touches the mind and the heart and creates a sense of intrigue in the search for the truth.

While sitting in the Rhu Inn in Scotland one wintry night, Willy Mitchell stumbles across a group of men in civilian clothes who are full of adrenaline—like a group of performers coming off a stage. To the watchful eye, it is clear the men are no civilians. As they share close-knit banter and beer, they are completely alert, and each of them checks him out and looks at his eyes and into his soul.

Mitchell learns in time that the group is referred to as call sign Bravo2Zero.

Operation Argus is a story of fiction based on true events. Five former and one serving Special Air Service soldiers converge on San Francisco for their good friend's funeral, only to find his apparent heart attack is not as it seems. A concoction of polonium-210 has been used, as with the assassination of Litvinenko in London years before.

Bikini Bravo

Bikini Bravo follows the adventures of Mitch; his daughter, Bella; and the team of Mac, Bob, and Sam as they uncover a complex web of unlikely collaborators but for a seemingly obvious common good: power, greed, and money.

Many years ago, Mitchell stumbled across a bar in Malindi, Kenya, and overheard the makings of a coup in an oil-rich nation in West Africa. Is a similar plan being hatched today?

Lord Beecham puts together the pieces of the puzzle and concludes that the Russians, along with the Mexican drug cartels and a power-hungry group of Equatorial Guineans, have crafted an ingenious plot to take over Africa's sixth-largest oil-producing nation in their attempt to win influence in Africa. The cartels desire to use the dirty money for good, and the Africans seek to win power and influence.

Bikini Bravo is another book of fiction by Mitchell that masterfully flirts with real-life events spanning the globe and touches on some real global political issues.

Mitch's daughter, Bella, is the emerging hero in this second book of the Argus series.

Cold Courage

Cold Courage starts with Willy Mitchell's grandfather's meeting with Harry McNish in Wellington, New Zealand, in 1929. In exchange for a hot meal and a pint or two,

McNish tells his story of the *Endurance* and the Imperial Trans-Antarctic Expedition of 1914.

According to legend, in 1913, Sir Ernest Shackleton posted a classified advertisement in the *London Times*: "Men wanted for hazardous journey. Small wages, bitter cold, long months of complete darkness, constant danger. Safe return doubtful. Honor and recognition in case of success." According to Shackleton, the advert attracted more than five thousand applicants, surely a sign of the times.

Following the assassination of Archduke Ferdinand earlier that year, at the beginning of August, the First World War was being declared across Europe, and with the blessing of the king and approval to proceed from the first sea lord, the *Endurance* set sail from Plymouth, England, on its way to Buenos Aires, Argentina, to meet with the entire twenty-eight-man crew and sail south.

Shackleton was keen to win back the polar-exploration crown for the empire and be the first to transit across the Antarctic from one side to the other.

The *Endurance* and her sister ship, the *Aurora*, both suffered defeat, and thirty-seven of Shackleton's men were stranded at opposite ends of the continent, shipless, cold, hungry, and fighting Mother Nature for survival.

This is a tale of the great age of exploration and the extraordinary journey these men endured, not only in Antarctica but also upon their return to England amid the Great War.

This is the story of the *Endurance*, the Imperial Trans-Antarctic Expedition of 1914, and all that was happening in those extraordinary times.

Northern Echo

Willy Mitchell meets an old friend in the Royal Oak, in the northern town they grew up in, for one last blast. Tiny Tim has terminal cancer, and at the end of the evening, he makes Mitchell promise to tell their story of growing up in the North of England during the punk rock era and of their dark secret from a trip to Paris.

There were dark clouds surrounding Great Britain at that time. The Provisional IRA was actively rebelling against the English, Arabic terrorism was on the rise, and Argentina invaded one of the nation's territories in the far-off South Atlantic.

Unemployment was at its highest level since the 1930s, and whole industries were being crippled by the trade union movement and strikes in every corner of industry. The Far Right was also on the rise, as was the Campaign for Nuclear Disarmament protesting the arms race that existed between the United States and the Soviet Union.

Society was on its knees; the middle class had given up, seemingly content to slide into obscurity, forgetting the victories and the pride of the past.

The youth of the time were disillusioned, with little prospect of jobs, careers, or a future, and as the punk rock scene spread across the Atlantic from New York, it changed into a movement and a commentary on the state of the country and the mood of society.

With no future and no rules, ripping up the rule book and starting again, the punk rock movement was an unlikely catalyst and contributor to change in Great Britain, with heaps of attitude, and it changed the nation for the better.

Mitchell, in *Northern Echo*, takes the reader on a sometimes humorous, eye-opening journey through one of the most interesting times in modern British history—a musical, political, and social revolution—and the story of two boys coming of age in their journey toward adulthood.

Gipsy Moth

Gipsy Moth is the tale of a young girl growing up with a privileged life in the North of England during extraordinary times, an era of extremes and pioneers, including the Wright brothers' first flight, the breakout of war across

Europe, and the burgeoning sadness of two parents both absent for different reasons.

Miss Boswell, the family's nanny, is the single point of continuity and has a profound influence on the lives of Nikki and her two brothers.

Nikki meets Amy, another Yorkshire lass, at school, and through their shared loneliness at home, they establish a unique and lasting friendship that takes them from Yorkshire to London and beyond, to places they've only ever dreamed of, and they encounter tragic twists and turns along the way.

Willy Mitchell tells the story his great-aunt shared with him after his own father's funeral, unearthing even more secrets in the Mitchell family history—secrets of happiness, times long gone, sadness, and tragedy.

The lives of Nikki Beattie and Amy Johnson collide as they meet through their fathers, who are successful men in their own fields of business. Their two pathways intertwine through friendship, school, university, and their discovery of the pioneering days of early aviation.

Together they get the flying bug and join the ranks of the most influential group of women in the history of British aviation. They become two extraordinary women, aviatrixes, true pioneers in the golden age of aviation.

Both are born just five months before the Wright brothers' pioneering flight in 1903. Nikki's best friend, Amy, becomes not just a celebrity in the evolution of flight but also a shining light for women's rights, a national and international hero. Amy reads about her rival from across the Atlantic, Amelia Earhart, who, in 1937, goes missing during a flight in the Pacific. Her body is never found.

In 1940, Amy and Nikki both join the Air Transport Auxiliary, and in 1941, Amy mysteriously crashes and disappears above the Thames Estuary. Her body is never recovered.

Just as many have their own and family skeletons, Nikki shares her story with Mitchell, including secrets long buried.

SS Indigo

An eclectic cast of characters from around the world and from different walks of life receive a mysterious invitation from Litions Industries to join luxury steamship *Indigo* at St. George's Caye in the Caribbean port of Belize City.

Sir James Parsons, chairman of Watershed Investments; Stuart Jacobs, a former RAF technician and regular in the San Francisco expat scene; Andrew Sheldon, a binman's son made good. Then there's Dr. Bronwyn Brown and Father Quentin Perkins, an art collector of sorts. Paul Bland is an Australian businessman, Angela Chalmers an American executive. A couple of military men, Simpson and Sharp, and Lady Helen Bailey and Sal Salmond, a pair of soulmates and adventurers.

Zach Carter, from Northern California, is the official tour guide, with experience in boats and the Caribbean. Perry and Kayla, the cook and the stewardess.

Captain Igor Bromovich, the ship's captain, qualified at Klaipeda Naval Academy, Lithuania.

Their invitations arrive from an N. Waring on behalf of the world-renowned but secretive investor Jemol Litions, and it was invitations from someone like him that these particular passengers found hard to refuse.

The twelve gather and set sail to Grand Cayman, and the mystery begins to unfold, one dark secret at a time.

The question is, Who is Jemol Litions? And why had they really been invited? What was the true purpose and destination of the cruise, and why is the passenger list depleting day after day?

A thriller mystery. Are you ready for the truth?

Printed in the United States
by Baker & Taylor Publisher Services